BLADES OF DESTINY

BEN COTTERILL

Published 2024 by Next Chapter

Edited by Elizabeth N. Love

Cover art by Lordan June Pinote

Part I

Prologue

CCXXI (X Years Ago)

Though only twelve years old, Rella couldn't remember ever being afraid of the dark. In fact, she couldn't remember being afraid of anything. The thought spurred her on, and she marched briskly with a confident sway of her shoulders. Close behind, the other two girls silently followed as she led them through the forest towards the Eye. The forest was dark at the best of times, and now it was night, she could barely see. However, the smell of bat droppings and the splashing of water beneath her feet told her they were passing the entrance to the caves.

A refreshing wind wailed through the warm night. She pulled her dark braid over her shoulder, double-checking that the leather strap was secure. Despite the wind thrashing strands of hair across her face, Rella savored the invigorating sensation it brought.

The reflections of the moon and stars shimmered slightly on the surface of the slow-flowing stream as it journeyed from source to sea. All they had to do to reach the Eye was follow it. The Eye was Rella and Elara's favorite spot, probably because both of them always had their eyes drawn to the stars. The best friends had never shared their special place with anyone, but Clare seemed trustworthy. Rella's father was friends with Clare's parents, who were new to the area and had brought special merchandise with them. Although Father had hushed up the specifics, he had a grin on his face while discussing it, meaning that it was something good.

Small animal bones crunched beneath Rella's felt boots and she remembered hearing stories of large cats and venomous snakes living within the woods. Regret for her earlier boldness surged through her, but she dared not show it in front of Clare, who was slightly older and showed no signs of hesitation.

"We shouldn't be out here this late," Elara then said, the youngest of them, twirling her red hair, blue eyes shifting to the forest around them.

"Of course, we should." Rella tried to sound confident. "But why do you say that?"

"Because there could be bandits lurking. They might rob or kidnap us and sell us as slaves." Elara had more knowledge of the woods than most; her people had lived in camps scattered around the highlands of Eden until Rella's father had invited everyone to live within the city as one.

"Father and I always target practice in the woods, and I've never seen any bandits." Granted, Rella only fired arrows during the day, but she decided not to mention that.

"That's with your father," Elara protested. "Things are different for children."

"I would simply command them not to rob or kidnap us." Rella gave a toss of her head. "Father says everyone must do as I say because I'll be Countess of Eden one day." Eating before morning prayers was a sin, but the palace servants would even serve Rella food if her stomach rumbled before breakfast.

"Bandits don't listen to orders. That's why they're bandits,"

Clare said, her voice always commanding and her head high, making her seem fierce and determined.

Rella straightened her back, trying to mimic Clare. If Clare wasn't afraid, she wouldn't be either. "We also don't listen to orders; we've left the city after bedtime. The bandits should be the ones who are scared of us."

The three girls giggled, and their worries seemed to fade into the night. As the stream got deeper, they decided to ascend the bank's edge. The recent downpour had made the soil loose and muddy. Rella slipped a couple of times, dirtying her white tunic. From the top, she and Clare pulled up Elara. The freckles all over Elara's face and the gap between her two front teeth made her look even younger than she was, inspiring Rella's protectiveness, as though she was her own little sister.

They reached a large clearing within the forest, close to the Eye. It was a stunning glade, full of lush greens and vibrant yellows. The Creator had blessed Eden with rolling hills and forested highlands, framing lakes, and lowland fields perfect for farming. Rella paused at the sight, her heart aflutter. As an only child, her destiny was to rule this paradise, every inch of it, right up to the neighboring territory of Tyrin, for Queen Shanleigh—the first monarch of Arcadia since the Omi's vanquish—had appointed her father as Governor of Eden.

Tyrin, on the other hand, was said to contain nothing but red rocks and sand. There were more territories beyond Tyrin, but its deserts stretched for thousands of miles and stories of what lay beyond were scarce. One day, Rella would explore all those lands to see them for herself.

They arrived at the Eye, and Clare stood still for a second in awe as both Rella and Elara had done when they first saw the construction. It was a round, domed building with a giant, metal cylinder protruding from the top, pointing towards the sky. There was glass on both sides of the cylinder, and if Rella looked through the bottom, the moon and stars appeared to be larger. Parts of the building had crumbled away. Though centuries old, the building's eye still worked.

The dome wasn't built from individual stones like the thatched cottages of the city or from bricks like Rella's palace. Instead, it seemed to be cut from one giant piece of rock, and Rella wondered what kind of technology the heretics must have had. Legend said it had once been possible to travel to different stars and planets, but such myths had been condemned as heresy during the Omi's reign. Rella wondered if there was life on planets other than Arcadia.

They took turns staring through the Eye at the stars.

"I wonder how many there are," Clare said.

"I counted nearly a hundred once." Elara smiled proudly.

"Be careful," Rella warned. "Count anymore and you'll be guilty of computing."

"Computing is no longer illegal," Clare replied. "I bet the heretics had a way of figuring out the number of stars, and we should have the freedom to do the same."

"Are you allowed to say that?" Rella asked, sometimes still unsure of exactly what could be said.

"So long as loyalists to the Omi don't hear us. My cousin Guin is a monk and he'd report me to the Monastery if he heard me express such thoughts."

"Why would he do that?"

"He says that the heretics allowed technology to run their lives instead of the Creator's doctrine, and that we can't do the same or we'll be condemned by the Creator as they were."

"Good thing the Queen has defeated the Omi," Rella remarked with a shrug, still remembering the freedom parades that occurred when it was announced that all territories of Arcadia were now free from the Omi's rule.

Elara wasn't interested in this discussion and went back to gazing out the Eye.

"The Omi may no longer be in power, but the Queen still

yields considerable authority to the Monastery," Clare said. "My parents think she's relinquished too much control, and as a result, the Monastery will pave the way for the Omi's return someday."

Rella scowled, not sure how to win this argument with Clare but also not believing her to be right. Father said the Omi were defeated, and he never lied about anything.

"Something's moving!" Elara exclaimed.

Elara stepped back from the Eye so Rella and Clare could take a peek. A metallic cylinder moved through the sky, getting closer and closer until Rella thought they might be able to see it with their own eyes. The girls dashed outside. At first, they couldn't see anything except for the moon and stars, then a giant, white object pierced through the sky. It fell towards the ground, crashing somewhere within the lowlands of Eden.

Elara inhaled a sharp breath, pointing to the sky. "I think one of the stars fell down!"

"That wasn't a star." Rella shook her head. "Didn't you see the color? It was white like snow. I must go tell Father."

"You can't," Clare said. "If you do, people will know we were out here."

"We have to tell people what we saw!"

"What will you say? That we saw an object—manmade looking—crash from the sky? That would be heresy."

"It can't be heresy if I just saw it with my own eyes!"

"Yes, it can. If you repeat this to anyone, then the Monastery or loyalists of the Omi will have you killed."

"My father is in control of Eden now, not the Omi." Rella stomped her foot, having heard enough of Clare's lessons. "No one will hurt me for speaking the truth."

Rella turned to leave, but Clare stopped her by grabbing her arm. "They could harm your parents too, Rella."

"Maybe we should listen to Clare," Elara said meekly.

"People will find the fallen object anyway. Why should we be the ones to cause trouble?"

That was true, Rella thought, and she didn't want to cause trouble for her father after how happy he was to become Governor. Rella nodded grudgingly. "Fine. I won't tell."

"We must swear an oath," Clare said.

"What kind of oath?"

"A promise to never speak of this," Clare explained. "If we never speak of it, it never happened."

The three girls formed a circle, and Clare extended her hand to the center. Rella and Elara placed their hands on top of hers, and together, they vowed to never reveal what they had witnessed lest the Creator strike them down.

Chapter One

I

CCXXXI (Present)

Rella lay fixed in the snow, her face succumbing to the same sensation of numbness as her fingers and toes. Her mind was still reeling from the elbow that had nearly dislocated her jaw.

"Do you think she's from the village?" one of the Enforcers asked.

Rella concentrated more on gluing her eyes shut and normalizing her breathing than on what they were saying. She couldn't let them know she was awake. She wasn't sure why these two Enforcers had attacked her on sight. Hunting was still legal under the Omi's law. All she had been doing was seeking some game on her way to Elara's house.

"We should kill her just in case."

"Maybe we should check with the general. She could be someone important."

"Don't be a fool, no one important lives in these hills anymore."

Rella stole a peek at the ground beside the Enforcers' feet. Her heart thudded in her ears. There, next to the Enforcers, lay her bow and arrows, along with the three knives that had been ripped from her belt and pockets.

She held her breath to keep from sighing with relief. They hadn't found the fourth knife in her boot. She still had a weapon. She could still escape.

She'd stowed the knife there on every hunt as a precaution against such assaults but had never imagined needing it to defend herself against the Enforcers. They had no business being in this section of the woods. Taxes weren't due for several more weeks.

Rella's stomach dropped as she thought of what that might mean. Elara's cabin was the only thing within miles in these parts of the woods, and Rella knew her friend had been struggling ever since her father's illness. Had she failed to pay her taxes? All Rella could do was make her escape and reach Elara's before any additional Enforcers appeared.

"Fine, we'll take her to the general and he can decide what to do with her," one said. "But you're carrying her."

She felt a feeble grasp on her ankles as her legs were hoisted into the air. She clenched a fist. Now it'd be too risky to reach for her knife. The man dragged her slowly across the snow, but before long, he had to stop for breath.

Rella opened an eyelid to see the other man halting his retrieval of her weapons and to look at his partner. "What's the hold-up?"

"She's heavier than she looks."

Her body stiffened at the remark, not that she'd ever admit to being vain or anything.

The Enforcer abandoned her weapons and went to help. "Are you kidding? You can't drag one little girl? Pathetic weakling."

Rella slowly reached for one of her knives in the leaves, careful not to cause a scraping sound against the white slush.

She was too late. A more powerful grip on her ankle hauled her away from her weapons.

Her back and head bumped against every rock in the forest. She bit her lip. It took everything she had not to groan out in pain. She looked up to see the handle of her knife sticking out from her right boot, while the two men faced forward. This was as good a chance as she was getting.

She lunged for her knife. The man yanked her away by her feet just before her fingers could get around the handle.

He stared at her, realizing she was awake. He reached for his sword, but she planted her boot directly in his face, flooring him.

She retrieved her knife and jerked her foot away from the other, much younger, Enforcer, who appeared confused as to what was happening. The second he reached for his weapon, she hurled her knife, aiming for the heart so his death would be quick.

Rella turned and sprinted for the pile of weapons they had left behind. The other Enforcer bolted after her.

With a snarl, he tackled her to the ground. Rella thrashed wildly to get free, but his weight held her down. He punched her, telling her to stop. Blood oozed from her nose.

With all her might, Rella drove her elbow directly into the Enforcer's ribs, feeling the jolt of bone against bone. He stumbled, losing his balance. Seizing the opportunity, she leapt up and darted for her bow and arrows, loaded the bow, and spun to face the Enforcer, firing at his chest just as he got back to his feet. This time, she aimed for a lung, and the impact of her arrow produced a dull, hollow plunk.

He rolled onto his back, choking on blood. Rella knew she should feel something watching him die. He was still human, even if he was Omi. But inside she felt as empty as the dying man's eyes. She picked up her things and wiped the blood trickling from her nose.

She continued on to Elara's house, now at a quicker pace.

She had to know if Elara was all right. She still wasn't sure the Enforcers were here for her, but why else would they be out this far in the forest? Then again, she could never understand anything the Omi did. Only the Omi could protect the territories from outer threats, they said, and only by being devout to the Creator could everyone be safe from evil. Really, the Omi were the only evil everyone needed protection from.

As Rella reached the outskirts of Elara's home, she feared the worst. Outside was a wagon not belonging to Elara or her father.

II

There were no footprints in the snow. No one had been out all day. Perhaps the Enforcers hadn't been here, but then whose was the wagon? The wagon was large enough to transport goods and it had a driver's seat mounted on the headboard, though the horses to pull the wagon were missing.

Rella took out her bow, getting an arrow ready to defend herself. She tiptoed across the snow towards the stone cottage. No matter how gently she crept, the sound of snow crunching under her boots was unavoidable.

She slowly creaked open the door. It was almost as cold inside as out. A fire hadn't been lit in days at least.

Rella heard something. Someone whimpering, shivering, and moaning—they sounded agitated, in pain, and in need of help.

A pale and shivering man rested in the main bedroom. It wasn't Elara's father. A crossbow and a large, blue jug rested beside him.

His skin stretched tightly over bone, little muscle remaining. He said through blue lips, his voice trembling, "Help. Please, you must help me. I have eaten everything from my cart. I need food."

"Where is Elara?" Rella asked.

"I don't know who that is, I swear. My cart got stuck in the snow and the horses ran off. Probably frozen to death by now. I came in here for help, but the place was empty."

Rella hadn't seen Elara at all this season, which was normal when the blizzards were as bad as they had been. Her father had been sick for some months, so it was possible Elara feared he wouldn't survive and had taken him elsewhere before the winter. However, the idea that Elara would leave without saying goodbye did not seem right.

She returned her attention to the starving man and thought about taking him home, but the distance was too great, and he would not survive the journey. Rella had only a squirrel and some dried fruits left on her but decided to part with the squirrel for the sake of the man. He needed something substantial, and quickly, so she told him she'd cook.

The man smiled faintly, and then he nodded off.

She lit the fire and placed one of Elara's pans above the flames, then started carving the squirrel. The pieces of meat sizzled as they reached the pan.

She had no trouble pulling the man out of bed; he was just skin and bone. His teeth chattered all the way from the bed to the fireplace. He immediately picked up chunks of meat and threw them into his mouth. He devoured every bit of meat off the bones. He looked at Rella and asked, "Are you not going to eat anything?"

"I'll have these." She held up the rest of her dried fruits. "You need the protein."

The man continued to gulp down everything he could. His haggard look and bloodshot eyes indicated he had been crying, likely from the pain in his stomach. Rella had never witnessed such extreme hunger before. Remembering her adoptive father's words about the healing power of tea, Rella prepared a cup for the man and offered it to him. "Here, drink this," she urged.

The man eagerly grasped the cup and gulped down its

still-burning-hot contents. "Thank you so much," he said, setting down the empty mug. "I was mere inches from death's door before you arrived."

Rella smiled at him in response, and he introduced himself, "I'm Kal,"

"I'm Rella," she replied.

"Where are you from, Rella? Do you live alone?"

"From a town on the other side of the forest."

"What brought you out here?"

"Hunting."

The winters here were bad, freezing lakes and rivers solid, covering the forests in a white blanket, and scaring most of the animals into hibernation. She and Alioth were running low, living off rations of dry food, so she had braved the icy winds and deep snow in search of game. Alioth had said the struggle of living in the wilderness would be good for her. He thought struggle was what made people strong.

"I planned on camping in the snow for a night or two, long enough to collect a good supply of food and still have some left over to trade in town. First, though, I was going to spend a night here, at Elara's house."

"Elara's your friend?"

"Yes, she lives here with her father. He was very sick, and she took care of him. I don't know where she'd have gone."

"I hope you find her."

"I had a run-in with a couple of Enforcers on my way here. I thought maybe they had come for Elara," Rella explained to Kal.

Kal shook his head. "No one's been here except me. How did you manage to escape the Enforcers?"

Rella showed him the two knives she kept in her trouser pockets, and that wasn't even all of them. "I can protect myself," she replied. It was true—ever since she was thirteen years old, Alioth had practiced with her every day.

"That's good. You have to be strong to live in these hills." The weakened man sat back in his chair and fell back asleep.

While he slept, Rella went out to track any sign of Elara or her father, but she found none. It appeared as though no one had been there in some time, other than Kal and his cart.

The following evening, Rella and Kal sat at the fire again, eating another squirrel Rella had caught. They drank more tea to stay warm and help Kal recover. His face had regained some color and he looked much healthier. Kal kept a jug by his bed, which he sipped every few hours. When Rella asked about it, Kal explained that it was fermented berry juice, but never offered her any. She was secretly relieved as the drink smelled more like acetone than fruit.

Kal was talkative and lively, revealing his true character. "Thanks to you, I feel a lot better. The weather is starting to warm up, so maybe tomorrow we can start a fire outside and send a signal to my people."

"Sure." Rella smiled. "You have people nearby?"

"My village is in the lowlands, but they'll have sent a search party for me. If we can get the smoke high enough, they should be able to see it. I look forward to getting back to my wife-to-be."

Rella leaned in. "You're getting married?"

He grinned proudly. "Of course. The women in my village couldn't resist a guy like me."

Rella found that hard to believe, as Kal was not at all what she would consider good-looking, what with his incredibly yellow teeth, uneven facial hair, inflamed eyes, and leathery skin. He clearly enjoyed a smoke of tobacco, and he looked like the perfect example of why it was a pastime better avoided. Nevertheless, she smiled politely and asked, "When do you plan on getting married?"

"As soon as I get back. I will have earned the right to marry in my village after venturing out so far for business. Not that I have had much success this year. The snow fell early and got me stuck! I had to eat my goods to stay alive!"

"What is it you bring back to your village?"

"Livestock," he said after a brief pause.

Rella furrowed her brows. "Small cart for livestock." He would only be able to transport poultry, she thought, not many goats and certainly not any cattle.

Kal nodded and then moved the conversation. "It's a beautiful village. You should see it. We love visitors."

"I'd like that."

The next morning, Rella and Kal woke to a shining sun, marking the start of summer. The sun was superbly close right from the beginning of the season, and so it didn't take long for the air to warm or for the snow to melt once the season started.

After they got a hefty fire going, Rella added some green for whiter smoke. Kal retrieved a damp blanket from Elara's bed and held it over the flames. As soon as the smoke ceased, he swiftly removed the blanket, resulting in a billow of white smoke rising into the sky. Kal started the process over again, sending several signals into the air.

While Kal was busy, Rella went to get more firewood. It could take a while for anyone to see the smoke signal, and so they could be at this for some time. As she passed the wagon, there was a pungent stench. Spoiled goods, she figured. Likely, some of the livestock had gone off before Kal had time to eat it all. The smell would attract insects and larger predators now the snow was clearing. The best thing to do would be to burn it as part of the fire.

She went to open the wagon to see what they were dealing with. Then a voice stopped her. "Don't," Kal said.

Rella turned to face him. His crossbow was pointed right at her.

"Don't do anything to make me shoot you. My people don't like damaged goods." Kal sneered, his yellow, decayed teeth on display.

Rella's stomach churned as the realization of Kal's intentions sank in. "You trade human beings?"

"Indeed, and many men will be starving for a woman's company after these cold winter months."

Cold fear washed over Rella, causing her hands and feet to turn numb.

"Now that I'm better, I must get back to work. You're young and healthy. Not beautiful, but pretty. You'll sell for a decent enough amount."

"You're doing this to me after I saved your life," she reminded him.

"Business is necessary," he replied with a shrug. "Now, throw down your bow and arrows!"

Rella unfastened her bow and arrows slowly and then let them drop to the ground.

"Now the knife."

"Which one?"

"All of them!"

Rella removed two knives from her trouser pockets and dropped them on the ground before slowly opening her coat to reveal another knife, which she reluctantly surrendered. "That's them all."

As Kal swaggered closer, Rella's heart raced with panic. But as he lowered his weapon slightly, she quickly drew the knife from her boot and threw it directly at Kal's face. The knife lodged itself into his eye, and he died almost instantly.

Rella shivered. She had thought that she was done for.

Turning to the wagon, she approached and opened the doors at the back. The smell grew stronger. The cart was full of people's clothes and skeletal remains, the bones stained dark with blood.

As she looked closer, she could see deep gouges in the bones where teeth had attempted to devour every bit of flesh. Rella felt a deep sense of horror and disgust. Among the remnants were the bones and skulls of children. It was the left-overs of Kal's goods—the remnants of those he had eaten.

III

All Rella could think about as she ran was whether or not Elara had been eaten by that monster. She dashed back through the forest to her village to tell Alioth of what had happened.

Since the return of the Omi, life was more fragile than ever, but Rella never imagined she would lose her only friend.

Even when teenagers, the two spent a lot of their time in the forest, climbing trees, learning to hunt, and talking about bringing down the Omi—they were both dreamers. Now older, they still hunted in the forest together sometimes. Elara was the only person, aside from Alioth, who knew that Rella's father had been the Governor of Eden.

The shrubs at Rella's feet were distorted, as though they had been flattened by something heavy. Rella knelt and studied the bushes and small trees. Many footprints had passed through the woods. Only the Omi's Enforcers traveled in such large packs.

Then, Rella had a terrible thought—the two Enforcers she had seen in the woods were heading to her own village, not for Elara's cabin.

She dashed the rest of the way at an even faster pace. But as she approached the outskirts of her village, Rella knew immediately she was too late.

The Enforcers had been there, and everyone now lay dead.

IV

His body was buried.

Rella fixed the shovel into the exposed mud and rested against it, sighing deeply. She straightened her back and wiped the sweat from her forehead, then grasped the wood marker she had carved with Alioth's name and stuck it into the soil above him.

Now that he was gone, Rella was lost in an impenetrable forest. He was the one who gave her purpose, and now for a second time, the Omi had taken everything from her. The Enforcers hadn't even spared the children.

Rella's heart sank with guilt, since it had probably been her the Omi were looking for when they came to the village. As the ex-Governor's daughter, she always feared the Omi would come looking one day to finish off her bloodline. Guilt was the only emotion melting the icicle in her chest. Death was becoming all too common, and now it only made her numb.

Fortunately, the Omi hadn't found what Alioth kept beneath his bedroom floorboards.

Her only hope now was that Elara was still out there somewhere. Perhaps she had decided to leave before winter with her father, and they had never even met Kal.

Rella scanned the green field surrounding the grave and decided there was plenty of space to dig the rest of the townspeople a burial spot. With the sun on her back, she picked up her bow and quiver of arrows, threw them over her shoulder, and walked to the main square.

The town was a small gathering of brick homes within an open valley. A large main square was in the center of town, where weekly markets were held, allowing people to sell and trade their goods. The valley was surrounded by an endless scene of trees and hills, as well as steep mountains, with rocky crags, which rose between beautiful lakes and streams.

A cooling wind blew between the empty homes, swaying open doors. The gust carried the stench of decomposing corpses. Bodies lay scattered across the courtyard in alleyways and doorways. Rella stood in the center of it, without another living being in sight.

She stepped across the cobblestones of the square, passing her old neighbors. She noticed the daughter of the baker, a young brunette girl who reminded her of herself, lying motionless on the ground in front of Rella's doorway. A deep gash, caused by a sword, was visible on the girl's forehead. Rella carefully stepped over her and pushed open the flimsy door of her home, entering inside.

Rella gazed at her reflection in the mirror, her cheeks flushed by the chilly wind. Her disheveled hair was in a similar state of disrepair to her clothes, which were tattered and stained. The latest addition to her soiled shirt was a hole, the result of a branch encountered on her last hunting expedition.

In the reflection of the mirror was the courtyard behind, including the lifeless body of the baker's daughter lying in front of her door. Suddenly, she noticed a man standing across the square, staring directly at her.

Heart racing and beads of sweat forming on her forehead, Rella grabbed the bow from over her shoulder. She pulled out an arrow from the quiver and spun to aim at the man in the square, ready to fire if he presented himself as any threat.

Standing on the cobblestones, he looked past thirty years old, dressed in an olive top and khaki pants, with dirty-blond hair. His face was flushed, and he walked with the aid of a cane. In his other hand, he carried a rolled-up rug, and something wrapped in a blood-soaked blanket.

"Who are you?" she yelled. "Are you Omi? An Enforcer?"

The man didn't flinch at the sight of the arrow aimed at his head. Instead, he held up the rolled-up rug and she realized it wasn't a rug, but a monk's robe. The monk replied in a gentle voice, "I'm looking for Elara. Does she live in this town?"

Her heart skipped a beat. What could a monk want with Elara? "She did. Everyone's dead now."

"I can see that." There was a pause. Then: "I'll be on my way."

The monk stepped back towards the alley from which he emerged. She was about to be alone again.

But Rella couldn't let him go just yet. Lowering her bow and arrow, she dashed after him, shouting, "Stop!"

He turned to face her.

"What do you want with Elara?" she asked.

"I came to take her somewhere safe from the Omi, but I guess I'm too late."

"Nowhere is safe from the Omi."

"I know a place."

Rella furrowed her brow. It was impossible that anywhere was safe from the Omi. Anyone who dared to ignore their laws ended up like her village, or worse, locked away in one of their torture camps.

"I heard the Enforcers were coming for her," the monk went on. "I was hoping to get here first, but I can see that I failed."

"How do you know Elara?"

"I'm looking for Countess Rella," the monk said, freezing her to the spot. It had been ten years since anyone referred to her as a Countess. "Elara is the only known connection to the Countess. They were friends as children."

Rella felt her mouth go dry. She pulled herself together and said, "There's no Countess anymore. Her father was executed by the Omi, and she's most likely now dead as well."

The monk flashed a slight smile. "I don't think so."

"What do you want with her?"

"I have something for her."

"What?"

"That's for her eyes." The monk then looked over his shoulders cautiously. "Is there somewhere else we can talk? I worry I may have been followed."

"Elara's house is just outside town," Rella told him. "It's empty now and secluded."

"Are you sure Elara's not there?"

"Yes, I just came from there."

"Would you take me?"

Rella studied him for a moment, and then nodded.

"I appreciate it," he said.

"Are you alone?"

The monk shook his head. "My companion is waiting for me on the main road. I came to request directions."

"I'll be right back, and then we'll go."

The man offered another smile, and Rella hurried back into her home. She went into Alioth's room, knelt down, and tore out the loose floorboards. Beneath them, there lay a wooden case—skinny and long—with rusty metal fastenings, which she retrieved and carried with her.

The memory of what happened last time she trusted a strange man flashed through her head, but she pushed it aside; her father had told her to never let the actions of a few lessen her view of humanity as a whole. Besides, she knew how to protect herself if the worst should happen.

"Let's go," she said, upon reuniting with the monk.

The man's eyes glanced towards the case she now carried, but he didn't enquire about it. She left the square and entered an alleyway. The monk followed her.

"I'm Brother Eric," he said, as they walked down the narrow passageway between the brick houses. "Thank you for showing me to Elara's home. Once I'm there, I won't stick around too long. I don't want to get you in trouble."

"Why would I be in trouble if you stuck around?"

"There are dangerous people after me."

"Who?" she asked.

"The Omi."

Chapter Two

I

XXX Days Earlier

Brother Eric slaved across the sands of Tyrin under the intense sun on his way back to the Monastery. He hadn't bothered to ask the name of the young novice by his side. They should have had a bodyguard present, but it was an expense the Monastery couldn't afford. Attacks by bandits were common in the deserts, though Eric took comfort in the fact that they weren't carrying anything of value and that it was punishable by death to place a hand on a monk under the Omi's rule.

Their trip to the villages had been completely futile. The task before them was to spread stories of the Creator's wrath, thus ensuring people lived in accordance with the Creator's doctrine and that they feared the consequences of doing otherwise. The problem was people were more concerned by their current existence than with what might transpire next. If a man was starving, he would rather steal some food than go hungry, even if it meant his soul would never reach the Holy World.

The Monastery claimed the purpose of monks was to educate, but Eric failed to identify any meaning to his life. Truthfully, if he was killed by a gang of bandits in the desert now, it would make no difference to anyone or anything.

"Brother Eric, I must confess," the young novice said.

Eric suppressed a groan. Some monks took pleasure in having a novice shadow their every step, but not Eric. If he had been traveling alone, he would have disrobed for some relief, but the novice seemed like the kind of pious dought who'd report any minor transgression.

"Only a senior monk can offer absolution," Eric replied. "Save your confession for Brother Guin or some other luckless sod."

"Please, Brother Eric. This is really wearing down on my chest. I will seek absolution later."

Eric sighed. "What is it?"

"I have sinned."

"Yes, go on."

"When we were at the inn, there was a pretty girl at the table next to us."

"And you slept with this girl?"

The novice shook his head. "No, Brother."

"What then?"

"Nothing. It was just something I noticed."

"What are you confessing then?"

"Lust is a sin."

Eric pressed his lips. "There is an important distinction to be made between actions and thoughts. You didn't act on these thoughts?"

"Well, later that night…"

"Yes?"

"I thought about her again."

"And?"

"I imagined what it might be like to be intimate with her."

"And you enjoyed these fantasies?" Eric asked. "You didn't try to rid them from your mind?"

"I don't think I had much control over the matter, Brother."

"Why's that?"

"I don't usually have control over my dreams."

"Dreams?" Eric gave an exasperated sigh. "You mean you were asleep?"

The novice nodded.

"Don't confess things that happen when you're asleep, halfwit."

"Why not, Brother?"

"If every monk confessed their dreams, the Monastery would be empty."

"Are you telling me that every monk is guilty of lust or of some other sin?" The novice crossed his arms. "I've never seen the abbot stare at a woman."

"You've never seen him crap either, but he does."

The novice furrowed his eyebrows and Eric couldn't tell if it was more out of disapproval or disgust.

Eric didn't much notice women, but he knew other monks did. Being a monk was easy for Eric, not because he was devout, but because he simply had no interest in typical temptations like sex, drugs, or alcohol.

Before the novice could say anything further, Eric stopped in his tracks and grabbed hold of him. There was a white figure ahead, ambling among the sand dunes.

"What is it, Brother?" the novice asked.

Eric shushed him and lowered him behind a rock. He peered over to see an old man dressed in white rags, with a cane and white beard. Immediately, he relaxed; the old man was unlikely to belong to a gang of bandits.

"It's just an old man." The novice stood and approached. "He may need shelter."

Eric went to stop him, but the old man had already spotted the novice. The Monastery no longer had the resources to provide permanent residence to newcomers as it once had for Eric, but it might be able to spare a bowl of watery soup and a bed for the night.

"Greetings," the novice said, "and many blessings to you."

The old man swung his cane up as if to use as a weapon, then relaxed once his failing eyes caught a good look at them. "Are you both men of the Creator?"

"Indeed, we are." The novice smiled. "What brings you out this way?"

"I'm on a mission. Perhaps two monks could assist."

"What mission?" Eric stepped forward.

"Wait a minute." The old man put out his palm. "How can I trust that you are who you claim to be and are not just disguised in monk's clothing? You could have attacked and ate two monks for all I know."

"We really are monks, good sir," the novice said. "We can take you to the Monastery for food and shelter."

The old man gripped hold of his cane and looked as though he might start dancing on the spot. "Really? You mean it?"

Eric nodded. "Besides, if we were bandits, we'd have attacked and killed you already."

"That's true," the old man replied. "Only monks would be stupid enough to greet and bless a stranger in these forsaken parts of the desert."

"So, what's the mission?" Eric asked.

"I'm delivering words of the Creator to the Omi's Sanctuary. First, though, I need to visit Eden to acquire the help of a Countess. She too is needed at the Sanctuary."

"I see, you know a Countess." Eric tried to keep from sighing. "These words, do they come from a voice in your head?"

"I'm not crazy," the old man snapped. "The message I deliver has been written down, and not by me."

"How do you know they're the Creator's words?"

"Look for yourself and you'll see there's no doubt." The old man pointed with his cane towards a small opening made of sandstone between the dunes.

"The words are in there?"

The old man nodded. "It's where I've been sleeping. I needed to rest before continuing my journey. I was out here looking for lizards for my supper when you spotted me."

Eric and the novice stepped towards the cave. Eric turned back to see the old man was not following them. "You aren't coming?"

The man rubbed his bony thigh. "My old legs have walked enough."

Eric peered into the cavern cautiously, but he could see no sign of snakes, scorpions, or other potential dwellers.

The novice clasped his shoulder and whispered, "What if it's a trap, Brother?"

"What kind of trap?"

"You heard the old man, he's starving. He may mean to trap us in this cave and then eat our starved corpses."

"You have a very suspicious mind," Eric replied. "I don't believe the old man wishes us any harm."

"Why not?"

"He seemed quite happy when you offered him soup and a bed at the Monastery. If you were in his position, would you rather not accept a bowl of soup than murder and eat two monks?"

"I suppose, Brother."

"And besides, the old man says that the Creator's words are inside this cave. That means the Creator is calling us here, and it's our duty as monks to answer that call."

"You're right, Brother." The novice lowered his head. "Please forgive me."

"Like I said, I can't offer you absolution. But I'm sure you'll recant it to Brother Guin."

"Do you think that's necessary?" the novice asked.

"That's up to you, but he'd rather hear about this than hear confessions over your wet dreams."

The novice went red with embarrassment, and Eric ushered him into the cave. As their eyes adjusted to the dimness, enough sunlight filtered through to reveal a tattered blanket on the ground where the old man had been sleeping, and a gold tablet placed next to it. The name *Marko* was embroidered on the blanket.

Eric reached down to pick up the tablet. It was about the size of a large book, and as he examined it, he could feel its intricate engravings under his fingertips.

"Those are hieroglyphics!" the novice exclaimed. "It's how they recorded the Creator's words in the Holy World. The old man was right."

"I know what hieroglyphics are," Eric snapped. "Unfortunately, I don't know anyone who can decipher their meaning."

"One of the novices can."

Eric narrowed his eyes at the young novice. "How would a novice monk know how to translate ancient hieroglyphics?"

"Aaron isn't training to be a monk," the novice said. "He's studying to be an architect at the Monastery, and he's about to become a master. I'm not sure where he learned to read hieroglyphics, but I know that he can. He's translated prayers for Brother Guin."

"Will you take me to him once we arrive back at the Monastery?"

The novice nodded. "Of course, but why? The old man said that it was his mission to deliver the tablet, not ours."

"I believe we were led to this tablet for a reason. And it's no coincidence that you happen to know someone who can translate hieroglyphics."

"You think this is part of the Creator's design?" the novice asked. "Why would he choose us to deliver His message?"

"Don't ask questions like that. We are led where destiny leads us."

Eric wrapped the heavy tablet in the old man's blanket and they exited the cave. They glanced over to where the old man had been standing, but there was no sign of him. Eric scanned across the sand dunes—the old man had disappeared without a trace. There weren't even any footprints to indicate which way he might have gone.

"Maybe he was an angel," the novice said as they walked.

"I've never heard of an angel needing a cane." Eric felt ready to collapse, carrying the weight of the tablet under his arm.

The novice frowned and they said no more on the subject.

Truthfully, Eric didn't care if the old man had been human or not. He had fulfilled his role by setting Eric and the novice on their path, and that was all that mattered. Still, Eric did not think the man had been an angel. He had said that his old legs had walked enough, and now Eric understood that the old man sent them into the cave not to have a look at the tablet, but because he needed someone else to take over his long and wearing journey. Plus, Eric didn't think angels were likely to have their names embroidered on their blankets. The lack of footprints could be explained by the wind or if the old man had simply walked on Eric and the novice's prints in the sand.

"Why do you think the Creator has entrusted us with such an important task?" the novice asked, eyeing the tablet under Eric's arm.

"I thought I told you not to ask questions like that."

"Sorry." The novice slumped his shoulders. "I just can't believe that He would choose me for anything special."

"Why is that?" Eric asked.

"My parents said I was too weak to work on their farm, so they gave me as a gift to the Monastery."

"Why would they do that?"

"They hoped the Creator would bless them with good fortune in return." The novice's lip quivered. "It was the only way I could be a blessing to my family. But instead, Brother Guin told them that I was a flawed gift and that the Creator punishes those who give flawed gifts. He said I was stupid and incompetent, and that my family would never receive His blessings because of me."

Suddenly, Eric felt guilt for insulting the novice earlier. "Brother Guin's an ass."

The young novice tried to suppress a smile. "You shouldn't say such things about a senior monk."

Eric shrugged. "Even if it's true?"

"How did you end up joining the Monastery, Brother?"

"I had no family. The monks found me out here alone in the desert and offered me sanctuary."

"You must have had a family at some point?"

"At some point, yes. They were heretics."

The novice raised an eyebrow. "I thought the heretics died centuries ago."

"Not all of them."

The novice still seemed confused. "What *is* a heretic, Brother?"

"Someone who is non-converted."

"You mean they don't follow the words of the Creator?"

"Some of them don't even believe there is a Creator."

This seemed incomprehensible to the novice.

The Monastery was now visible in the distance, and Eric couldn't help but marvel at its size. Built into the side of a mountain range, the sandstone buildings included a grand place of worship, workplaces for the monks and nuns, a learning institute where students became masters of their chosen trade, and enough dorms to house thousands of people.

Just then, Eric heard a whooshing noise. His heart sank; he knew exactly what it was. He looked to see two bandits had appeared atop a sand dune beside them. In the desert, bandits wore colors representing their clans, and these two were no exception. They donned light brown armor and leather, along with hooded purple shawls, and brown masks to retain moisture, a common practice among desert dwellers. One of them swung three weights in the air tied on the end of three interconnected ropes, known as bolas, used to capture animals and entangle big birds. The other bandit held a bone knife, poised to attack.

Locking eyes with Eric, the knife-wielding bandit slid down the dune in pursuit. Eric told the novice to run. The novice looked over his shoulder and gasped in fright. The weight of the tablet slowed Eric down, so the novice quickly sprinted ahead.

The bolas whizzed through the air and ensnared the novice's legs, causing him to trip and fall face-first into the sand.

Eric quickly helped him up and told him to keep running.

"We can't outrun them," the novice said. "Maybe we should try and reason with them."

"No," Eric said firmly. "We must protect the tablet at all costs."

The bandit's knife suddenly plunged into the novice's jugular. Eric recoiled in horror as the young man's body fell to the ground, the bandit swiftly retrieving his weapon.

The bandit demanded to know what was inside the blanket.

Eric tried to make a run for it, but the bandit lurched with his knife. Eric slammed the tablet against the bandit's arm and the knife dropped to the sand. The bandit bent to retrieve it and Eric brought the tablet down on his head as hard as he could, then again and again until the sand was painted with the bandit's skull and blood.

The other bandit watched from atop the sand dune. Eric picked up the knife and held it into the air to show that he was now armed, while the bandit was not. As he hoped, the bandit thought twice about attacking and he disappeared down the other side of the sand dune, possibly to get reinforcements.

Eric sprinted with all his might, holding the tablet tightly against his chest, the blanket now soaked in blood. The Monastery wasn't much further. He glanced over his shoulder at the novice's body and wished he was able to take it for a proper burial, but he couldn't risk the bandits catching up and stealing the tablet. Eric was now surer than ever that delivering this tablet was his destiny. He had just committed a terrible sin. For the first time in his life, he had taken another person's life. If he lost the tablet now, then his sin and the novice's death had all been for nothing.

The ground beneath him broke away. Eric fell through a hole into a small underground cavern. He felt his ankle pop and he yelled in pain. He felt it to check whether it was broken. Luckily, it was only sprained.

His eyes drifted to the tablet, which lay before him in the small ditch. As he reached for it, a bee whizzed past his hand. Eric looked closer. The bright tablet was attracting several desert bees and he realized he was lying at the entrance to their nest. Within seconds, dozens of them had landed on the tablet.

First the bandits. Then his ankle. Now the bees. Eric realized his faith was being tested. He could crawl out of the cave to safety and leave the tablet behind, but he would never fulfill his destiny. The bandit's friends could be close behind and they would be the ones to recover the tablet if he didn't take it now.

Eric reached for the tablet and a bee flew up and landed on his face. It crawled across his cheek and stung him. He clenched his teeth and groaned, but he didn't have time to lick his wounds. A couple more bees came to rest on his face. The pricks from their tiny stingers increased in number and intensity. He punched through the swarm to grab the tablet, enduring more stings as he did so. Eric leapt to his feet with the tablet in hand and pulled himself out of the ditch.

He crawled to the surface and swung his arms around like a mad man to scare away the bees. Eric attempted to run to safety, but he nearly collapsed to his knees with the pain from his ankle. He could barely hobble. For a moment, he thought he was going to be sick. He clenched his hands in the sand, willing himself to move forward.

Eric inched himself closer and closer to the Monastery, the bees still following and stinging him, his ankle throbbing. A fierce wind wailed across the desert from a small sandstorm, blowing sand into his eyes and knocking him from his feet, but at least it propelled the bees away. He stared up into the sky and saw a couple of vultures circling overhead.

Not today, he said to himself.

He didn't have the energy to stand so he dug his hand into the sand and dragged himself forward for what seemed like hours. The Monastery was now only a stone's throw away. No matter what happened next, Eric was ready for it, because finally his life had been given a purpose—he was going to deliver the Creator's words to the Omi's Sanctuary.

II

Eric slowly sank into a chair in Brother Guin's office and squirmed in discomfort. The masters of medicine had applied an ointment to his skin, causing his robe to cling uncomfortably to his body whenever he sat down. Eric placed down the walking stick he had been given and turned his attention to Brother Guin at the other side of the desk. Despite being of similar age, Brother Guin appeared as if he could be Eric's future self, with his fair complexion and wispy blond hair, albeit now mostly bald.

Brother Guin's deep blue eyes stared Eric up and down. "You have blood on your robe."

"The novice's blood. We were attacked by bandits upon our return."

Eric didn't tell him about the bandit's blood. It was a sin to lie, but Eric would ask the Creator for forgiveness later. If he told Brother Guin about committing murder, then he would be forced to repent via months of isolation. Eric didn't have time for that; he had a mission to fulfill.

"You escaped these bandits?" Guin asked skeptically. "How?"

"I suppose the Creator has something else in store for me."

"Don't mistake coincidence for fate." Brother Guin didn't tolerate self-importance from monks, perhaps because he himself had hoped for a higher position by now. He had assisted the Omi with their rise back to power in hopes of becoming a bishop, but none of his dreams had come true. "I suspect you simply got lucky."

Eric nodded, feigning agreement with Guin's bitter remarks as if they were pearls of wisdom.

"Anyway, why did you want to see me?"

"I found something in the desert." Eric unwrapped the gold tablet from the blood-soaked blanket and presented it to Brother Guin. "Words of the Creator."

Brother Guin inspected the tablet with mild curiosity on his face. "How do you know it's words of the Creator?"

"Those hieroglyphics are from the Holy World." Eric pointed to the engravings. "Also, there was an old man in the desert who told us they were the Creator's words. He instructed us to deliver the tablet to the Omi's Sanctuary. Then he disappeared." It was close enough to the truth.

Guin placed down the tablet. "What do you mean he disappeared?"

"I don't know how else to explain it. He was there, and then he wasn't."

"Are you suggesting that this man was an angel?" Guin looked as though he was on the verge of laughter.

"He was a messenger sent by the Creator, that's all I know," Eric said.

Brother Guin's expression remained doubtful. "And how do you know that for certain?"

"Afterwards, I was tested. That's why the bandits attacked us. They wanted the tablet, but I refused to give it up. Then I sprained my ankle and was attacked by bees. Then there was a sandstorm."

"Maybe the Creator didn't want you to have the tablet, after all."

"No," Eric argued. "The Creator was testing my commitment to my mission."

"What mission?"

"To deliver the tablet to the Sanctuary."

"You'll do no such thing," Brother Guin said sternly.

Eric felt a knot in his stomach. "Why not?"

"You're needed here, and monks are told what to do and where to go by their superiors, not by old men in the desert who may or may not be angels."

"But the tablet must reach the Sanctuary so it can be studied and protected."

"And it will," Guin said. "The Omi sent a party of Enforcers to Eden's highlands in order to retrieve a Pure Blood."

"A Pure Blood?" Eric didn't think there were any Pure Bloods remaining.

"Yes, a young woman. She's been hiding within a town called Culloden."

"Never heard of it."

"Exactly. The Enforcers will be passing through here on their way back, and they will require monks to assist with the sacrifice. You can deliver the tablet to them as a gift on our behalf." With that, Guin threw the tablet back to Eric.

"The Creator has chosen me for this mission," Eric asserted.

"Frankly, I am not convinced. Bandits, bees, and sandstorms hardly seem like clear signs from the Creator. Your desire for glory is a sin, Brother Eric, and I order you to reflect upon this before confession. After you confess your sins, I will devise appropriate repentance. Now, return to the dormitories. We're finished here."

Eric stood with the help of his walking stick and left with the tablet, but not to go to the dormitories.

Chapter Three

I

CCXXI (X Years Ago)

Aaron stood outside his father's sitting room, gathering the courage to knock on the door. His father Robert Walden did not like to be interrupted. If Aaron entered to collect his papers, he was likely to cause an uproar. Even at the age of fifteen, Aaron was afraid of his father, who could bellow so loud that half of Eden could hear him.

His father was a successful man, but not an educated one. He had fought valiantly for Queen Shanleigh against the Omi, helping her take control of Eden. Aaron too would have liked to become a warrior, but he had neither the strength nor stamina of his father. He struggled to even carry a heavy sword and he had lost just about every fight he had gotten into with the local children. This was much to his father's disappointment. Aaron's brother Elijah, on the other hand, was two years younger and was already both taller and stronger. Their father would always celebrate Elijah's victories in fights. Aaron had to remind himself that at least he was smarter than his brother, whom he could always outwit in an argument, much to Elijah's frustration.

Once the war was over, Robert had been awarded a home within the City of Eden for him and his family as thanks for his service. Robert had not wanted to move there, but Aaron's mother Claudia had convinced him on the account that she'd feel safer within the walls of a city than living in the countryside. Claudia was a redhead, meaning she was most likely a Pure Blood—those whose ancestors arrived from the Holy World. During the Omi's regime, Pure Bloods had been caught and slaughtered as sacrifices to the Creator for certain rituals. They, therefore, traditionally lived in camps together for protection around the highlands of Eden. Queen Shanleigh had put an end to this barbaric practice, and Aaron suspected that was what motivated his father to fight for her, as he had never shown much interest in religious freedom.

Currently, Robert was having a discussion with Walter Ifran, one of the city's newest arrivals. Aaron's family made their money these days by sourcing wool and selling it to the city. At first, everyone had a need for new clothes following the war and the move to the city. However, things were not as prosperous anymore, and they could no longer afford meat for every meal like they used to. Walter had come from the lowlands of Eden, further than Aaron's family currently sourced. Robert was curious to hear if the place was worth exploring to acquire cheaper wool.

Aaron took a deep breath and gently struck the door.

"Come in!" his father roared.

Aaron stepped inside. Both men sat by the open window, enjoying Robert's homemade beer. Walter wore a richly colored tunic, a cloak, and jewelry to show his wealth. He had clearly brought sought-after merchandise with him to the city. It was quite a shame that Robert was a clothing merchant, yet his tunic was noticeably more worn and faded than Walter's.

"Oh, it's you. What do you want?"

"Sorry to disturb you, but I just came for my papers." Aaron pointed shyly to the desk, where a few scraps of paper resided.

"Well, hurry up and get them."

As Aaron dashed to collect the papers, he noticed Walter scan his sketches. The guest crouched forward. "What have you got there?"

Aaron pressed his papers to his chest and shuffled his feet. "It's nothing, sir."

Walter gently pried the drawings from his hands and examined them. "Looks like plans for a sundial."

Robert shook his head, clearly mystified as to why such a successful man would take any interest in his son, a boy who was strange to even him. "Be gone, Aaron. Mr. Ifran has no interest in your childish pictures."

"Actually, I'm quite interested." Walter laid the drawings out on the table. "Can you explain them to me, Aaron?"

Aaron cleared his throat. "It works similarly to a sundial, but it's better because it won't rely on shadows to indicate what point of the day it is. So it'll work even if it's cloudy or during the winter."

"People use sandglasses during winter." Walter shrugged as though he wasn't impressed. "In fact, in the lowlands of Eden, I've even seen people use candles to tell time. They make markings on the candles and then know what time it is based on how much of the candle has burned away."

"Now that's a clever idea," Robert remarked.

Aaron stopped himself from rolling his eyes. "I plan to build a tower, a large one, where a dial will move along the face, indicating the time of day. A bell will also ring at specific intervals, so even those who can't see the tower will know the time. It's a more convenient and accurate way to tell time than relying on candles and people won't have to go home to check their sandglasses."

Robert dismissed the idea with a scoff, but Walter leaned in with interest and asked, "How will the dial move?"

"It will be powered by a water wheel located at the bottom of the tower." Aaron gestured to his sketch. "The water will be collected in buckets, and as the weight of the water increases, the dial will move accordingly."

"That's amazing." Walter turned his attention to Robert. "That son of yours has a grand talent. What school does he attend?"

"The local one, of course."

"That's no school for a genius."

Aaron thought his father was going to choke on his beer. "My son is not a genius, Walter."

"The boy should be educated properly," Walter said. "My sister's son is a monk at the Monastery. I could put in a good word for Aaron so he could be enrolled at their school. There, he could become a master of his chosen craft, and learn to read and write at an advanced level."

"For what purpose?" Robert asked. "My son is to become a wool merchant."

"Nonsense." Walter waved him off. "The boy is clearly destined to be an architect, and for that, he must become a master."

Aaron was thrilled to have someone pay him so much attention. He wondered though, if he was to become a master at the Monastery, would he have to restrain himself from sex as the monks did? He decided to save that question for another time.

"Tell me, Aaron, what are you doing this afternoon?"

Aaron shrugged. "I was going to play with my brother, sir."

"Do you and your brother fight?"

"No, sir. He just wins if we fight."

Robert smiled at this.

"Then what do you play?" Walter said.

"I like to tell him stories, sir."

"Stories?"

"Yes, sir. About the Omi's war and about the heretics."

Walter tilted his head and narrowed his eyes. "What do you know about the heretics?"

"I believe they must have had a means of telling time that was more precise than candles."

"I think you're probably right." Walter gave a sly smile, and Aaron almost forgot that talking about the innovations of the heretics was still considered by some as heresy. "Do you like stories, Aaron?"

"Yes, sir. Very much."

Robert shook his head. "A true man makes his own story. He doesn't indulge in fantasy."

Aaron didn't understand his father's statement at all. He found no greater joy than in stories; it was his means of understanding and connecting to the world.

Walter seemed to ignore Robert's comment and said, "In my home, you will find a great number of stories. Would you like to visit there with me?"

Aaron furrowed his brows, confused, yet intrigued. "Yes, sir. I'd like that very much."

That afternoon, Walter Ifran led Aaron to his home in the palace grounds. Walter's home was almost as large as the palace itself and was built from newer bricks. Aaron found it unusual that the Governor would permit a merchant to build upon his land, then realized that the Governor must immensely value the worth of whatever Walter was selling. Both Walter's home and the Governor's palace were protected by a moat, and Aaron and Walter had to cross a wooden bridge to reach there. Aaron noticed that the bridge appeared delicate and concluded that it was probably intentionally designed to be dismantled swiftly in the event of an attack.

Observing the windows on the exterior of the house, Aaron deduced that the residence had two stories, and he began to speculate on the number of rooms it could contain. At least eight, he counted. From what he had heard, Walter only had one child, and so he wondered why the family would require so much space.

They stepped into a small entrance hall with doors and hallways branching off in every direction, along with a staircase leading upstairs. Sitting atop the staircase was a girl reading silently, whom Aaron presumed was Walter's daughter. She was the most beautiful person Aaron had ever seen. Her eyes were a mesmerizing shade of green, and she had sleek brown hair that shimmered in the light. Her tunic was turquoise and costly, but she sported actionable leather boots rather than the pretty fabric shoes favored by most girls. It hadn't rained in several weeks, but Aaron noticed some dried mud on her soles that could have only come from walking along a riverbank. He wondered what a noble lady would be doing out in the forest. She glanced down briefly, and their eyes locked for a second, during which Aaron realized it was as if he had dreamed of this girl before, even though he had never met her until now.

The girl, only a little younger than him, quickly snapped her book shut and dashed upstairs out of sight. There was something unusual about the book she had been reading. All the books he had seen were related to the Creator and were published by the Monastery. This book looked older, and it seemed to have a navy hardcover rather than the normal black leather binding, though it may have just been the light playing tricks.

Walter led him past the staircase, down the labyrinth of hallways. "You must be careful whom you tell about what you see here, Aaron. There's still a lot of people in Eden who won't like it." With a creak, he opened a door, unveiling a vast hall filled with nothing but tightly packed bookshelves.

Aaron couldn't believe his eyes. He didn't think there were this many books in the whole of Arcadia. The shelves were brimming with books of every size and color.

"What is this place?" Aaron asked.

"It's the first library within the highlands of Eden," Walter said with a proud smile.

"What's a library?"

"A collection of stories."

"I don't understand. Are all these books about the Creator?"

Walter shook his head. "Not all books are related to doctrine. These are stories like the ones you tell your brother. They're tales of history and fantasy. Every book serves as a gateway to a different world, providing new insight into the human experience."

"How old are they?" Aaron rubbed his forehead. "Where did they come from?"

"Most of these books were written by heretics before the Omi's reign. When such books became illegal, most were burned. However, some were fortunate enough to be saved and hidden in underground libraries across the lowlands. Now that knowledge sharing is permitted again, these books can be distributed to anyone who desires them."

Aaron felt Walter's eyes on him, but he wasn't sure what to say. He was frozen in wonder over how that many stories could exist, and he wanted to start reading them all immediately.

Walter grabbed him by the shoulders. "If those still loyal to the Omi find out about this library, they will burn it to the ground. That's why you must be very careful about who you tell, Aaron."

"Why do you trust me?" Aaron found himself asking.

"I need to trust people if I'm going to distribute these

stories, and you seem hungry to know about more than just what lies within these city walls. Once enough people have these books, the Omi's followers won't be able to stop the spread of these stories. They will live on in people's minds and hearts."

"You want me to have one?"

Walter nodded.

Aaron shuffled forward. "I don't know where to start."

"Then let me make a recommendation." Walter took a worn book with a green hardback from one of the shelves and handed it to him.

Aaron clutched it tightly and rubbed the thin layer of dust from the cover, realizing this book had survived hundreds of years so that generations could enjoy its story. It had well outlived whoever wrote it, allowing his or her soul to live on.

"What's the story about?" he asked.

"A village boy's attempts to build a bridge across a river."

Aaron thought back to Walter's comments about him becoming a Master of Architecture at the Monastery, realizing that Walter was trying to motivate him, especially after he heard about Aaron's plans for the time tower. "What lies beyond the river?"

"A girl from a neighboring village," Walter said. "The boy has admired her beauty from across the river for too long and builds the bridge so that they can meet and fall in love."

Aaron thought about the girl atop the staircase and his heart skipped a beat. "It sounds perfect, sir."

II

CCXXXI (Present)

A teacher rang a bell to signal noon and prompt everyone to pause work and gather with their families for prayer. It was two hundred and thirty-one years since the Omi had won the Great War. According to history lessons, their reign had gone uninterrupted during that time. After all, if the Omi were defeated once then they could be again, and so Queen Shanleigh's rebellion was an event that the Omi preferred to erase from people's memory.

Aaron viewed services as a distraction from his education and the only family he had was his mother. Both his brother and father had died heroically in defense of Eden against the Omi. Their deaths had been in vain: The Omi had still returned to power.

Later that night, the other novices would celebrate by drinking whatever beverages they had managed to acquire on their occasional trips to town. Aaron could not afford such luxuries. Instead of being paid for the work he did, the learning institute housed and fed both him and his mother. Claudia spent most of her days in the nunnery, teaching the youngest girls to read and write. Luckily, her hair had turned white long ago, so no one could tell she was a Pure Blood.

Aaron never felt like he was missing anything by not having money to spare like the other novices. After all, he had come to the Monastery's learning institute to learn and secure a better future, not to waste money on meaningless celebrations.

There were only a few weeks left of his noviceship and then Aaron would become a Master of Architecture. All that was left was the ceremony in which he would swear to use his knowledge to benefit society and then be rewarded with a yellow silk cape. This would grant him the freedom to work as an architect anywhere within Arcadia, and Aaron eagerly looked forward to leaving behind the restrictions imposed by the Monastery. Although he wasn't required to take vows of poverty and celibacy like the monks, all novices had to pledge their obedience. Morning and evening prayers were obligatory even outside the Monastery, but that was a law Aaron would happily break if there was no one around to notice.

Aaron's sole desire was to go back to Eden and search for Clare Ifran. He had been in love with her since the first moment he saw her. During their brief time together, he had been painfully shy, but, luckily, she hadn't shared his inhibitions. She had told him that she found him interesting and attractive, and one day, he had gathered enough courage to kiss her. Soon after that, the Omi had invaded and Aaron's mother had taken him away from the city and to the Monastery for safety.

Aaron felt his heart in his throat whenever he thought about these memories. The only time he prayed was when he retreated into his head and wished that he could relive that time of his life over and over again.

Since arriving at the Monastery, Aaron had tried to get to know other girls, but none had been able to shake his longing to return to Eden and search for Clare. No one else seemed able to replicate the feeling in his stomach that Clare had given him. With her, it had been as though his gut was wiggling and burning, but in a thrilling way that made him feel alive and walk with a bounce in his step.

Of course, Clare could have married someone else by now, and might barely remember him. If that was the case, it would hit him hard but at least he'd have the comfort of knowing she was happy. It was the unknown that was driving him out of his senses.

Before joining everyone else at services, Aaron gave the new dormitory they were building a final inspection. As the senior and most experienced novice working on the site, it was his responsibility to ensure that all the tools had been stored away safely. This was particularly crucial today, given that there would be several inebriated novices roaming around later in the night. The last thing Aaron wanted was for a careless drunk to pick up and play with any tools he had neglected to spot.

Satisfied that everything was appropriately stored away, Aaron turned to leave when he found a monk standing at the doorway. The monk's face was reddened and blistered, and he supported himself with the use of a cane.

"Are you Aaron?" the monk asked.

Aaron nodded hesitantly, worried he might be about to get in trouble for missing services. Monks seldom approached him, and he generally tried to steer clear of them. It wasn't that he disliked them, but their pious nature made him uncomfortable.

"I'm Brother Eric. I was told I might find you here."

"What can I help you with?"

"I was told that you've translated hieroglyphics for Brother Guin, and I was hoping you might assist me with something." Brother Eric unwrapped and presented a gold tablet from a blanket soaked in something red.

Aaron stepped closer. "You want me to translate this?"

"Yes, please." The monk handed him the tablet rather hurriedly. A bead of sweat dripped off the monk's forehead as he gave a wide grin. Aaron couldn't tell if the monk was nervous or excited.

Aaron had translated scrolls for Brother Guin, but never a tablet. Normally, the translations were of ancient prayers or hymns, but this one was different. It contained a picture of three columns, followed by a series of instructions: *Center. Underground. Right. Left. Left.* As he read through them, he realized that the tablet was actually a map.

"Well?" the monk exclaimed impatiently. "What does it say?"

"It's a list of directions."

The monk's eyes lit up. "To what?"

"I'm not sure." Aaron shrugged. "But the start point is three columns, arranged in the shape of a triangle."

"I've never seen such a structure."

"Me neither." Aaron handed him back the tablet. "Sorry I couldn't be of more help."

"Maybe it's at the Sanctuary." The monk's smile didn't drop. "You see, I found this tablet in the desert. An old man was supposed to be delivering it to the Sanctuary, but he tasked me with the job instead."

"Good luck," Aaron said, only because he wasn't sure what else to say.

The monk grabbed Aaron by the arm to stop him from leaving. "Wait. By your accent, I'd say you're from Eden. Am I right?"

Aaron nodded.

"What can you tell me about the Countess there?"

"Eden has no current Countess. The Governor's wife died long ago in childbirth, and he has only two sons."

Eric's smile dropped and he seemed to think deeply about this. "That can't be right. I'm supposed to be meeting with a Countess there before going to the Sanctuary. The old man said so."

Aaron couldn't tell if the monk was talking to him or to himself. "Sorry, but that's the truth. There hasn't been a Countess of Eden since before the Omi's takeover."

Eric's smile returned and his eyes lit back up. "Who was she?"

"Her name was Countess Rella."

"What happened to her?"

"Her father was executed by the Omi, but she was allowed to live. Killing a twelve-year-old girl for the crimes of her father would not have inspired loyalty to the Omi from her former subjects."

"Where is she now?"

"I'm not sure anyone knows."

"Who were her friends?"

"She was friends with a girl I knew, Clare. Her best friend was a Pure Blood called Elara."

"A Pure Blood?"

"Yes, they were different times. Before you ask, I don't know where Clare or Elara are either. I lost touch with everyone after leaving Eden."

"Don't worry. I know where to go now."

Aaron eyed him for a moment. "You know Clare? Or Elara?"

“The Omi's Enforcers are on their way to collect a young woman—a Pure Blood—from a town called Culloden in Eden. I suspect that's this Elara that you speak of.”

“Could be, there are barely any Pure Bloods left, but how can you be so sure?”

Eric only smiled, and Aaron assumed the monk was guided by faith or something equally incomprehensible. He could never understand how monks could be so sure that everything happened for a reason. In his opinion, people created their own destinies.

"Thank you for your help," the monk said.

Aaron furrowed his brows, ready to leave.

"There's just one more thing," Eric called.

Aaron turned back to face him. "What's that?"

"Brother Guin would like you to accompany me to Eden and then to the Sanctuary."

"What are you talking about?" Aaron asked shakily. It could be considered a crime to question the authority of a monk, but he couldn't possibly leave the Monastery. "Why would Brother Guin want me to help with such a task?"

Eric shrugged. "It's what has been ordained."

"I want to speak to Brother Guin."

"He's quite busy at the moment, and we don't have the time. He wants us to leave immediately."

"What about my mother?"

"What does she do?" Eric asked.

"She teaches at the nunnery."

"Don't worry, the nuns will look after her while you're gone."

"I can't leave the Monastery now," Aaron said. "In three weeks, I will become a master."

"Three weeks?" Eric asked. "That means you've already completed your training and exams. All that remains is for you to take your final vows."

"That's right."

"Then I can oversee that for you right now."

Aaron stepped back. He stammered, "I need to take these vows before an audience in a place of worship."

"Those things are immaterial." Eric waved his hand in the air. "All that matters is that you take the vows in front of a holy man. Now, you must swear to never teach what you've learned to anyone. All learning must occur within the Monastery and under the eye of the Creator. It is a sin to reveal knowledge outside the Monastery. Second, you must swear to only ever use the knowledge that you've been taught and to only ever conduct your work exactly as you remember having learned. It is a sin to compute or to have thoughts that weren't transpired by the Creator. Finally, you must swear to be content with your life as it has been given to you by the Creator and with the knowledge that you have been given. It is a sin to want more. Do you swear these things as I have said them?"

Aaron stood frozen for a moment. This wasn't how he imagined this happening, but he couldn't argue with being made a master or with being offered a chance to travel to Eden. "Yes, Brother. I swear to them."

"Then congrats and all that shit, you are a master."

Chapter Four

Sin gazed up at the night sky. The coffered dome covering the Omi's council chamber provided a central opening through which Sin could observe the cosmic display, a maze of bright stars, each of them showcasing just how small Arcadia was—nothing more than a grain of sand in a vast spiral galaxy.

Sin wondered, as he often did, whether his ancestors hailed from any of those celestial bodies, but like many non-human species, he had encountered very few of his own kind and had no knowledge of their origins. According to the Creator's texts, non-humans had always existed on Arcadia, but some held alternative views. Some believed that non-humans arrived on Arcadia during the era of the heretics or that the heretics themselves brought non-humans to the planet from the heavens. During the Omi's reign, it was heresy itself to say the heretics or that non-humans had been capable of such technology.

The council members were quietly conferring amongst themselves when Sin stood to face them. With his green-grey hand, he grasped the gavel and slammed it on the table several times, ending their conversation. The councilmen turned their attention to him.

Standing before them, Sin tried to look confident and strong, keeping his feet fixed to the floor, and hiding that his weakening legs often had the shakes these days. As the principal of the Omi's council, he couldn't afford to appear frail, even though the council had become just that. His face was covered in deep wrinkles and had become mottled, and his large, round eyes were weary and bloodshot, making the stress he had experienced all too evident.

"Order!" he addressed. "Meeting is now in session. Let's try and keep this quick. Monaro, we'll start with you."

Everyone's eyes turned to Monaro, the councilman in charge of tax collection. The Governors tallied taxes locally; Monaro was merely contacted by Governors to say if taxes had been collected.

"Vox is behind on taxes, sir," Monaro replied through his fabric face mask, something he wore due to his propensity for getting sick. He was also fully coated in an armored suit that protected his fragile body. "Shall we send a Security detail to fix the problem?"

Sin shuddered at the thought. Security were chosen as children and transformed into ruthless killing machines through relentless preparation. Their aim was to dispose of any threats to the Omi, jobs they did without any qualm of conscience, their training having long rid them of any compassion.

"Our only course of action is to inform the Omi's Head," Sin replied. "Depending on the amount of unpaid taxes, Security will be dispatched, or the Governor will be instructed to handle the matter personally."

"It's because Vox has nothing to offer," said Guid Neck, a blue creature in charge of overseeing the manufacture of weapons. His kind were knee-high and had the bodies of human babies, yet heads almost as large as that of a fully formed adult. Like the puzzle of how a bee's wings can carry such a heavy insect, it was equally wondrous how the tiny bodies of Guid Neck's species could support their heads.

"That is no excuse," said Commander Straumme, an elder human in charge of the Omi's army of Enforcers. "We should make an example out of them. If we do nothing, other territories will follow suit, and the Omi will soon lose its grip on power. Can you imagine the chaos? Revolts at every turn. It would be the end of the Omi. We must take action—"

Sin silenced him with a few slams of his gavel. "Will you hold your tongue, Commander Straumme? There have been no rebellions in a decade, precisely because the territories are largely unaware of what's happening in other regions, and it's best to keep it that way. Making an example out of an entire territory will only draw unnecessary attention."

Commander Straumme glared at Sin with seething anger. Sin was aware that the commander harbored a personal grudge against him. Straumme was not accustomed to taking orders or being talked down to. Unfortunately for him, giving orders and talking down to people gave Sin great pleasure. It was the only source of power he had left, and he held all the power within the council chamber.

"Which leads me to my point again. Why must I continue to oversee the manufacturing of weapons, when there is simply no more use for them?" questioned Guid Neck.

"We will continue to do our jobs until we are ordered to stop," Sin replied, not losing his assertive tone.

The large-headed non-human shook his face from side to side, unsatisfied with the answer, and each time he did, Sin thought the neck might give way.

"Has the situation within Tyrin improved?" Sin asked.

Monaro shook his head. "No, sir. There are still complaints of raids across the land."

"Not raids," Guid Neck said. "No crops, livestock, slaves, or treasures were taken. The people of the towns in Tyrin were merely slaughtered, along with everything else, and then their villages set ablaze."

"Perhaps it is local disputes over food or land," Sin suggested.

"Who cares?" Commander Straumme asked. "So long as the anger of these towns is with each other and not with the Omi, I consider it a blessing."

Sin shook his head at Straumme's callousness. "Is Security not taking care of it?"

"Apparently not," Monaro said. "But it's not local disputes. It's a sole attacker doing this damage, leaving behind only one survivor for every town they destroy. The survivors report a crazed warrior dressed in navy leather armor."

"Well, I'm afraid it's out of our jurisdiction. It's up to Security to deal with such matters. Our only job is to ensure these towns continue to pay taxes and follow the laws of the Omi," Sin replied.

"If an entire town is slaughtered, how are we supposed to ensure they pay taxes?" Straumme asked.

"I said it's out of our jurisdiction!" Sin too was frustrated with the lack of involvement from the Omi's Security, but he didn't dare say anything. He feared the Omi's Head as much as anyone, and he had never doubted the possibility of the meeting chamber containing a spy.

"Speaking of Tyrin, I have something else to share," Commander Straumme said.

"Yes?" Sin asked. "What is it?"

"Brother Guin has reported a monk gone rogue from the Monastery."

"A rogue monk?" Sin wasn't sure if he wanted to laugh or cry. "Is that really what we've been reduced to? Tracking down runaway holy men?"

"Apparently he took something with him of great value," Commander Straumme went on.

Sin waved his hand in the air. "I think this is a matter the Monastery can take care of themselves."

"The stolen object was a tablet with ancient writing. It was supposed to be delivered to the Omi's Sanctuary. The monk has since thought to have crossed into Eden, meaning this is a global issue. Brother Guin has insisted we take care of it immediately."

Sin kept himself from sighing. He was principal of the Omi's council—a council consisting of former world leaders and war legends—yet he was subordinate to a mere monk in the Omi's new age. "Very well. Commander Straumme, can I trust you to take care of the situation?"

"I'll make sure the monk is terminated and the tablet is reclaimed before the monk even knows I'm coming for him."

"I'm not sure there's any need for that. Just arrest him." Sin took a deep breath. No one dared break the silence. Then he spoke again: "So, Commander Straumme will keep us updated. For the meantime, meeting adjourned."

He slammed his gavel. The meeting was over.

Commander Straumme walked off with a grin.

"Did you hear me, Commander? Don't create a frenzy!" Sin yelled after him.

The elder commander kept walking, however, smiling to himself defiantly. When it came to enforcing the Omi's laws outside the chamber, Straumme was the one with the power.

Chapter Five

I

CCXXI (X Years Ago)

Rella gazed at her mother, a mix of confusion and fear clouding her thoughts about the uncertain days ahead. Her mother battled a relentless illness, and the outcome appeared to be bleak. Her skin was dry and lifeless. She was constantly thirsty, and no amount of water seemed to replenish her, likely because she was constantly vomiting.

Walter Ifran's nephew Brother Guin had arrived from the Monastery to look after her. He was a Master of Medicine, and he quickly dismissed the local elders, who had been providing Mother with home remedies. Rella thought Guin still had the face of a boy, yet his blond hair was already thinning. Like all monks, he wore a brown robe with a thick piece of rope tied around his waist. He dampened Mother's skin with a sponge from a bucket of hot water. She looked at Rella and smiled, but Rella could tell it was forced.

"I heard you leaving the house during the night," Mother croaked. "Where did you go?"

Rella worried Mother would know if she lied, but she couldn't tell her about what she had seen from the Eye; it would only cause her more stress. She decided it was best to tell part of the truth. "I was out playing with Elara and Clare. We were stargazing."

"How is my cousin?" Brother Guin asked.

"Clare?" Rella shrugged. "Fine."

"The Monastery has heard disturbing rumors about her father."

"What rumors?" Rella's father stood from his armchair in the corner of the room.

"That he's been spreading heretic knowledge."

Father's eyes shifted around the room, prompting Rella to speculate once more about what Clare's family had brought with them to the city and why Father had permitted them to build on his land within the moat's protection.

"Unfortunately, I wouldn't be surprised if the rumors were true," Guin said. "My uncle has always been outspoken, and my cousin never has known her place. She never wears dresses and she speaks without reserve as though she were a boy."

"What's wrong with not wearing dresses?" Rella asked.

"They are the appropriate attire for ladies."

Rella furrowed her brows and crossed her arms. "Who says Clare has to be a lady?"

"It is how the Creator has ordained it," Guin snapped.

Rella was about to argue some more but she caught sight of her father winking, indicating that she was wasting her breath.

"You should invite Elara for dinner," Mother said, probably trying to break the tension, her voice only getting more and more hoarse.

"Excellent idea," Father concurred. "There's no better company than that of children."

Brother Guin scrunched up his face as though he was sucking a lemon. He probably thought children should be seen and not heard as it was in the times of the Omi.

"I'll go and invite her." Rella went for her coat.

"Bring some cheese or honey as a gift for her family," Mother said.

Father always stressed the importance of assisting those we can when we can, so Rella nodded with a smile. When Rella inquired about why Elara's family was less fortunate than theirs, Father had explained that Elara's family, who were all redheads, had fled their camp during a raid on Pure Bloods, escaping with only the clothes on their backs. Thankfully, all redheads and Pure Bloods were safe under Father's protection in the City of Eden.

"You're welcome to stay for dinner too, Brother Guin," Father said.

"That is very gracious. Since I arrived from the Monastery, I've been surviving off the gruel they are serving at the local abbey," Guin replied. "That said, I already have plans to visit my family tonight."

"Shouldn't you be here looking after my mother?" Rella asked.

"Rella, don't be rude," Mother said. "Brother Guin has to eat."

"I'm here at your father's command, Lady Rella." Brother Guin gave a small bow. "However, your mother must be given time to rest. She will need it after I drain her blood."

"Drain her blood?"

"The infection resides in the blood. I must drain the blood if I'm to have any chance of saving your mother."

"Will you save her?" Rella asked.

"It would be presumptuous of me to predict the decisions of the Creator. All we can do is what we can. The rest is up to Him."

"Maybe we can do more, but we just haven't learned what that is yet."

"All the knowledge we require is within the texts of the Creator." Guin pointed his finger at her as though he was giving a lecture. "There is no reason to learn anything else."

"The heretics had to know something of importance," Rella argued. "Look at the structures they left behind. Even with the Creator's texts, we don't understand things the heretics did."

"That is insolence, Lady Rella, and you're dangerously close to spreading heresy. You may be the Governor's daughter, but I am a Master of Medicine and representative of the Creator. That means my words are His words."

"My daughter didn't mean to offend," Father quickly said. "She's just a curious child."

"She should visit the Monastery sometime and learn a few lessons."

"Or maybe I will seek out my own information. Then, I might be able to help people in my own ways." Rella turned to her mother and hoped for that to be her calling. But Guin laughed shrilly, covering his mouth with his hand. She pursed her lips. "What's so funny?"

"You're a lady, and your destiny will be to follow the commands of your husband," Guin said smugly.

Rella felt herself going red. She wanted to slap the arrogant smile off Brother Guin's face.

"Then maybe I won't marry," she said.

Father's lip quivered. "You must marry, Rella, or who will rule the land of Eden once you have gone? You must find someone to help you rule and to ensure our family lives on."

"I think it's time you went to get Elara," Mother instructed.

As Rella left the palace, she saw a teenage boy leaving Walter Ifran's house. He was carrying something under his coat. Clare watched the boy leave from the window of her upstairs bedroom. Rella made eye contact with Clare, and she disappeared from the window, perhaps too feeling uncomfortable over the oath they had sworn the previous night.

Rella wished she could be more like Clare, wearing what she wanted and not caring what people thought of her. Rella cared too much about embarrassing her parents, and she wanted to make them proud more than anything.

She collected Elara and returned home. Every time Rella brought her friend to the palace, Elara seemed in awe of the multiple stone floors, wooden frames, and gigantic dining hall. As they entered, the smell of fresh seafood and spiced vegetables passed into their nostrils.

"It smells glorious," Elara said.

Elara had probably never had seafood before, Rella realized. Only the rich could afford to import it from the shores.

As Rella and Elara entered the dining hall, they found it deserted. Suddenly, a servant rushed in. "You must visit your mother at once, my lady."

Rella's heart sank, fearing the worst. She hurried upstairs and saw Brother Guin standing outside her parents' bedroom, holding a bowl of blood. "I did everything in my power, Lady Rella, but the Creator has decided that it is time for the Countess to leave this world."

Rella wept and pushed past the monk, flinging open the door. Her mother's eyes were closed, and her complexion was so pale that she could have been mistaken for a ghost. Father stood beside her. Rella collapsed on her knees beside her mother's bed and clutched her lifeless hand.

"She's dead?" Rella asked, struggling to speak over her sobbing.

Father nodded, burying his head in his hands.

"I don't understand. Mother survived for days under the care of the elders. But Brother Guin arrives to look after her and she dies within hours."

"It seems he was not as skilled as he believed himself to be."

"Then why did you listen to him?" she yelled, louder than she meant.

"Life often faces us with difficult decisions to make we are unprepared for," Father said. "That's why knowledge is important. After Brother Guin leaves, I have something to show you."

"What is it, Father?"

"A collection at Walter Ifran's house."

"A collection?" she asked.

"Yes, of stories and knowledge. If you want to know more about the world so you can help people, that's what will happen."

"Really, Father?"

"You're the Countess of Eden now," he said. "You can do whatever you want to do."

Father rested his face in his palms and wept. Rella realized she had never seen her father cry. He was the Governor of Eden and a war hero, the strongest and most powerful man she knew. Seeing him cry made her think that what Clare had said last night was true, that they might never be safe, and that there were things even her father couldn't protect people from; the world was both dangerous and unpredictable.

Brother Guin entered the room. "Governor, please accept my condolences. I'll take Lady Rella downstairs and give you some privacy with your late wife."

"I'm not going anywhere with you." Rella stood. "I'm the Countess of Eden. And I'll never be told what I can or cannot do again."

II

CCXXXI (Present)

Upon returning to Elara's cabin, Rella felt a chill run through her body. Kal's wagon was still parked outside, but his body was missing, likely taken by animals. Inside the cabin's kitchen, she sat with the monk and his companion. The companion wore a master's cape and looked vaguely familiar, though she couldn't place where from.

Rella rested her bow and arrows on the table but kept them within reach. "You said you knew the Omi were coming for Elara. How did you know this?"

"A senior monk at the Monastery told me," Eric said. "He said Enforcers were on their way to retrieve her and take her to the Sanctuary for a sacrifice."

As the monk spoke, Rella felt a sense of hope rise that Elara could still be alive, even though she knew her friend was likely doomed. With Alioth dead, Elara being alive was Rella's last chance of finding someone she knew and loved.

"I'm sorry about your town," the young master said, speaking for the first time since they met. "What will you do now?"

"Survive."

"Alone?"

Rella glanced to the box at her feet, thankful no one had enquired about it. "Maybe. Or maybe I'll find another town."

"I've seen a lot of towns and none of them are much different than yours." The monk shook his head. "If the people aren't dead in body, they're dead inside."

"There has to be a place better. Life is always beautiful," she said, more to herself than to the men at the table.

Her father had told her that right after the Omi's invasion. No one had taken the Omi's rise seriously, thinking the attacks upon other territories had nothing to do with them. Her people stood idly as foreign homes were destroyed. But, eventually, the Omi came for them too, sending an army led by General Karmeeleon. Loyal to the Omi's Head, General Karmeeleon was in charge of spreading terror throughout Arcadia and destroying all threats to the Omi's reign.

Amidst the panicked crowd, Rella and her father had watched as Karmeeleon and his troops made their way to the palace. Karmeeleon stood upright on two legs, resembling a human, but with lobster-like claws at the end of his scaly limbs. It was the first time Rella had seen a non-human, having previously believed they were only myths. Karmeeleon had fierce, bright red eyes on his reptilian head and his bulky green armor covered most of his dry green scales. A cape, gleaming in the light, trailed behind him.

Visions of the general still haunted her sleep. The sight of her people lying dead, their city destroyed.

After her father's execution, she spent days in the forest alone. Eventually, she found Alioth, an old friend of her father's. She was near starving. When he asked her what was wrong, at first, she was too consumed with grief to speak, but eventually, she opened up to him. Over the years, he taught her to hunt, and she discovered she had a talent for it, having perfect aim. Her father had given her archery lessons as a girl, but never had she shot moving targets.

It wasn't long before Alioth asked her to live with him, and she readily accepted. He looked after her, raised her, and cooked her meals. In return, she hunted their food. It was the perfect arrangement. They got on well, and Rella grew to love him and his town.

"You said you had something to show the old Countess," Rella said to the men at the table. "What is it?"

The monk and master shared a brief glance, and then the monk unwrapped a gold tablet from his blanket and placed it in front of her. It was engraved with hieroglyphics. "We've been instructed to deliver this to the Omi's Sanctuary. Countess Rella is supposed to join us."

Rella raised her eyebrows, not sure what to say.

"Our instructions come from the Creator," Eric went on.

Rella gave a look that made sure her skepticism was evident.

"I don't understand it myself. But it's not my duty to question orders, only to follow them."

"That might work for you," Rella said, "but not everyone blindly trusts orders claimed to come from the Creator. And not everyone trusts monks either. Most of us struggle to survive, while monks are fattened up in return for nothing but prayers. On top of that, they pretend to have all the answers and justify selfish decisions by claiming to be in service of a being they don't even understand. They're usually lazy or corrupt, if not both."

Eric blinked a few times and then looked away.

"I'm not a monk," the young master then said.

"Yes, I can see that," she replied. "Who are you?"

"My name is Aaron, and I used to live in Eden when Countess Rella's father was the Governor."

Upon hearing his name, Rella's memory jogged. She recalled that he was the son of a wool merchant and friend of Clare's. She also remembered that he had a habit of avoiding religious services whenever possible. "You don't believe what the monk is saying, do you?"

Aaron shrugged. "I follow the Monastery's orders. Whether those orders come from the Creator or from lazy and corrupt monks, I don't know. What's important is that this tablet is taken somewhere safe."

"Is that all?"

Aaron shuffled in his seat. "I'm also looking for someone. I'm hoping Countess Rella will be able to point me in the right direction."

"Someone special to you?"

Aaron nodded.

"Clare?"

Aaron's eyes snapped up and stared right at her. "How did you know?"

"I remember you," Rella replied. "Clare used to speak of you all the time. I'm afraid I don't know where she is now. Last I heard, she moved south following the Omi's invasion."

Aaron's eyes widened in realization before he looked down at his feet, processing the news about Clare.

"You're the Countess," the monk observed.

"I'm not a Countess anymore."

"You need to come with us."

"I don't need to do anything," Rella made clear.

"Elara is your friend?" Eric asked.

"My best friend."

"If you come with us to the Sanctuary, we might be able to help her."

"How could we help her?"

"Even if we are lazy and corrupt, being a monk still carries a lot of authority."

"No one even knows where the Omi's Sanctuary is."

"Monks do," Eric replied. "Escort us safely to Tyrin's capital, and I'll lead the way from there."

"So, the Sanctuary is in Tyrin?" Rella raised an eyebrow.

Eric gave a sly smile. "Without a monk's help, finding it is an impossible task."

Rella sighed. "There's something you should know. When I arrived, there was a man staying here. A human trafficker. Elara and her father may have been killed before the Omi even arrived."

"Enforcers would not have left a man here alive if that was the case," Eric argued. "He must have come after Elara had already been taken by the Omi."

Rella nodded in agreement. In the end, all she had to cling to was the small chance that Elara could still be saved from the

Omi's clutches. She remembered her father's words, that life was always beautiful, and knew that in order to believe them, she also had to believe that Elara was still alive.

"So, you'll come with us?" Eric asked, his grin growing large.

"I'll journey to the Sanctuary to rescue Elara, but I'll do it alone," Rella replied. "I won't help you deliver some tablet."

"You'll never find the Omi's Sanctuary without us."

"If you won't tell me, I'll get the information from some other monk."

"Monks make a vow to never reveal the Sanctuary's location. And most monks would die before breaking their vows."

"But not all of them." Rella eyed him with a smile.

"Aaron and I barely made it here from the Monastery alive," Eric pleaded. "It will be a far longer and more dangerous journey to Tyrin's capital. You seem like someone who can handle herself. Please, we need you."

While the idea of a monk dying in the desert didn't trouble her much, Clare had always spoken highly of Aaron, describing him as gentle and kind-hearted. If she could prevent them from being slaughtered by bandits during their journey, she might as well. "Guess I have nothing to lose if we travel together. Let's be clear though: I only care about helping Elara. I'll get you safely to Tyrin's capital. Then, you show me to the Sanctuary. You can deliver your tablet, and I'll save Elara."

"We'll both save Elara," Eric said.

Rella studied him for a moment, and he didn't react. She presented her elbow and they tapped on it in agreement.

III

Before their journey, Rella went out to hunt while Aaron and Eric gathered enough firewood to keep Elara's cabin warm for the night. Despite Rella's reluctance to spend another moment in the cabin, it was getting late, and it made sense to sleep there and begin their trek in the morning. The journey to Tyrin's capital was long, and they could be without a bed for weeks.

As Rella hunted, she remained vigilant, not only for food but also for her safety. While hunting in the forest was legal, predators roamed freely, and there were other dangers such as oversized insects, venomous snakes, and traps left by other hunters. The woods had always been dangerous. However, Rella had an advantage over other food seekers with her rare bow, crafted by Alioth, a former weapons craftsman. Rella often had food to spare, which she used to sell in town. Really, she had always been fortunate in comparison to most citizens, considering starvation was the main cause of death.

When Rella was first taken in by Alioth ten years ago, he was hesitant to teach her how to use his weapons. Instead, he tried to convince her to let go of her anger and hate for the Omi. He said it would make her bitter, and the Omi would have succeeded in taking her life as well as that of her father.

Eventually, he realized there was no convincing her. She even once ran away, in hopes of finding Omi Enforcers to take her anger out on, so she could at least make a small difference. Alioth went after her and saved her from certain death. He told her about his past; before the Omi, he built weapons for the Queen's army. Since then, he had been in hiding, thinking his purpose was over. Through Rella, he found a new meaning to his life. Over the course of ten years, they had daily classes and he taught her how to use his blades, once used by the Queen's army.

Her thoughts were interrupted by a squirrel leaping from a nearby tree. Rella froze and drew her arrow. She aimed for the top of the squirrel's skull. Suddenly, she heard voices carried by the wind. She stopped and lowered her bow. It was coming from Elara's cabin. She dashed against the wind and knelt into the foliage. Bandits. Three of them stood outside Elara's house, encircling Eric with wooden spears in their hands. Aaron lay unconscious on the ground. At least, she hoped he was unconscious. There was no blood.

The bandits were like vultures, drawn by the scent of death to scavenge whatever they could.

Eric put his hands in the air. "I already told you, we don't know anyone called Kal!" he yelled. "We only just got here."

So, these weren't bandits, they were Kal's people. They must have seen the smoke signals and come looking. That made them even more dangerous. Bandits would have looted what they could, but probably let them keep their lives. These savages, if anything like Kal, wouldn't be so generous. Rella aimed at one and launched an arrow straight through his heart. The other two darted behind Kal's cart for cover.

One of them peered over and caught sight of her. "It's just a girl. We'll grab her and take her back to our village."

"And the monk?"

"I'm not killing a holy man."

They thought taking her would be easy. Well, they were wrong. One of them hurled a spear at her, but Rella rolled away just in time, causing it to get stuck in a nearby tree. The men lunged out of their hiding spot and sprinted towards her. The attacker who had thrown the spear picked up his comrade's weapon as he ran past his fallen body. Rella fired an arrow at him, but he deflected it with his spear. There was no time to load another. One of them smacked her across the face with their wooden weapon. Rella fell back into the grass, and they pulled her by the feet, dragging her from the foliage.

Rella struck one of them across the face with her boot and then leapt to her feet. She stood between them, waiting on one of them to make the first move. The two men looked her up and down with a grin that made her sick to her stomach. Eric attempted to intervene by hitting one with his walking stick, but the man simply floored him with a quick boot to the stomach, telling the monk to stay out of it.

One made a run for her. She spun and picked up the spear from the ground, then slammed it into his elbow just before he could grab her. He cried out in pain, and she slid the spear up through his neck. His body dropped with a thud.

There was no time to yank the spear back. She could hear the other man charging from behind. Rella jumped out of the way, only just missing the point of his spear. Rella and the attacker stood once more, staring at each other. She half expected him to lob the spear her way, but he knew if he missed, his weapon would be lost. Instead, he charged at her once more. This was her chance. Unfortunately for him, she was more confident in the accuracy of her throw. She grabbed a knife from her belt and hurled it at him. It hit his stomach and he fell to his knees with a spray of blood.

Rella jerked her knife back and finished him with a quick cut of his throat. She cleaned her blade on his clothes and then sheathed it.

Eric was back on his feet, standing over Aaron's body. She dashed over and checked he was still breathing. Thankfully, he was.

"What happened?" she asked.

"Blow to the head," Eric replied.

Rella stared down at the unconscious man, thinking her life was about to get even more complicated. She straightened anyway. "Let's get him inside."

Chapter Six

I

CCXXI (X Years Ago)

Every day that week, Aaron looked out for Walter Ifran's daughter, whom he had since learned was called Clare. She barely seemed to leave the upstairs of her house, other than to attend assembly at the palace's chapel and occasionally wander in the woods. Why would she need to go out when she had all those stories at her disposal? Aaron had devoured the book Walter gave him in little over a day.

Aaron couldn't stop daydreaming about Clare, but fantasies weren't enough. He wanted to meet and talk to her. Problem was, even if he did approach her, he had no idea what to say. He had hoped that Walter's book might have given him a few ideas, but the story didn't have a happy ending. Instead, it finished with the couple never being united, as all the boy's attempts to build a bridge continuously failed. It hadn't been what Aaron was hoping for; he was expecting a message about persistence. In the end, he really wasn't that sure what the meaning of the book was, but maybe that's what made it interesting.

That day, Aaron had seen Clare go into the woods, and he decided he was finally going to speak to her. He tried rehearsing conversations in his mind, but every time it was his turn to speak, his mind drew a blank. Just seeing her made his head spin and caused a fluttering feeling in his stomach. As pathetic as he knew it was, he was afraid of her, more so than he had ever been afraid of anyone or anything.

It was odd because girls had never really interested Aaron, but there was something different about Clare. She didn't seem to care what anyone thought of her, and she was clearly drawn to a quest for knowledge as Aaron was. That made her fascinating.

They both also seemed to enjoy the forest. While most people only entered the woods to hunt, Aaron loved to go for a long walk and admire nature. The countless number of different birds and the working of the insects were all amazing. Being among the trees also offered an escape from people and allowed his head to think clearly. Constantly being around people made him feel suffocated and kept him worrying about how to behave and what to say.

Aaron followed Clare's bootprints along the riverbank. At the other side of some bushes, Clare sat at a bend in the river. She wore a short white dress with long lace sleeves, and a thin brown belt around her waist. A book rested beside her, and a sheet of paper lay in front of her as she wrote. At first, Aaron thought she might be practicing calligraphy like many wealthy women did, but once she moved her hand, he realized that the characters she was forming were a mix of symbols and pictures.

Aaron was so amazed he forgot about his anxiety, and he stepped through the bushes. "Those are hieroglyphics!"

Clare jumped, though her features relaxed when she saw him. "You scared me."

Aaron felt a fool and fidgeted with his hands. "I'm sorry."

"What are you doing out here?"

His throat went dry, and he responded with a mere shrug. They stood in silence for a moment, each passing second feeling like an eternity. Aaron wished he could disappear, his heart pounding in his throat.

"I saw you with my dad," Clare said at last. "He speaks about you often. Says you have a brilliant mind."

"Your father speaks too highly of me."

"It's good he speaks of you at all, otherwise I'd know nothing about you."

"Do you help your father with distributing the books?" he asked.

She nodded. "Mm-hmm."

"Aren't you afraid of what the Monastery will do if they hear?"

"Even if I am, people deserve the right to knowledge and the freedom to think for themselves."

Aaron was taken aback by her bravery. He pointed to her paper. "What are you writing?"

"My father says it's an ancient language." Clare picked up the sheet of pictorial writing and showed him.

"It *is* an ancient language!" Aaron said excitedly, happy to have something to talk about. "My mother comes from a camp of Pure Bloods. They read and write with hieroglyphics."

"Do you think it's the language of the Holy World?" she asked.

"My mother thinks so," he replied. Truthfully, Aaron wasn't so sure such a place as the Holy World existed. The stories in the Creator's texts seemed no different from any other stories, imaginative and fictitious. Claudia had taught him to keep such thoughts to himself, so he asked, "Can you understand the pictures?"

"I'm trying to. Some are obvious, like the picture of a bird, but others not so much."

Aaron could not believe it; he was actually talking to her. His heart got faster as he tried to think of what to say next. "Um, do you know what that story's about?" He pointed to her book.

"I'm not even sure if it is a story," Clare admitted. "I can't work out the meaning of most pictures. Maybe your mother could help me."

"Or I could help you," Aaron suggested.

"You understand the pictures too?"

Aaron nodded. "My mother taught me."

Clare smiled and handed him the book. "Tell me what it says then."

Aaron was so happy to see her smile that he thought his knees might give way. She sat down and indicated that he should sit beside her. He did so and realized they had not only been having a conversation, but one that only they could have. He looked into her eyes and smiled, then he read her the story—the tale of the Pure Bloods first settling on Arcadia from the Holy World—and she seemed engrossed by every word he said.

II

CCXXXI (Present)

Aaron's dream began to fade.

His eyes felt heavy, as if the lids had been glued shut. He could still picture—though now only faintly—him and Clare by the river reading the hieroglyphics from her book. A feeling of frustration came over him; a sense that what he was dreaming wasn't real. Something was wrong. His eyes shot open.

Aaron looked around. He was no longer by the river with Clare. Instead, he lay on an old and tattered bed. Not his own bed. He was within a small wooden cabin. His heart pounded. Was this the dream?

"Clare," he shrieked. His voice sounded like a stranger's, too stifled to be his own. "Clare, are you there?"

All he could hear was the pounding of his head. Only then did he notice someone else in the room: a blond man with reddened skin and thinning hair, making him appear older than he probably was. Aaron thought he recognized the man but couldn't place where.

The man spotted Aaron and turned to the open door of the cabin. "He's awake!"

A young woman ran into the room. She could have passed as an older sister of the Governor's daughter, but Rella had no sisters, and this woman wasn't dressed like a noble. Instead, she wore a ragged leather vest over a soiled shirt and patched brown trousers. A silver necklace shaped like wings hung around her neck, looking oddly out of place. She greeted him with a friendly smile. "Hello, there. How you feelin'?"

Aaron looked around and mumbled, "Wh…" He closed his eyes and took a deep breath before trying again. "Where am I?"

The woman appeared quite perplexed at his question, and she didn't answer him. She put a hand to his bruised head. "Does that hurt?"

He nodded gently. Even the gentle sway of his neck going up and down caused his head to ache. "Where's Clare?"

"Clare isn't here," she replied. "I'm sorry, Master Aaron."

"Why did you just call me Master?" he asked. "And I don't understand, Clare and I were just by the river."

The young woman squinted at him, looking confused.

The blond man approached the bedside. "You're a Master of Architecture, Aaron. We just came from the Monastery together."

Aaron stared at them both for a moment, trying to figure out if this was some sort of joke. "That's impossible."

"What's the last thing you remember?" the young woman asked.

"I was by the river with Clare. We were reading from her book."

The two strangers shared a look.

"Why are you looking at each other like that?" he asked.

The brunette sat on the bedside. She said gently, "You've suffered a head injury. I'm sorry to say this, but the truth is, you haven't seen Clare in almost ten years."

"What are you talking about?" He had just been with Clare; it wasn't a distant memory. It was as vivid as everything else that had happened that day, including morning services and having bacon and eggs for breakfast with his family. Despite the pounding in his head, Aaron got out of bed and declared, "I've had enough of this. You're talking nonsense."

He brushed past the brunette and headed for the door to see what was going on. As he did so, he caught sight of himself in the window's reflection. Then, he realized they weren't talking nonsense; they were telling the truth.

Chapter Seven

Commander Straumme's squadron of Enforcers marched to Eden's border across Tyrin's barren desert, blending into one moving dull-grey mass. The only color on their uniforms was the royal red stripes on their arms that represented their loyalty to the Omi. Straumme led the way, his own grey tunic only separated from the others by his commander badge, a reward for all his impressive victories that dated back to decades before even Queen Shanleigh's rebellion.

When Commander Straumme was younger, the adventure had excited him, his victories had fulfilled him, and his skills had given him great pride. Looking back on his victories, however, wasn't enough to make him feel accomplished. Wrinkles, gray hair, and medals were all he had to show for his life. There was no one to carry on his name, to share his stories with, or to give him companionship. His frail body gave the impression that the slightest breeze would be enough to push him over, but anyone who thought as much would be wrong. He had nothing to lose except his reputation. That, despite all appearances, was what made him the utmost level of danger to any criminal.

A group of Security was ready to greet them at the border.

Three men, dressed in their customary red, stood in a line, blocking his path. A brunette woman stood in front of them, bronzed-skinned and with her long hair in a bun. Her name was Talitha and she served as one of Zylina's Security squad leaders within Eden.

Talitha stepped forward. "Commander Straumme," she said, stone-faced. "What brings you to Eden?"

"I'm pursuing a rogue monk from the Monastery," he replied. "Now, let me pass."

"If the monk is within Eden, I have jurisdiction. Though I could use some of your men."

Straumme's blood boiled. This was his chancc to prove he still had a purpose within the Omi. He wanted to show he could still do his job and eliminate threats to the Omi's peace. Instead, he was being turned away, and by a woman.

There was nothing he could do about it. While he was Commander of the Enforcers, his army was outranked by Captain Zylina's Security who dealt with more direct threats to the Omi. In their official roles, both he and Zylina held the titles of Lord and Lady of Peace, their positions equal in significance. Nevertheless, they were obliged to respect the distinct responsibilities of their respective armies. They both answered only to two other lordships—other than Develon, of course—General Karmeeleon, Lord of Justice; and Principal Sin, Lord of Order and head of the Omi's council.

It had been Develon's idea to let women and non-humans work for the Omi. Why could things not remain as they had always been? How much humiliation must Straumme suffer? Develon saw no reason why both men and women shouldn't serve the Creator, but this was just wrong. He would have liked to grab Talitha by the neck and strangle her with his bare hands. But that wouldn't go down well with Develon, and Straumme still wanted a chance to prove he had the skills and usefulness of his younger days.

With a slight growl, he ordered four of his men to go with

Talitha. Then, he spun around and led the rest of his men back across the deserts of Tyrin. Behind him, he sensed the Security's mocking smile, but he would show them. He may look as though his best days were behind him, but that wasn't the case. He'd catch the rogue monk to prove it, and consequences be damned.

Chapter Eight

I

Eric led the way along the lonely dirt road, surrounded by boggy grassland. There were no longer any reminders of winter. The snow had melted, and so had the ice from the mountains. It had dripped down the mountainsides, flooding the fields. He tightened his grip on the tablet, feeling a surge of pride. He was finally doing something meaningful.

The smoothly sloping highlands were covered in green grass, and beneath the summits were valleys and lakes hidden by deep forests. Beyond the trees lay the miles of grass fields that currently encircled them. The road twisted and turned around the edges of the fields. Above them, clear blue infused the cloudless sky.

"Your land is beautiful," Eric said.

"It's not my land," Rella replied. "It belongs to the Omi."

"The land belongs to no one, but you live off it and look after it."

"Well, my people did," she said solemnly, looking over her shoulder in the direction of her murdered town.

Rella had eyed the tablet in the blood-soaked blanket

several times. He was surprised she hadn't asked about it, but it was probably so he wouldn't ask about what was inside the box she carried. She clutched that thing so tightly it was as if she was worried he'd steal it from her. Eric decided to respect her privacy and not ask about it. Not that he was interested; he was focused on his quest. He felt at long last that he had found his calling.

Of course, he was also happy to be helping reunite Rella with her friend. Maybe there was more to life than finding a personal meaning to one's existence.

Aaron ambled behind them, glancing around as though he was seeing everything for the first time. They had convinced him that he might as well travel to Tyrin's capital with them, in hopes of finding some clues as to Clare's location. Hopefully, his memory loss was only temporary.

"How exactly do the Omi now rule Arcadia?" Aaron asked, catching up and interrupting Eric's thoughts. "Queen Shanleigh brought peace to the territories. My father fought in her war."

"The Omi reclaimed the territories from Queen Shanleigh in a second war," he replied. "They then appointed their own Governors to rule over the territories of Arcadia."

Aaron looked down at his feet. "My parents used to tell me that the Omi were just a part of history better to never speak about. I'm not even sure how they rose to power in the first place."

Rella seemed to shy away, but luckily this was a story Eric loved to tell. "A thousand years ago, there was a war between the Ichu and the Omi. The war went on for centuries and no one thought that it would ever end. Both sides fought for power over Arcadia. Eventually, the Ichu were defeated; their chief was destroyed, along with most of his army. The survivors either retreated and hid or were caught and executed. The Omi took control. They ruthlessly crushed any dissent and purged the world of the heretics—those who had chosen pursuits in science over faith in the Creator's texts."

"The Omi's reign went unopposed for over two centuries," Rella added. "Eventually, the people revolted against them, led by Shanleigh and her army. She created the first monarchy of Arcadia and restored freedom to the territories by appointing Governors who actually cared about the people."

"So how did the Omi return?" Aaron asked.

"Everything was destroyed by a non-human named Develon, an Omi leader who survived the fall. He returned, murdered the Queen and her army, and spread terror and destruction across the territories. Now, he rules over all of Arcadia."

"No one has tried to fight against him?" Aaron asked, appearing to be questioning what he had got himself in for.

"Impossible," Rella replied. "There is too much Security. The Omi have made weapons illegal. Besides, people have to worry about surviving and not starving to death."

If Aaron wondered what Rella meant by Security, he wouldn't have to for long. They halted, as a wall of four Enforcers stepped in front of them, dressed in their dull grey uniforms with royal red stripes. Behind them were three male members of Security, far more intimidating. Standing apart from the group was a brunette woman, unmistakably the leader of the squad. Her unwavering gaze fixated on them, and a faint hint of a smile flickered across her lips.

"Get them!" she roared.

II

They were probably looking for Eric. He had said he'd stolen something from the Omi. Rella couldn't take the chance though; they might be looking for her. She glanced at the box in her arms.

The squad's leader had ordered her men to attack. That's

all Rella needed to hear. Since she spotted them, Rella had been waiting for them to make a move. Now that they had, Rella dropped her case to the ground and kicked it open.

Inside were the three beautiful shining blades that Alioth had given her, with golden hilts, and rich crimson rubies embedded in their golden branches.

Now, Rella's training with Alioth would be put to the test.

She pulled the three swords out of the case and turned to Eric. "Can you use this?"

He nodded. She threw the blade towards him. Eric caught it with one hand and smiled. Clearly, he had learned at least something about protecting himself even as a monk.

Rella turned to Aaron and presented him with the third sword. He shook his head, appearing greatly alarmed, as if she was asking him to cut off one of his own limbs. She tossed the sword back into the case. Aaron would have to either surrender or she and Eric would have to protect him.

Rella raised her sword and held it out in front of her, her eyes reflecting in its silver steel. She had been waiting for this moment for a long time. Now, it was either kill or be killed.

She leapt at the nearest Enforcer and shoved her blade through his neck, just under the chin, before he even had a chance to defend himself. Rella pulled the sword out just in time to block an attack from another soldier. The clash of their swords resonated in the air, sparkling under the sunlight. He lifted his sword into the air for a second attack, but she was too quick and slashed him across the chest.

Rella drew near the remaining two Enforcers. They ran at her together, but she dodged the swings from their swords. She swiftly slashed one of them in the leg, causing him to cry out in agony and drop his defense. With his guard down, she swiftly slit his throat, crimson blood spurting as he crumpled to the ground. She parried an attack from the other one and plunged her sword through his chest.

She looked down at herself in shock, surprised by the

sharpness and speed of her moves and reflexes. Sure, she had been trained since a child and her sword was one of the finest upon Arcadia, used by the very people who ended the Omi's First Empire, but she had just taken out four soldiers in seconds. Eric and Aaron had not moved, but Eric smiled, impressed by her victory. Aaron still had the same look of shock as when she presented the swords.

Her victory was short-lived. The three Security males strode towards her, responding to orders from the brunette woman, who watched with calculated patience. Security personnel were an entirely different breed from Enforcers. They were sheathed from neck to toe in dark-red formfitting outfits to hide any splatter of blood, made from reptilian skin. The three Security males in front of her, with their blank expressions and cold stares, appeared not even human-like.

Rella wouldn't be able to fight these three by herself. Aaron would be of no help. She turned to Eric. "Can you really fight?"

"I've taught myself the basics." Eric waved around the sword in a way that'd make him more likely to take out his own eye than kill anyone.

"Just do what you can, and I'll look out for you," she said.

Eric threw his walking stick to the ground and limped towards one of the Security, who brandished a sword of his own. As their blades clashed, Eric strained with every ounce, emitting a determined grunt. One of the other men held up a firearm and shot at Eric. He was met with an agonizing zap of electricity. Eric convulsed in pain.

There were rumors that the Omi had stockpiled weapons made by the heretics, as well as the technology used to make them. *Hypocrites*. The Omi would argue they were using technology only to make sure no one else did.

The man aimed for Rella. She rolled to the side, dodging the attack. She jumped to her feet, but the third Security member grabbed her arm. He kneed her in the gut, knocking her to the ground.

He spun around to kick Rella, but she grabbed his foot and caused him to tumble. She jumped up and ran at the fallen Security member but was blasted by the other member's gun. Rella flew and landed hard on her back, the electricity zapping through her body.

At first, she was too stunned to think straight. As her mind cleared, she wondered why the Security were using taser guns. Then, she realized—they were trying to take them alive. Perhaps, to make an example of them, or maybe to interrogate to see if they were part of a rebel group. Whatever the reason, Rella now knew a weakness to exploit.

She sprang to her feet and charged at the one with the gun. Like a raging bull, she tackled the man to the grass. They rolled across the ground, her arms wrapped around his neck. With a sharp pull of her arms on the next roll, she snapped his neck.

Rella wasted no time and took his gun. She glanced to see one of the Security running for Eric and fired. The man dropped to the grass near Eric's feet. Eric pierced his blade through the Security's throat, apparently knowing the perfect kill spot.

Eric took another shot and hit the ground. Rella turned to see the third Security member, carrying another taser gun. She raised her sword but was too late. He fired at her too.

As she sprawled on the ground, Rella felt the crushing weight of the Security member's boot on her neck. She started to choke. Panic surged through her as she struggled to inhale, her desperate gasps for air stifled. As she stared into the Security member's cold and empty eyes, she thought she was going to die.

Just as darkness encroached upon her, the weight disappeared. She took a deep breath. Her eyes shifted to the fallen Security member, a sword embedded in his back. Eric had saved her. He offered out his hand and helped her to her feet. They shared an uncomfortable smile, Rella not quite ready to express any more affection than that. Even if he had saved her life, he was still a monk, like the one who had killed her mother.

Rella rubbed her aching neck and turned to where the squad's leader had been. However, the brunette woman was running off into the distance. Rella picked up one of the guns and fired in her direction, but the woman was too far away.

She would surely send more Security after them.

Chapter Nine

For the past ten years, Sin's council had controlled and monitored the Omi's territories. They met in the globular chamber regularly to discuss matters of importance, but with no uprisings in a decade, they found little worthy of discussion. Three seats in the chamber had sat empty for years now, gathering dust. One belonged to Develon, the Head of the Omi, while the other two were reserved for General Karmeeleon and Captain Zylina. The meeting chamber was now nothing but the Creator's waiting room for deteriorating souls. Then, a rogue monk and his two traveling companions had taken out a squad of Security, and now the council found themselves with plenty to discuss.

Principal Sin faced away from the council, staring up through the central opening of the chamber's dome at the night sky. When they heard that news, the council probably expected an outburst of anger from Sin. Instead, he had stood facing away ever since, staring silently. He was thinking back on his quest for power. He'd always craved political control, a dominating influence over his subordinates, and a respected expertise. As he stood there, he wondered why. He concluded that to be without power would be like sitting stranded and alone in the dark.

The power had certainly taken its toll on him, and he thought back to the day he made a deal. The deal changed his life forever. It happened when he served as a representative for Queen Shanleigh. Lord Develon, a trusted aide of the throne, had requested to meet with him.

Develon was an aquatic humanoid insect with leathery pastel-red skin. There was a short layer of grey hair on his otherwise bald, pink scalp. Sprouting from his skull were two elongated antennas that curved inward, while six short, stout tentacles hung from his mouth, perpetually moist with droplets of saliva.

When Sin asked why Develon had called him, he warned Sin that a change was coming, but that he was giving him the chance to profit from it. He promised power, treasures, and anything Sin's heart desired. Sin had asked what he would have to do. Develon explained he would need a group of people to control and maintain aspects of Arcadia.

Sin quickly realized that Develon wanted to bring back the times of the Omi. He had little choice other than to accept; Develon had powerful friends, who would be sure to silence him if he refused. Or maybe that was just how Sin justified it to himself.

Whether Sin accepted Develon's offer out of fear or greed, he now felt tired of it all. His friends who had also assisted in Develon's uprising had fallen, either due to the stresses of the job or Develon murdering them out of paranoia. Sin had lived looking over his shoulder, and pushing his luck, for too long; if the stress didn't do him in soon, Develon or some rebels would. At this point, there was no chance of defect and so, Sin had resigned himself to the fact that his role as principal of the council would end with his death.

He spun around to face his council and noticed the slight smirk on Straumme's face. "What are you smiling about?"

"Those criminals were not to be underestimated. I should have been allowed to handle the situation, instead of being pushed aside by Security."

"Then maybe you should have done something, instead of rushing back here with your tail between your legs."

Straumme strained his face in embarrassment.

Sin sighed. "There's no need to panic. Security will continue to pursue them and have them taken care of. Just wait and see, Commander."

"It is too late. The Omi will hear of your failure, and I wouldn't be surprised if General Karmeeleon's already on his way here."

"Ridiculous! Develon trusts me!" Sin spoke confidently, but it didn't match the tremble in his hands.

Straumme scoffed with contempt. "I doubt he trusts you now, if he ever even did. I should be thanking these criminals. I was beginning to forget why I took this job, thinking that I had wasted my years. But they have vividly reminded me why I dedicated my life to serving the Omi. The poor used to leech off the rich; now the scum is contained, to rot away in their slums like animals. The successful can prosper and take as much power as they want, without being compromised by the slothful and imprudent."

"You're overreacting, Commander."

"Overreacting?" said a familiar voice.

The room of councilors turned to see he had been standing in the shadows. Green scales rapidly appeared on the edge of the room, revealing the full form of General Karmeeleon.

The giant lizard walked towards them on his two feet, dressed in his impressive, bulky green armor, his cape trailing behind him. Sin couldn't keep his eyes off the lizard's giant tail that slithered behind him, like a ginormous snake, so wide in diameter that it was larger than Sin's whole body.

"Once people hear of this, it will spark more of these

menaces. They'll breed quickly and eat away at our perfect system," Karmeeleon said.

Sin bowed respectably, sweating and stuttering. "General Karmeeleon, we are honored to have you here."

The green general stepped towards him and spoke calmly. "This isn't intended to be a pleasurable visit."

Commander Straumme stood. "General Karmeeleon, I ask that you send me and my army of Enforcers after these criminals."

"Sit down, Commander. You and Talitha both let the monk slip away because of your petty territory dispute and your injured pride. There are consequences for all our sins, and now you will face yours."

Straumme sat back down, his wounded ego all too clear by the expression on his face.

"I have everything under control," Sin assured.

The council, all looking in horror at their guest, quickly nodded in agreement with Sin's statement.

Karmeeleon's glare filled with contempt. "You are in control of nothing. The Omi has long questioned if there is still even a need for an imperial council, and you have proven yourselves to be just as ineffective as I'd have imagined you to be. I will be dealing with these criminals henceforth, so they are no longer of your concern. Your meeting is over." Karmeeleon headed for the door.

"Yes, sir. Please give Develon my regards," Sin called after him.

The general gave a snort of amusement, and then exited. Sin collapsed in his chair, panting.

"Are we really getting out of this in one piece?" Straumme asked. It was the question on all their minds.

Sin did not answer. Instead, he sat in his chair and stared up to the black and vacant sky. Now, he was truly alone in the dark.

Chapter Ten

I

CCXXI (X Years Ago)

Over the next few weeks, Clare met Aaron nearly every day by the river to hear him read one of the stories. He had translated so many of them now that Clare was sure she knew the meaning of almost all the hieroglyphics. Their meetings provided a good distraction from Clare's worries about her situation with Elara and Rella.

Clare hadn't spoken to her two friends since the night at the Eye, and she figured it was best that way. There had been no news of the crashed object. A part of her wished she had been braver and that she had told people what she'd seen, but her family would have been investigated by the Monastery and their library would have been discovered.

She should never have sneaked out during the night, she knew, but she had a terrible habit of being recklessly impulsive and breaking the rules. She often got into trouble for saying just whatever was on her mind instead of thinking it through.

Not like Aaron, who seemed to overthink everything to death. Sometimes, though, she wished he would be more impulsive. She knew Aaron found her attractive from the looks he gave her, but he hadn't made a move yet to kiss her even though she had given him several signals.

Clare had liked a few boys before, but not in the way that she liked Aaron. He was more thoughtful and brilliant than any boy she had met, and he had taken her interest since she first saw him with her father. Not to mention, he was also handsome, with wavy hair that fell down to his ears, the color of aged mahogany. His chestnut eyes had mesmerizing swirls, deep enough to captivate one's soul.

Whenever Aaron read her a story, he was very expressive, and she liked that about him most of all. He was clearly angered by stories of oppression and injustice, and he seemed to feel the emotions of the characters he read about in a way she'd never seen before. Like Clare, he believed in the fundamental rights of individuals—to seek happiness and to think and believe freely.

That day, Clare knew she would arrive slightly late for her meeting with Aaron due to the arrival of her aunt. Aunt Anais was visiting from the lowlands and their servants had prepared a luxurious lunch for her arrival. She was the mother of Brother Guin, and she was equally pious. She always wore black, as if she was in a permanent state of mourning and was frighteningly pale. When Clare was very young, she used to get a spanking from Aunt Anais for misbehaving until Walter found out and made her stop. She was always imposing her own rules and beliefs onto others, and Clare was sure that Guin must have felt suffocated growing up.

If Aunt Anais expected a tour of the house, Clare worried how they'd stop her from seeing the library. But the moment she entered the house, she sat in the sitting room next to Clare. "It's time we spoke about your future," she said.

Clare felt her brows bump together in a scowl. "What do you mean?"

"You're nearly fifteen years old, Clare. Have you given any thought to what you will do as an adult?"

Clare's parents too sat down with serious expressions, and Clare had a bad feeling about where this was heading. "I haven't decided yet, but I've learned to read and write at a high level, and I believe I want to do something that will make use of those skills."

"A pretty girl like you doesn't need to learn such things." Aunt Anais waved her off. "As long as you can recite your prayers, what more could you possibly need to know? Besides, you are from a rich family so you will marry well and have no need to work."

"I want to learn such things," Clare said sternly.

Aunt Anais didn't seem to hear her, or at least pretended not to. "I've brought someone with me whom I'd like you to meet. His name is Lord Patrick. He's the son of the Governor and Countess in Tyrin."

"What?" Clare stood and turned to her parents. "Is this some sort of ambush?"

"He's outside waiting to speak with you," Aunt Anais went on, "and I think you should invite him inside."

"I won't!"

"Think about it," her mother said, "if you marry Lord Patrick, you'll become the Countess of Tyrin."

"Marry him?" Clare thought she was going to be sick. "I don't even know him, and I will not be a broodmare just so that our family can become aristocrats."

"I would never ask you to marry someone you don't love," Walter said. "But you're getting to the age when it's appropriate to find a suitor, and there's nothing wrong with meeting men who might make a good match. There's no harm in speaking to him, is there?"

Clare sighed. Her father was always so gentle and reasonable that he made it impossible to refuse him. Clare ignored Aunt Anais' victorious smile and nodded in defeat. She stepped outside and closed the door so she could at least speak to her potential suitor with some privacy.

To her surprise, Lord Patrick was a tall man with pasty skin and light blond hair, even though she had heard that those in Tyrin were typically dark in complexion. He wore a purple tunic and a ridiculous-looking circular purple hat with a golden feather sticking out. If his goal was to stand out conspicuously, then he had succeeded even more than a juggler at a funeral.

Clare knew she should bow but she didn't dare; if Lord Patrick was to be her future husband, he had better get used to the fact that she'd be no typical lady.

"Lady Clare," he said. "My name is Lord Patrick. After hearing of your beauty from your aunt, I've come all the way from Tyrin just to meet with you."

He beamed with pride, as though she should feel the luckiest girl in the world for what he had just said and should collapse at his feet. Instead, Clare sighed and asked if he'd like to walk her into town. He agreed.

On market day, the bustling streets were a jungle of people and stalls. Farmers came from all over the highlands to sell their produce, and the poor gathered to haggle for good deals. As Clare and Lord Patrick ventured through the vibrant chaos, she noticed Aaron's parents at a nearby stall, offering their wool for sale. Next to them, another stall dealt in the trade of farm animals, mostly chickens and goats. Patrick didn't seem to be very interested in what was on sale, but Clare found talking about the market to be a welcome alternative to discussing marriage.

The atmosphere was alive with energy, enriched by street performers and merchants from Tyrin offering exotic foods and trinkets for sale. The air carried the delightful aroma of hot pies, freshly baked bread, and ale. It wouldn't take long,

Clare knew, before the street would grow rowdy from men overindulging in alcohol.

Two men seemed to already have a head start on their ale consumption and were busy launching punches at one another in the street. They seemed to be fighting over a woman, though Clare could barely decipher their muttering. One of the men pushed the other back and he bumped right into Patrick.

The man spun round, ready to hit whomever he had crashed into, but stopped when he noticed Patrick's attire. His expression turned to dread.

"Injudicious swine," Patrick shrieked. "I should have you flogged for this."

"Begging your pardon, sir," the man stuttered.

"I am not a sir." Patrick had gone red. "I am Lord Patrick of Tyrin, and you will address me accordingly."

"Yes, my lord," he groveled, bowing his head. "A thousand apologies, my lord."

Patrick made eye contact with Clare, and only then did he notice how uncomfortable she was. He seemed to suppress his anger and the redness drained from his face.

"Don't let it happen again," Patrick warned the man, and then they kept walking.

"Why were you so harsh with him?" Clare asked.

"Peasants need to know their place or our entire system falls apart. Respect is what keeps them in line."

"And you think fear earns respect?"

"At times, yes."

"The Omi once thought as you did."

"The Omi weren't all wrong."

Clare stopped in her tracks. "How can you say that?"

"My father was the Governor of Tyrin even during the Omi's reign," Patrick said.

"Then why did he fight against them for Queen Shanleigh?"

"He saw that the Omi were losing and so he thought about what would be best for his people."

He wanted to save his own skin more like.

"Enough politics." Patrick held up his hand. "Such discussions are meant for men. Besides, it's not what I came to Eden to talk about."

Clare bit her lip. "Then what did you come to Eden to talk about, Lord Patrick?"

"You and me."

Clare turned away. "I think we should discuss something else."

Patrick spun her back to face him. "I'm serious. You're the most beautiful woman I've ever seen, and I want you to be my wife."

Clare batted his arms off her. "Absolutely not!"

Patrick furrowed his brows in pure confusion. "But I love you."

"You don't even know me!"

"I don't understand," Patrick said. "If you were to marry me then you would become Countess of Tyrin. That's the dream of any woman I've ever met."

"Then perhaps you should marry one of those women."

"I won't take no for an answer." Patrick grabbed her wrists and tightened his grip. "You will be my wife, Lady Clare, and you will have a league of servants at your feet to follow your every order."

He pulled her towards him despite her squirming and kissed her on the lips. His tongue entered her mouth, prompting Clare to bite it. He yelled in pain and let go of her. She slapped him hard across the face. By this point, everyone in the street had stopped to stare at the sight. Men and women were trying hard to contain their amusement. Blood was dripping from Patrick's mouth, and he rubbed his reddened cheek from where she had slapped him.

"I will never marry you," she declared.

Clare could hear people snickering and gossiping as she ran off. She left the city and entered the forest to meet Aaron at their usual spot.

Aaron was already there when she arrived, reading with his back turned. She stood for a moment to study him, dressed in his simple blue shirt and sandals. He must have heard her rustling in the bushes because he looked over his shoulder to see her and smiled.

"I'd like to read today," she said. "I know most of the pictures by now."

Aaron handed her the book, and she took off from where they last finished. In the story, a red-haired princess led her people across the wilderness of Arcadia. With the help of a knight—her lover—they fought off evil spirits. The knight had a special blade made of metal from the Holy World, where, like all Pure Bloods, they had come from. Together, they built a prosperous community upon the highlands of Eden.

Once the story was over, Aaron leaned in suddenly and kissed her as if without thinking. At first, she was stunned. Then, she eyed him and smiled.

"Took you long enough," she said.

She grabbed him by his shirt and kissed him back. Her mother's teachings on maintaining modesty around boys faded into the background as raw passion coursed through her veins. She ran the tip of her tongue along his lips, then opened her mouth and thrust her tongue between his lips. His tongue responded eagerly.

Clare removed her tunic and guided his hand to her breasts. Instead of touching them, he slipped his hand awkwardly down the side of her chest.

"You've never seen a girl naked before, have you?" she asked, as if in explanation.

Aaron shook his head. He seemed startled, yet excited.

"Waiting for the right person, like the boy in the story you told me about?"

"You think we're right for each other?" he asked.

She nodded.

"How can you be so sure?"

"Things have their own secret plan," she replied, "even when we don't understand them. Sometimes, we just have to follow what seems right."

Aaron too got undressed and she put her arms around his neck. They lay down together, Aaron on top of her, resting his weight on his elbows. She stared at him, never wanting to forget the look of his face, his smell, or the heat of their bodies. They lay naked together and she whispered that he could do whatever he liked.

II

CCXXXI (Present)

Aaron felt the stone in his pocket, happy to find it still there. He rubbed its smooth surface. Doing so during times of stress and worry was a compulsion, dating back to when he was very young. He never went anywhere without it.

He wasn't entirely sure why the white pebble brought such comfort. Maybe it was because it offered something that he could control, giving some order back to the universe. He always had a need to organize and sort the world around him, but sometimes he'd face something he couldn't control, and then at least he had his rock.

Rella had asked him to recall what he remembered several times now. He was still trying to make sense of everything. It can't be real, is what he kept thinking. *These people can't be real. The Omi can't be back. Clare can't be gone. I'm actually still with her by the river.* But every time he opened his eyes, he was still walking through Eden's woodlands with the young brunette and blond monk.

The woodland mirrored how he remembered it, yet there was also something in his head that told him things were different. Dry, green trees surrounded them and there was a constant smell of composting leaves. Branches crackled under their feet as they walked. A gentle breeze brought with it the delicious scene of honey-sweet flowers. The scene was beautiful—too beautiful, like a dream so perfect it's obvious it can't be true.

If this was a dream, it was the most elaborate dream Aaron had ever had, filled with details such as the soldiers dressed all in red. Rella had called them *Security*.

"Any idea why we're being hunted down by Security?" Rella had asked Eric.

Eric held up a gold tablet. "They're after this."

"I thought you said you'd been asked to deliver it to the Omi's Sanctuary."

"Oh, I may have lied about that."

"You may have lied about that?"

"No, wait, I definitely lied about that."

Rella crossed her arms. "Explain."

"Nothing's changed," Eric said. "I was told to deliver this tablet to the Sanctuary by a messenger of the Creator, just not by the Monastery. The plan is still the same."

Rella flew her arms into the air. "What are you talking about? What messenger?"

"An old man in the desert."

"Do you realize how insane you sound?"

"The Creator provides the jigsaw pieces. As a monk, it's my duty to put them together."

Rella conceded with a sigh and suspicious stare. "Tell me, how did you become a monk, Eric?"

"I was given as a gift to the Monastery by my parents," he said after a pause. "They said I was too weak to work on their farm and so giving me away to the Creator was the only way I could bring blessings."

"I'm sorry to hear that."

"My parents thought my life would be one without meaning, but they were wrong. By following the Creator's path, my life will have purpose."

They decided to camp for the night. Aaron's head was spinning with all the information. He rubbed his pebble and thought back to the stories he had read to Clare, if only so the universe would make sense again for a moment.

He limped around, looking for firewood, which was about as much as he could contribute. He felt guilty that he was more of a burden than a help to Eric and Rella, but he didn't understand this world. His head was racing with too many questions. Rella had told him that his father and brother had been killed during the Omi's invasion and that Walter's library had been discovered. It was too much to take in. There were ten years missing of his life. If he hadn't seen Clare in that time, why was she still dominating his thoughts?

When Aaron first saw his reflection, he was disappointed. He always thought he'd grow to be bigger and taller like his brother and father, maybe just at a slower pace. Instead, he looked almost the exact same, except for some slight stubble and wearier-looking eyes.

No matter what he was dealing with though, he had no excuse for how he had stood idly while the Security had almost choked Rella to death; he truly was a coward. He rubbed the surface of the rock in his pocket, knowing that only by having Clare at his side could he be brave.

He was frightened that the Security would return for them, even though Rella had led them in a different direction so they wouldn't be found. Rella's efforts though would mean a longer walk to Tyrin's capital, and a longer time until he found Clare, if he ever even would.

They sat around the campfire. At the edges of his sight, he could make out Eric, staring into the fire, looking as though his eyes were struggling to stay open. Eventually, Eric stood and said goodnight, retiring for the evening. Rella had dug them each a shelter within the dirt hillside, telling them it would probably get cold once it was dark.

Aaron felt Rella's eyes on him. The conversation had pretty much ended when Eric left. He was the one who wanted to know more about Rella. He bombarded her with all sorts of questions. She and Eric had spoken more about the Ichu and Omi, the source of their war, and how Develon's reign had begun. Meanwhile, Aaron had stayed quiet, not caring about anything they had to say.

Just then, Aaron lost control. He rested his head into the palms of his hands and sobbed, thinking not only of how he had lost Clare but grieving for the lives of his brother and father. The death of his brother wore heavier on his heart than he ever thought it would; they drove each other crazy, but to lose his little brother made him feel as though he had failed at protecting him.

Rella walked over and put her arm over his shoulder, trying in vain to comfort him. "I think it's time we got some sleep too."

"I'm going to sit by the fire a little longer."

"Very well. Good night, Master Aaron."

She walked off, leaving him to sit by the flames alone. He knew he wouldn't be able to get any sleep. The drastic change was too much to feel any hint of relaxation.

He closed his eyes, seeking some rest, but to no avail. Insects and birds chirped, cheeped, and tweeted in the woods. A high-pitched whistle then interrupted his thoughts. He sat up and concentrated his hearing. Again, there it was—a faint whistling in the background. Thinking it was probably just a bird, he closed his eyes and tried to ignore it. The sound continued. Eventually, he stood.

Aaron walked away from the fire, towards the edge of the forest. He looked around for the source of the noise, but it had stopped. Something didn't feel right.

He could sense something.

Something from behind.

Someone.

He turned around, but it was too late. There was a smack against the back of his head. Then, all he saw was darkness.

Aaron's eyelids fluttered open, only to be met with a disorienting dizziness and a pounding headache. With each blink, his vision gradually sharpened, revealing his surroundings. He found himself situated in the heart of the forest, his hands stretched behind his back. As he tried to get up, his wrists throbbed with pain, a thick vine digging into his skin, and his back forced against a hard tree.

He was tied up.

Aaron scanned in front of him to find who could have done this, and he found them. Sitting a few feet away, holding onto a hand-crafted whistle, was Eric.

"Eric? Eric, what are you doing? Untie me!"

Eric didn't react to his cries, too focused on the small, wooden whistle in his hands. "This whistle was made from an elderflower tree. It's actually very easy to make your own whistle. I made this one with Brother Thomas, and I've carried it around ever since." Eric's eyes finally looked up to meet Aaron's. "Do you know anything about elderflower trees, Aaron?"

Aaron was flabbergasted. "What?"

"Amazing trees. They're used for food, drink, craftsmanship, and medical uses. But a thousand years ago, they had a far more spiritual cause. Back at the Monastery, I almost became a Master of Medicine. Never completed the training, but I took particular interest in the history of elixirs. The Ichu believed elderflowers could be used to summon demons in order to fight against the rising Omi. The Omi sought both the persecution of the Ichu, and also the extinction of elder-flower trees, because they represented a supernatural worship which the Omi couldn't understand. The beliefs over this tree's magical abilities were nonsense, of course. Yet, the tree is still used at modern weddings as a symbol of good luck. I guess we will always need something which is beyond the comprehension of the human mind. Something which can give us an unknown source of hope and comfort, which can neither be unproven nor confirmed. An unknown world of possibilities."

The dribble that was trickling from the man's mouth astounded Aaron. "What are you talking about? Never mind all this tree nonsense! Why the hell did you tie me up?"

Eric crouched down to face him. "I see it as my job, Aaron, to see that you're set on the right path."

"What path? Why did I even agree to follow you to Eden?"

"I told you that Brother Guin ordered you to join me, but that was another lie. I apologize, but your ability to decipher the tablet's hieroglyphics made it crucial for you to accompany me. We have all been chosen to fulfill a role."

"What role?"

"I don't know all the specifics yet. But I do know it can't be coincidence that I was told about a Countess of Eden and that you knew a connection to her. The three of us are meant to help each other. There's a plan set in motion that ends with us all getting what we want."

"All I want is Clare," Aaron cried, his frustration turning to anguish.

"And I want to help you find her. But first, you need to be strong. I know it isn't easy for you to be strong, Aaron, because you're enduring a lot of suffering."

"You have no idea."

"I know more about suffering than you might think. At least you loved. I don't know which is worse, the pain of grieving or the pain of loneliness. When the monks took me in, I was all alone. I didn't even speak their language. Brother Thomas taught me the ways of the monks and looked after me. He told me that I was meant for something great. It wasn't always easy to believe, but knowing that something bigger was awaiting me got me through difficult times. Suffering is how we are prepared."

Eric stood to his feet and took out a bottle of clear liquid from his pocket. He splashed it over Aaron's face, causing him to groan. It soaked through his skin and dripped down his face.

"What is that?" he asked.

"An elixir, containing elderflowers among other ingredients."

"Why are you doing this to me?"

"I am doing it because it's for your own good, Aaron, and for the greater good of all of us."

Eric walked away towards the bushes. Aaron shouted after him, "Wait! Are you just going to leave me here?"

"Man can survive in freezing cold, flourish in the depths of jungles, and conquer the highest mountains. You can surely free yourself, Aaron. The height of a task is only determined by one's state of mind."

Eric departed through the shrubs.

Aaron was alone.

He leaned back against the tree, thick vines coiled around the trunk, constricting tightly around his arms and chest. He tried to wiggle free, but their tightness burned and ruptured his skin.

Aaron stopped, wondering what the use was. There would be no reward for his struggles. He had nothing to live for. His brother and father were dead, and Clare was probably gone. He may as well die too.

Defeated, he lifted his gaze. The sun was ascending, painting the sky a vibrant blue. Rays of light filtered through the canopy of trees, and the forest came alive. Birds chirped in the sky, insects buzzed around, and larger creatures stirred in the underbrush.

Suddenly, another figure emerged, and his gaze locked with theirs in bewilderment. In front of him stood Clare.

Aaron's eyes widened as he beheld Clare's image, but she didn't look like herself. She wasn't smiling. She stared at him with dead eyes. Her skin was bruised and bloody.

"Clare?" Aaron said, his voice mixed with shattered spirit and childlike astonishment. Yet, Clare offered no response. She simply turned away, venturing back into the depths of the forest. Aaron's eyes remained fixed on the spot where she had stood. He screamed after her, his voice filled with desperation, "Clare!"

In an instant, Aaron found himself fueled by an entirely new determination.

He had to follow her!

With every ounce of strength he possessed, Aaron strained against the constricting vines, wincing in agony as they pressed against his thin bones. Clenching his teeth and summoning every ounce of willpower, he forced his hands upwards, disregarding the searing pain, until his fingers reached the knot cinched tightly behind his back. He tugged at the vine, gradually loosening its grip. He had unraveled one knot. A mixture of relief and anguish escaped him in a breathless exhale as he continued to loosen it, allowing the vines to cascade down and fall to the ground. He was free. He ran after Clare, not even bothering to rub his aching wrists.

Adrenaline flowed through Aaron's body, surging at the weight of what he had just seen. Well, what he thought he just saw. He realized he could have been hallucinating. Clare couldn't possibly be here, could she?

A scream filled the woods.

It was undeniably Clare's voice.

Aaron ran after her. He began to lose his footing and his bearings, stumbling around in circles. Coming to a clearing, he was surrounded by dense forest. He stopped. He had no idea where he was. He looked around, whispering, "Clare?" under his breath.

He spun faster as he called, his voice growing louder and louder. "Clare?"

He spun so fast he made himself dizzy. "Clare!"

There was nothing but complete silence. Too silent. No insects. No birds. No rustling in the bushes. Just an eerie silence. And the sound of his own breathing.

Aaron stood paralyzed, rooted in the heart of the forest. However, he soon realized that he was not alone. His breath hitched in his throat as a sound reached his ears—a sound that was too close, too near. Behind him.

He whipped around, ready to catch whatever he had been following. But to his dismay, there was nothing but the familiar sight of the woodland. Aaron crumpled to his knees, his hands clutching his head tightly. He was breaking apart! This couldn't be real!

A snapping twig jolted Aaron's senses, causing him to whirl around just in time to catch a fleeting glimpse of someone darting through the forest.

Aaron ran, pushing leaves aside. He could make out Clare not too far ahead. As he came close, she halted in her tracks. Aaron stopped too. She turned and faced him. The blood had vanished from her face. She looked as beautiful as ever, wearing the turquoise tunic she had worn when he first met her. A smile played upon her lips as she said calmly, "Hello, Aaron."

"Clare?" It was all that Aaron seemed able to say.

"Yes, it's me. I love you, Aaron."

"No…" Aaron's realization struck him with sudden clarity. This couldn't be real. He could see it in her eyes, in her presence.

"Kiss me, Aaron," she beckoned, leaning closer to him.

"This isn't real."

"Sometimes illusions are better than the truth. They can give us what reality cannot."

Perhaps an illusion was what Aaron wanted. He felt so weak and lonely without Clare. This could be his chance to find solace and recapture the companionship and joy that had slipped away. Now that Clare was here, he could return to a world where things made sense and didn't fill him with anxiety.

Clare pressed her gleaming lips forward, and Aaron trembled, a tear escaping his eye.

"Agghhh!"

Another scream rang out. This time it was the real Clare. It had to be. It was her voice. She sounded in trouble. It came from behind. Aaron didn't contemplate not answering it. He turned and ran in the direction of the scream, leaving the illusion of Clare behind.

The scream persisted, unrelenting.

He was close. It was coming from just the other side of the shrubs. Aaron pushed them aside.

His heart dropped.

It wasn't Clare. But someone else was there—Eric. Sitting on a fallen tree, waiting for him.

Rage overcame Aaron. He threw himself at the blond monk. They tumbled to the ground, Aaron clutching him tight. Eric lay on the ground, and Aaron sat on his chest to prevent him from getting up.

"What the hell did you do to me?" Aaron demanded.

Eric's eyes squinted in a condescending manner, as though expecting Aaron to already know the answer. And Aaron did know—the elderflower water that Eric had flung in his face. The visions hadn't been real. He had been hallucinating. He hadn't seen Clare.

"What did you see?" Eric asked.

Aaron didn't answer; he was aware that Eric already knew, and he wasn't one for answering rhetoricals.

"Be strong," Eric said. "Use the strength that Clare gave you, even though she isn't here right now, and that strength will help you get her back. I promise."

"How can you be so sure?" Aaron crawled off the blond monk.

Eric stood with a smile. "Because it's all part of the plan."

Chapter Eleven

I

CCXXI (X Years Ago)

In her bedroom, Rella sat at her desk, trying to recreate the object she had seen in the sky on paper. She grabbed hold of the wing-shaped necklace around her neck as she thought, an heirloom that had belonged to her mother.

When she heard steps behind her, she assumed it was her father, but was disappointed to see Brother Guin standing at her door.

"I'm going back to the Monastery now and came to say my farewells, Lady Rella," he said.

She turned back to her drawing. "Goodbye."

His steps drew closer.

"I didn't say you could enter my room," she said, twisting back to face him.

"What are you drawing?" he asked, ignoring her comment.

"It's nothing."

His pale eyes narrowed in on her desk. "It looks sort of like a mechanical bird. You must have quite an imagination, Lady Rella."

"You said goodbye," she snapped. "What else do you want?"

"I just want to give you a friendly warning," he said, crouching to face her. "You may be the Governor's daughter, but you should be careful how you speak to representatives of the Creator. Governors come and go, but He will always be there, and so will His followers. For example, if you were to let anyone see that drawing of yours, they might think such a thing actually exists, and then you would be guilty of spreading heresy. Then, not even your father could protect you. Better to hand it to me now, just to be safe."

Immediately, she knew it was a mistake, but, afraid, she handed the piece of paper to him. He folded it carefully and placed it into his pocket.

"That's a good girl."

Brother Guin left with a wicked smile. Somehow, in that moment, Rella understood everything she knew was destined to collapse.

II

CCXXXI (Present)

Rella awoke to an empty campsite. When the two men returned after sunrise, they said they'd gone for a morning walk. She didn't know what had happened during the night and didn't press it, but Aaron seemed different. It was as though he was mentally with them, rather than simply trailing behind like a stray puppy.

She could tell Aaron still felt scared and confused, maybe even a little guilty that he was of little help. But Rella didn't hold what happened with Security the previous day against him. Violence was frightening for some. In fact, she respected those for whom killing didn't come easy. It hadn't been easy her first time either, and she wished it were still not easy, even when it came to those who likely deserved it, like Kal.

They had left behind the forests and highlands. Now, the lowlands stretched before them, a sea of green and yellow meadows that seemed to never end. A cloudless, blue sky hung above them.

Rella studied Aaron as she walked. There was a sadness about him that interested her. It wasn't just that he was missing his memories and was confused, but something deeper.

"So, Master Aaron, tell me about what you like to do," she said.

"What do you mean?" he asked.

"Clare used to say you liked designing and now you're a Master of Architecture. Tell me about that."

"I don't know what you want to know," he said bluntly.

"If it bothers you to talk, I can stop."

"It doesn't bother me."

Blunt again, she thought. "Are you sure? It seems as though it bothers you."

"I'm sure it doesn't bother me."

"Why do you design buildings?"

His eyes widened. "That's quite a question."

Rella shrugged. "I simply want to understand why you do what you do."

"I still don't recall being a master, but I design constructions because I understand them more than I understand people… well, real people."

"What do you mean *real people*?"

"I read a lot of stories," he explained.

"You understand characters from stories better than real people?"

"People are confusing and inconsistent. They say and do things they don't mean, and you can only know what they want you to know. You don't get the same understanding and intimacy as you get with characters in stories. Characters, like buildings, go through a clear and logical journey, beginning with establishing the foundations. The only real person I truly understood was Clare."

"That is sad, Master Aaron."

"Will you stop calling me Master Aaron?" He sounded rather annoyed for the first time since she met him.

"What should I call you?"

"By my name, of course—Aaron."

Rella smiled. "Very well, Aaron."

Aaron nodded towards Eric, who led the way ahead. "You don't call him Brother, so why call me Master?"

"My father taught me to reserve titles for people of importance who have truly earned them," she replied. "Monks don't earn their titles. Not like my father. He fought, served, and sacrificed to become Governor of Eden."

"I'm not someone of importance," Aaron replied.

"You're a master, but not Omi. That means you gained your title through hard work. My father said that such a man should be respected. Then again, my father said that everyone deserves respect, yet I think people should have to earn respect. For example, I wouldn't—"

Aaron raised his palm. "I get it. Not everything warrants a conversation."

"So, in that instance, talking *did* bother you?"

"A little."

"People *are* confusing and inconsistent," she agreed.

A smile grew so briefly on Aaron's face that she assumed he let slip, because he made it disappear as quickly as it had appeared.

After allowing a moment of silence, she asked, "Do you think about Clare while we're walking?"

Aaron nodded. "Mostly, yes, as well as try to make sense of this strange world."

"Do you remember anything else yet?"

He shook his head. "Let's not talk about that. What do you think about as we walk?"

"A little while ago, I was thinking about what I'd do if a group of bandits attacked us, or if Security showed up. If they came from behind, I'd pull out my sword and spin around, before letting them know that I knew they were there. I'd stab the first one, then step back before another had a chance to strike. What I'd do next would depend on what they did next. If they tried to strike me overhead, I'd twist their hands back and pin them down. If they tried to strike underhand, I'd kick their hands. If they were to plunge their weapon forward, I would jump to the side, probably to the right, so I'd be close to you, Aaron, in case another tried to hurt you."

"You don't have to protect me," Aaron replied. "But it's very interesting hearing what you think about, albeit a little frightening. I guess you're always on the lookout for danger."

She was glad Aaron was opening up, but there were some thoughts of her own she hadn't shared, such as the dream she had last night. She had dreamed of feelings that she had long tried to forget; feelings about the only man who had ever made her heart flutter and her stomachache. When she told Elara about him, she had said that was what love felt like, but Rella hadn't been so sure.

As a child, Rella had been talkative and curious. It pleased her to see this side of herself resurface again with Aaron. Perhaps it was because she hadn't seen him since childhood, and he took her back to that time in her life.

Eventually, Rella, Aaron, and Eric saw a giant open crater in the distance. As they grew closer, they noticed several specks dotted around the ginormous pit. They were circular stone houses. Around them were people in the nearby fields, picking crops. The open pit was some sort of mine, around which the town was meticulously constructed in the shape of a perfect circle. The mine was so deep that the bottom was hidden from sight.

"There's a village here," Rella said, not quite able to keep the shock from her voice. "I had no idea."

"What is that?" Aaron pointed.

"I don't know. Clearly, they're mining for something."

Upon entering the village, the townspeople gathered from their houses and eyed the newcomers. Among the dozen or so dwellings, there stood a larger rectangular building, likely serving as a communal space for gatherings. Timid children peeked from their doorways while the adults clustered together at the town's center, eager to meet Aaron, Eric, and Rella. Almost every adult carried a blue jug. An older man, who reminded her of Alioth with his big belly and bushy beard, stepped forward, clutching a blue jug of his own.

"Hello travelers," he greeted them. "I'm the chief of this town, and it's my honor to welcome you."

"Thank you," Rella replied. "We saw the pit from some distance away. Did your village mine it?"

"We did." The old man beamed with pride. "And we continue to mine to this day."

Rella noticed over his shoulder people were hauling barrels of rocks and dirt away from the pit.

"What are you digging for, if you don't mind me asking?"

"Our village has always dug the pit. It serves as a unifying force. We take pride in detaching ourselves from the chaos that exists outside our borders. We pay our taxes, but other than that we spend every second of every day doing our work."

"You mean that you aren't mining the pit for any specific purpose?" she asked.

The man shook his head. "Our forefathers dug the pit and now we follow in their steps. Their motivations, whether it was the pursuit of ancient remnants, access to a hidden world, or great treasures, have been lost to time. So, now, we dig just to dig."

"To what end?"

"Do you not live a life doomed to end?" the man asked in turn.

Rella paused, a little taken back. "I suppose."

"Thus, our existence is just as meaningful as yours, is it not? For what do people typically strive for in life? They chase after wealth that cannot accompany them in death, and they pursue love that will inevitably fade away. Life is ugly, but digging the pit gives us purpose and structure as we pass the time."

Rella was shocked. She dreamed of a life without the Omi so life could be enjoyed, yet he was telling her life was inherently bleak. Sure, things gained in life would always eventually be lost, but experiencing them was what gave life meaning.

As she glanced around the faces in the village, she found it odd that there were a lot more women than men. What was more unsettling was that only the men carried weapons, mostly spears and crossbows.

"I would like to invite you all to stay the night," the village chief said.

"We couldn't impose like that," Rella replied immediately. "We merely wish to pass through."

"Nonsense. It will be dark in a few hours and there isn't another town for hundreds of miles. Please, it is our custom to welcome guests. We will all eat and drink together."

"That's a very generous offer," Eric said, stepping forward. "And we'd be fools to refuse it."

"Wonderful. Let me get you all some water to drink. You must be thirsty," the village's chief said. Eric and Aaron followed him.

Rella stepped after them, uneasy. It didn't seem right that a small village would have enough food to share with visitors, but perhaps the Omi and her experience with Kal had just made her skeptical of people. The village's chief opened his blue jug and took a swig. Even from a few feet away, Rella could pick up on the strong smell of acetone. She recognized the aroma. It was the fragmented grape juice that Kal had been drinking in Elara's house.

This was Kal's village.

III

Eric wasn't sure what was wrong with Rella. She seemed distracted and had been quiet since they arrived in the village. Other than the strong smell of the grape juice that was being drunk by everyone, the village seemed very pleasant.

After reviving themselves with water, Eric and Aaron were invited to join the men of the village on a hunt. Despite not being asked, Rella also came along.

Eric had never hunted deer, only reptiles and rodents in the desert, but he was interested to watch. He doubted Aaron had ever hunted anything in his life; he also opted to merely observe.

After walking several miles, they spotted dozens of hinds grazing in the woods farther ahead. Rella retrieved her bow and arrow, as did the other hunters in the group. The chief, who was red-faced from the walk, put out his hand, indicating they should all keep still. In a soft whisper, he told them to wait for his order, and each of the hunters selected their target deer. It was important they all fired together, Eric guessed, as the deer would all run off as soon as one was shot.

At the chief's directive, a flurry of half a dozen arrows was unleashed towards the herd. The majority of the hunters hit their intended targets, although a couple only managed to wound their prey and had to chase after it to finish it off. Rella's shot was perfect, striking the animal right in the heart.

As they made their way back to the village with their

spoils, a few of the men offered their congratulations to Rella for her impressive kill.

"Why are there no women on the hunt?" Rella asked.

"Men are the hunters, and women mend the gardens," one of the men replied.

"Why don't you bring the boys on the hunt to teach them?"

"Peter teaches the boys to hunt." He pointed to one of the men. "They don't join us on hunting trips, as children must miss out on things. It makes it more likely they will one day follow our traditions if it is something they long to take part in."

Rella nodded, but the furrowed expression on her forehead hinted at her dissatisfaction with the response. "What about the pit? Do only men dig?"

"Yes. To be recognized as an adult, a boy must first break stone. But breaking stone is hard work. My son is yet to do so. He must learn soon; otherwise, he will bring shame upon our family. My daughter even has more strength than he does."

"They could exchange jobs."

"Huh?"

"She could break the stone, and he could tend to the crops," Rella explained.

"Don't be absurd! No one would stand for it," the man replied, eyebrows crossed, and then he marched on.

"Their insistence on following tradition makes you angry," Eric said in observation to Rella.

"I wouldn't expect a monk to understand," she replied. "When I was a girl and my mother was sick, I wanted to learn how to help people, but the monks said it would be improper. Joke's on them though; I became a warrior and a hunter. Is there a labor the monks would consider more manly than that?"

Eric grinned. "Probably not."

She studied his smile curiously. "Doesn't my defiance of tradition anger you?"

"The early monks had to take risks when constructing their monastery. At that time, not everyone knew there was such a thing as the Creator. When spreading His texts, the monks had to endure rejection and ridicule. To be true though, one must do what they believe to be proper, even if the world says otherwise. It's easy to lecture from a seat of power. How many of today's monks would continue their duties if they were stripped from their warm beds and were attacked for sharing their beliefs? Most monks don't know what it's like to be an outcast."

"And you do?"

Eric nodded slowly. "I was something of a pariah at the Monastery. When I first got there, I didn't speak their tongue and I represented the unknown. That made me frightening."

"Lonely, too, I imagine."

"Yes, though I probably didn't help myself. The more the other monks excluded me, the more I rebelled. The more I rebelled—"

"—the more they excluded you."

"That's right. For instance, there was one senior monk who always had it in for me. He would constantly berate me in front of the other novices and took great pleasure in teasing me for my limited grasp of the language. One day, I'd had enough, and I snuck some bowel evacuants into his food from the medicine closet. He was shitting his pants for nearly a week. I got the cane twenty times for that one."

They shared a chuckle, and Eric thought she was maybe warming to him. A few philosophical beliefs aside, they weren't too different after all.

Eric watched the hunters curiously. They walked in silence, seeming completely aloof. There was no look of enthusiasm on their faces when they caught their food and they showed no curiosity, even though, as a monk, Eric was usually asked many questions when he traveled.

Just then, Peter asked flatly, "So, where are you from?", his eyes looking in Rella's direction. Though he was wearing the same brown fabric as the other villagers, Peter's skin was darker, and it was clear to Eric that he descended from those nearer Tyrin, as opposed to those in the lowlands of Eden.

"I'm from a nearby village," Rella replied, turning to him, surprised.

He nodded.

"Are you from this village?"

"No," Peter replied. "My village was destroyed, so I sought refuge here."

"Destroyed how?" Eric asked.

"By Cyllene, the fierce warrior who has been terrorizing this area."

"Cyllene?" Rella asked. "What happened?"

Peter's eyes stared off. "We had heard of her before, the witch who destroys towns and leaves one survivor. Unfortunately, when she came to my village, I was the person she spared. Our huts burned. Smoke clouded everything. Only screams could be heard. Women and children ran, but Cyllene slaughtered them. The men tried to fight back, but she killed all of them. All except me. As I lay on the ground, leg bleeding from where she had slashed me, the bodies of my fellow villagers all around me, I saw her emerge from the smoke.

"Cyllene rode towards me on her horse, only after making sure everyone else was dead. I crawled for my sword. Then a laced navy boot slammed down. I looked up and saw her face. She was laughing; her long, frizzy hair spilling in her face, and her crazy green eyes lit up with glee. She stroked my cheek and whispered in my ear, 'Spread the word of what happened here. Tell the people to fear me—Cyllene.' After she left, I found my wife trapped in our hut, killed by the flames."

His story finished, Peter lowered his head.

The village's chief said, "Luckily, he found us, and we were only happy to offer him a home." Peter, however, didn't appear as though he felt very much at home.

"I'm sorry to hear about your wife," Aaron told Peter, speaking for the first time since they arrived in the village. Eric eyed him, realizing Peter's story probably resonated.

"It has taken a long time to get past it, but I'm getting there," Peter replied, glancing at the village's chief.

"I can't imagine how. I've recently been separated from someone, and the pain is so intense that I can't even sleep," Aaron added.

"The nights are the worst. It takes a long time before the pain lessens enough for you to think about sleep. For a long time, I didn't even want the pain to lessen. I wanted it to fuel my anger so I could draw Cyllene's blood. But I gave up on hunting for her when I came to this village."

"If we give into our lust for revenge, it compromises our very selves," Rella chimed in. "Hate is a vicious cycle. If you let it consume you, then you merely pass more hate on and allow it to take more victims."

"You speak as though you have experience," Peter said.

"When the Omi invaded Eden, General Karmeeleon destroyed my home and executed my father."

"Ah, we all share hatred against the Omi," Peter replied.

Curiosity tinged Rella's tone as she probed further, "So, you abandoned the pursuit of revenge when you arrived here, because the people welcomed you?"

"No, that's not why I no longer hunt Cyllene." He lowered his head, and Eric took note of the sadness in his eyes. It was as if Peter meant something was keeping him trapped here and stopping him from carrying out his true desires. After a pause, Peter raised his head, and asked where they were going.

"We are heading to the capital of Tyrin," Aaron replied. "I

hope to reunite with someone there, and Eric is on a mission to the Omi's Sanctuary."

Peter turned to Rella. "And how do you fit into this journey?"

"I am assisting the monk in his mission, and in return, he has offered to help me find a dear friend."

"I hope that each of you finds what you seek."

The man who had engaged in conversation with Rella earlier took a sip from his blue jug and then extended it towards her, offering a drink. Rella politely declined. The man offered once more, but Rella still refused. Eric wondered why no one offered him or Aaron any of the grape juice and noted how disappointed the village chief looked when Rella declined.

Eric didn't like the feeling in the air. There was an indescribable disquiet, a feeling that something was amiss with the villagers. Was that why Rella had seemed distracted all day? Did she sense something wrong with this village before he did?

As soon as they arrived back at the village, Eric asked the chief if they could be excused to wash before dinner. They were told to make their way to the guest quarters—a building they could sleep in.

"What's wrong?" Eric asked Rella as soon as they reached the privacy of their own quarters. "You've seemed off since we arrived here."

"I think this is Kal's village, the human trafficker I found inside Elara's house."

"What makes you so sure?"

"The grape juice. Kal too had a jug of it."

Eric contemplated this, and then said, "All right, let's go. We'll be quick and get far away before they realize we've left."

Rella nodded in agreement.

There was a creak at the door. Rella drew her sword and pointed it at the intruder—it was Peter.

"Stay back!" she warned. "We're leaving!"

"As you should," Peter replied. "I came here to warn you."

"Why?" Eric asked.

"They've decided to make Rella a member of their village. The rest of you are no good to them and will be killed."

"Why Rella?"

"We are low on females this year since one of our suppliers didn't make it back from the winter. Our women aren't treated well here. They're owned by their husbands. You shouldn't stay."

"I don't want to," Rella replied.

"What would they do if she refused to join?" Eric asked.

"They'd force her with this." Peter lifted a jug. "There's a strong toxin in this drink, the samc one once used by the Chief Ichu. It's how he kept his army in line. The toxin dampens your mind and makes you dependent on more. That's why you were offered a drink during the hunt. After only one swallow, you would become completely addicted and you would do whatever they demanded in exchange for a continued supply of the drink. The men are told to dig the pit in order to keep receiving their share. There is a well in the village where the juice is fermented and has been since the days of the Ichu. Some say that the Chief Ichu blessed the well a thousand years ago, and that is how it got its magical abilities. Regardless, the well is the only place where the juice can be found.

"The village elders believe that if they continue to drink the juice as the Ichu once did, they are honoring the Chief Ichu's memory and carrying on the hope that he will one day return with his army of eternal slaves to defeat the Omi. Drinking the grape juice does not grant eternal life—only the Chief Ichu could do that—but it does make you a slave."

"Stories say that the Ichu were even worse than the Omi," Rella said.

"The village doesn't see it that way. They hope to discover

the Holy World and require the Ichu's help to do so," Peter explained.

"That's just a legend."

"They believe the Holy World is real," Peter replied, "and that it is located in the heavens. It was from there that the Creator created life and now He watches over us. The village believes that the Chief Ichu once created the formula for immorality and offered the secret in exchange for eternal service, exploiting the weak and power hungry. For some of them, he didn't even need to use the grape juice to make them his slave, as the mere promise of never aging sufficed. Then, with his army of slaves, he engaged in war with the Omi. Since the Great War, objects belonging to ancient civilization have been found, thought to have been brought to Arcadia by the Pure Bloods from the Holy World a thousand years ago, all marked with their mysterious writing."

Eric felt his heart begin to flutter. He unwrapped the tablet from the blanket and presented it to Peter. He pointed to the hieroglyphic engravings and asked, "Writing like this?"

"Yes." Peter gasped. "Exactly like that. Where did you get that?"

"It's what I'm bringing to the Sanctuary."

"You can bet it came from the Holy World a long time ago."

"Why are you helping us?" Rella asked Peter.

"They would hunt me down if I was to leave. They don't want anyone to learn of the well. A few days ago, they captured some Pure Bloods passing through and are planning to sell them. That's when I decided I can no longer bear being a part of this village."

"Pure Bloods?" Rella's voice perked up. "Are they being held in the village?"

Peter nodded. "Yes, as prisoners, until the villagers can find a buyer."

"Take us to them."

IV

They crept through the village streets in darkness, Peter leading the way. *It has to be Elara and her father,* Rella thought. *They must have been traveling south when they were captured by the village.* If Rella didn't have cause to hate the village beforehand, she certainly did now.

As Peter brought them to one of the stone houses, there were two villages with spears stationed outside. They eyed them suspiciously, then Peter pulled out a knife and stabbed one in the chest, pinning him to the wall and covering his mouth to stifle his cries. Rella followed by example and took care of the other one. Peter then rummaged through their pockets, searching for keys.

Inside the house, there were three men and two children, all helplessly shackled to the floor. Sure enough, they were all redheads and pale-skinned. However, there was no sign of Elara or her father.

The tallest of the men regarded them with caution. Meanwhile, the children, a girl and a boy of similar age, cowered behind the older of the men, clear from the wrinkles etched upon his forehead.

Rella stepped forward and put out her hands. "We don't mean you any harm. I'm Rella. We're here to help you escape this place."

The tall man hesitated for a moment, and then replied, "I'm Lukas. If you free us, they'll come after us."

Peter dashed forward with the keys and freed the prisoners from their chains. "There are some horses nearby that you can all take."

Lukas looked to the older man, who, after taking a second to think it over, nodded in acceptance.

They all followed Peter outside and down the street to some tied-up horses.

"Now, all of you must go," Peter said. "They will be almost

finished cooking the deer and then they will discover you are missing. During dinner, they will try once more to get Rella to drink the grape juice. Only this time, they won't give up so easily."

"Come with us," Rella said.

"Thanks for the offer," Peter replied. "But I'm staying here."

"Why?" Eric asked.

"I refuse to give up on the children that I teach. Maybe I can give them the chance for a better future, one where they think for themselves and don't tediously follow traditions. I'll make sure they don't continue digging that awful pit, and that they work to live, instead of live to work."

Rella nodded, and then tapped his elbow with her own. "Thank you for helping us."

Eric and Aaron also tapped Peter's elbow and said good-bye, before following Rella's lead and jumping on a horse. The Pure Bloods did the same, Lukas and the older man each pulling up one of the children to accompany them. Rella unleashed her blade and cut free the other horses so the villagers wouldn't be able to follow them.

They all galloped towards the tree line. As they left, Rella looked over her shoulder and gave the mining town one last stare.

Chapter Twelve

The Omi's Sanctuary was concealed within Anubai, the Omi's secret capital, home only to officials of the Omi.

Within the capital, General Karmeeleon ran the Palace of Justice, a monumental temple that stood in the heart of the city. It contained various chambers of courtrooms where crimes against the Omi were taken, but they were all empty. According to public perception, there were no crimes against the Omi. Yet, execution rates across Arcadia were astronomical and jails were full, holding elderly people who once worked for Queen Shanleigh or young people guilty of questioning the Omi's rules or breaking their laws.

The citizens of Anubai lived their lives in bliss, completely ignorant to the crimes. Like the poverty faced by many in the Omi's kingdom, crime was out of sight and, thus, out of mind.

General Karmeeleon made his way to the interrogation room in the Palace of Justice, the sound of his bare feet echoing through the stillness of the stone corridor. His scale-encrusted arm reached for the door and pulled it open. His cape trailed behind him as he entered, and the cold stonewalls caused a chill to run down his reptilian spine.

Within the room, a small circular pool of water occupied

the center. Submerged within its depths was Talitha, the squad leader who had failed in capturing the criminals of Eden and, even worse, had fled after her team's defeat. Her brunette hair was neatly tied up in a bun, and she remained in her uniform. Her head and arms were bound by chains, attached to a wooden post behind her. She stared, eyes wide and piteous, as General Karmeeleon entered the room. The other Security members in the room turned their attention to him as he approached the pool, bowing in respect.

"I'm sorry I failed you," Talitha squeaked to him in a pitifully frightened tone.

"It's not that you failed me that fills me with such ire," he replied. "It's that you ran away from your assignment. Cowardice is the worst trait that Security can have. Now, I must make an example of you. However, you can make things better for yourself by being of some usefulness to me."

"Anything, my lord."

"Where were the criminals going?"

"They were traveling south, my lord."

"To where precisely?"

Her eyes watered. She shook her head, trying to hold back tears. "I don't know," she sobbed.

Karmeeleon felt the rage build inside him. Giving into emotions was a weakness that had to be eradicated within Security.

He pulled a piece of rope from the stone ceiling. Talitha shook her head and cried, begging him not to. But it was too late. The water in the pool gurgled, releasing steam into the air. Talitha screamed as the water scorched her skin.

Once he had heard enough of her cries, he released the rope. The water gradually cooled, causing the bubbles and vapor to disappear. Talitha panted, her heart struggling to continue and sweat dripping off her as if she was in a sauna.

"Tell me about the criminals," he ordered, his composure remaining undisturbed.

"The monk was accompanied by a woman and a man," Talitha replied, her voice strained as she struggled to catch her breath. "The woman was a native of Eden and had long brunette hair. She was the one who owned the blades."

"Blades?"

Talitha took a deep gasp of breath. "Yes, my lord. She carried a chest, which concealed three weapons. She gave them out to the others, but only the monk fought with her. The other man was dressed as a master. He must have journeyed with the monk from the Monastery."

He rolled his eyes in disbelief. "So, one woman and one monk managed to defeat your entire squad. How is that even possible?"

"The woman fought well, my lord."

"Tell me about the blades," he instructed.

"I didn't get a close look, my lord, but they were three silver blades."

"Did they reveal any information over where they were going?"

"No, my lord. I wish I had more information to give you, but I don't."

"Very well, Talitha, thank you for your assistance."

"Please, my lord," she begged, "I've told you all I can. Please, be merciful."

"You still have to be punished for your sins, Talitha," he replied. He reached for the rope. "Don't scream this time. It will only worsen your fate."

The squad leader closed her eyes and braced herself for what was to come, muttering for grace under her breath. General Karmeeleon pulled the rope, causing the pool to boil once more. As he expected from a coward, Talitha screamed as she writhed in the scalding, bubbling depths.

After dealing with Talitha, General Karmeeleon made his way from the Palace of Justice to Develon's palace. Making his way through the main hallway adorned with vibrant royal red walls, the floor beneath him cushioned by a luxurious carpet, he passed by an assortment of treasures and antiques collected from all corners of Arcadia. With a brief knock, he announced his presence and confidently entered Develon's throne room, well aware that Develon awaited his arrival.

He kneeled before Develon's golden throne. Develon's face was covered by a gold mask, engraved with hieroglyphics, their meanings unknown to almost anyone but the ancient inhabitants of the lost Holy World. Some say he wore the mask to hide his non-human features, and others claimed he had been horribly deformed in combat when overthrowing Queen Shanleigh and her followers. The mask emitted a radiant glow, accentuating Develon's piercing blue eyes, while a voluminous crimson robe enveloped his entire form.

"Your Highness," General Karmeeleon addressed Develon, "I have dismissed the council as you instructed. I made it clear to them that Security and I will personally handle these three particular fugitives."

"The entirety of that council has become frail and useless to the Omi."

"Perhaps they should be retired."

"Indeed. Have Principal Sin imprisoned for his failure. He and Commander Straumme were unaware of whom they faced. Do not make the same mistake."

"Understood, Your Highness," the general replied. "The Security squad I dispatched failed to capture the group. However, the squad leader did catch a glimpse of them and provided a report. There is one woman and two men, all armed with blades of silver."

Develon sat back in his chair, sighing. Mention of the blades clearly filled him with even greater worry, much as it had General Karmeeleon when Talitha shared with him the news.

He knew even better than Karmeeleon that these three particular criminals were indeed a great threat. The news that they had taken out an entire squad of Security was frightening enough. The information regarding the blades, however, changed everything. If these were indeed the blades that Karmeeleon and Develon believed them to be, it suggested their greatest fears were a reality.

"Find these three, swiftly and quietly, before this goes any further," Develon ordered him.

The general rose from his kneeling position and bowed. He traveled alone to the lowlands of Eden, mounting a particularly large kappatora, over seventy feet in length. He felt uncomfortable using a fellow lizard species for transport, but they were obedient, and their long strides and strong limbs made them exceptionally fast options for transfer over long distances.

He inspected the area where Talitha's squad had found them, discovering a discarded walking stick. Karmeeleon sniffed the cane to pick up on the scent of the owner. Next, he inspected the footprints in the grass, made during the scuffle. One of the criminals wore heavy boots, but the other two wore sandals, the kind issued by the Monastery. Talitha had said one of them was dressed like a master. If he still wore Monastery-issued sandals, he had likely only just graduated. He could ask at the Monastery to get the man's identity. Maybe there were family or friends who would be useful to him.

Karmeeleon followed the scent and footprints. Talitha had reported that the group was traveling south. They were, in fact, now heading southeast; they had probably slightly changed their paths in hopes of not being tracked. Karmeeleon knew there was a nearby village in this direction —the one with the giant pit.

Once he arrived at the village, he recognized the scent of the grape juice once used by the Ichu, containing a toxin now forbidden under the Omi's rule. He remembered words from the Creator's texts: "A man who does not follow the laws of the land will be burned".

The residents recognized him as a threat and prepared to attack, picking up bows and spears. They fired arrows, but those did little against his thick armor. Three men with spears crept up behind him, but he tripped them over with the tail that slithered behind him.

In that moment, a primal instinct surged within him, tempting him to unleash his sharp teeth and claws upon his fallen attackers. However, he recalled as a child being punished for biting or walking on all fours because it was non-humanlike. This was back in the days when his species had been exiled by humans, before he helped the Omi with their conquest. Karmeeleon took no pleasure in reminding himself of those times; he could not behave like some uncivilized creature and had to control his primitive instincts. Instead, he unsheathed his large sword and cut through the villagers like twigs, keeping only one of them alive to interrogate.

Meanwhile, in the vast fields stretching for miles, the women had taken to fleeing in the opposite direction of the village. Karmeeleon grabbed the small flamethrower he kept attached to this belt, fueled by naphtha and quicklime. He fired at the crops, then watched as the flames spread rapidly across the fields, engulfing all in their path. The women's terrified screams pierced the air.

The survivor, a fat man who was likely in charge of the village, was crawling away. Karmeeleon picked him up and dragged him to the edge of the open pit.

"I'm looking for two men and a woman. They may have passed through here recently. Have you seen anyone you didn't recognize?"

"They were here," he said immediately.

"Do you know where they are going?"

"They are going to Tyrin's capital."

Karmeeleon felt a smile grow on his face. He thanked the

large man and then tossed him into the pit. Karmeeleon peered inside but the drop was too deep to see the man's body.

There was a sound of rustling from the tree line. Without thinking, Karmeeleon dropped to all fours and dashed towards the noise. Behind the bushes, a man stood with a group of children. The man went to lift his spear, but Karmeeleon sliced the man's neck with his claws before the spear even cleared his waist.

As the body dropped to the ground with a thud, the children gathered round and watched the spread of blood, not looking all that particularly horrified by the sight.

Karmeeleon noticed a bag on the man's back and then realized the children were all carrying clothes and other belongings, as if they were about to go somewhere.

"Who was he?" Karmeeleon asked the children, pointing to the dead man on the ground.

"Our teacher," one of the older boys replied.

"He was taking us away from the village," a girl added, "so we could start to do things differently."

"Oh, no," Karmeeleon said. "Things should remain as they are."

One of the smaller boys picked up a blue jug from near the body, inspected it curiously, and took a sip. He passed the jug around and all the children took a swig. The children scrunched up their faces, sickened by the toxin that was seeping into their systems, but to do what they thought was proper, they persisted.

Karmeeleon walked away, knowing the children wouldn't last long on their own. Another errant community had met their demise, and all that would remain of them would be a meaningless relic, much like the heretics.

Better than that, he knew where the troublesome group was going, and he would have a surprise lying in wait for them at Tyrin's capital.

Chapter Thirteen

I

Stone columns came into sight, marking the border between Eden and Tyrin. Beyond them, Rella could see the ground growing dryer and dryer until there was nothing but pale brown sand. The desert stretched south for tens of thousands of miles.

Apparently, Lukas and the other Pure Bloods were part of an even larger group. They had been collecting water for their camp when they were captured. Rella and the others had offered to escort them safely to their people.

Proving he was telling the truth, Rella soon observed that the sand was scattered with footprints indicating a herd of people had recently passed through, including adults and children of all ages and sizes. Alongside them, hoofprints indicated the presence of horses and goats.

"Why are you traveling through the desert?" Rella asked Lukas as they trekked. "Don't you know there's nothing for thousands of miles?"

"We had to leave our home. It wasn't safe there anymore after we had been discovered."

"Where is home?"

"The uncharted lands, north of Eden," Lukas replied.

"There's nothing north of Eden except mountains and ocean."

Lukas smirked. "Oh, there's more than that."

The Pure Bloods walked ahead, and Rella, Aaron, and Eric followed them the rest of the way to their camp. As they walked, Rella was mystified by the lack of green and streams. Since entering Tyrin, they had only seen a handful of trees, all of which were less than a third of the size of those in Eden.

Eventually, they came across a camp in the desert, consisting of a couple dozen tents. Rella couldn't believe it—they were all redheads. It was a community of Pure Bloods. Rella didn't think there were this many of them left in the whole world.

It was a traveling village, and they soon found themselves in the center of it as the members came to investigate the strangers and huddled around them. The community happily greeted Lukas and the others, clearly overjoyed by their safe return.

"Thank you for escorting us safely," the older man said. "I'm Chaikou, and this is my son Rikka."

Chaikou pointed to the boy who had walked with them and he grinned happily. Rella smiled back.

"Most people prey upon our community, simply because they can, but you chose to help us. Why?"

"I have a friend who is a Pure Blood," Rella replied. "So, I'm familiar with your struggle. It makes me sick how the Omi hunts you."

Eric stepped forward and opened up his arms. "Make no mistake, we're not all morally corrupt. The Creator teaches us to care for our fellow human beings."

"Yet monks hunt us just the same as everyone else." The man's stare turned cold.

Eric shrugged. "I don't."

"But your brothers do."

"Most of them, yes. They are under the illusion that spilling holy blood will persuade the Creator to reveal His Holy World."

"Is this monk to be trusted?" Chaikou asked Rella.

Rella had no idea. He had previously saved her life, but her own survival was currently to his benefit. "Either way," she said, "it's dangerous for a community of Pure Bloods to travel through Tyrin. Lukas told me that you have come from north of Eden."

Chaikou nodded. "That's correct. Our people have lived there in camps since the Omi's return. Hiding. It wasn't easy, living between the mountains, but we made it work. We fished from the sea, and we scaled the mountains—thousands of feet tall—to catch birds and eggs. Things got easier once we discovered the mountain goats; they gave us milk and meat. The conditions were freezing, but we lived in tunnels made by the heretics."

"The heretics?"

"Yes, there are a great number of remnants there from their civilization."

"How do you know the tunnels were made by the heretics?"

"The tunnels were smooth to the touch, and there were long, thin tracks on the ground —like iron, but not quite. No living people we know possess such technological prowess, and only the heretics held such knowledge. Witnessing those tunnels, I became certain that the tales of the heretics were true. Centuries ago, humankind possessed secrets that have since become lost to us. That's why the Omi want us to never speak of those times. They fear that if we remember, we might learn. And if we learn, we might uncover a way to defeat the Omi."

Rella thought back to the tasers Security had, knowing the Omi had knowledge they were keeping secret.

"Where did the tunnels lead?" Eric asked.

"We don't know. They went for miles and miles, and we were never able to follow one to the end."

Eric and Aaron looked skeptical of the man's story, but Rella needed no proof. She had known the stories about the heretics were true ever since she was a little girl and had discovered one of their observatories. As a girl, she had called it the Eye. From there, she, Clare, and Elara had seen a metal container crash from the sky. The girls had sworn to keep their secret hidden, vowing to bury it in the depths of their memories, but Rella had never forgotten; she often wondered about who might have discovered the strange, metal object.

The man held up his palm. "Enough talk for now. It is rude to not welcome guests appropriately. We may not have much to offer, but we would be honored to serve you each a cup of our exquisite tea."

They agreed readily, though their stomachs were hungry for more. A place was cleared around a campfire. A select few of the elders sat down, leaving enough space for Aaron, Eric, and Rella. They took a seat, and the aromatic tea was carefully poured into small clay cups that were then passed around.

Rella took a sip, experiencing a taste that was both bitterer and sweeter than the tea Alioth used to make. As the liquid trickled down, it settled her growling stomach and infused her insides with a comforting warmth.

"Is this all your people?" Rella asked.

"No," an old woman replied. "Some of our kin settled in Eden, but we wanted to get as far from the mountains as possible."

"Why?"

"We were not alone there," an elder man added.

"You were discovered by the Omi?"

The old woman shook her head. "Not the Omi."

"Then by who?"

"The Ichu were living there. That's why we had to escape."

"The Ichu are extinct," Eric said. "They were killed by the Omi in the Great War."

"You're wrong," the old man said. "We saw them. They've been living there for centuries, hiding from the Omi, praying for their Chief's return."

"They would howl in the night." The old woman trembled.

"Howl?" Eric asked.

She nodded. "They're like animals. They wear the skin of men and women, but they are not human. They have become something else entirely. The Chief Ichu once granted them eternal life for their service. Do you know what it's like to face something that never dies? Their skin has paled, and their eyes are lifeless, but they walk all the same. They devour raw flesh because they don't have to worry about getting sick. They walk around the mountains in bare feet and ripped clothing, impervious to the biting cold. They don't bleed. They leave no tracks."

"Did they attack your people?"

"They attacked Kathe's camp—the girl you freed. The Ichu murdered all of her people, but she escaped. She came and warned us. Told us they were coming. She's a special girl."

"No more of these depressing tales." The old man stood slowly. "We are hosting guests and that calls for celebration. Tonight, we shall revel in life and cast aside thoughts of death. Bring forth the drums. It is time to dance."

The community erupted into cheers, and the elders stood up in unison. Men swiftly retrieved the drums, and the rhythmic beats filled the air. Everyone began to move in sync with the music, dancing joyfully around the crackling fireplace. Eric wasted no time before bouncing up and jiggling his arms and head. Rella thought he looked like a demented monk undergoing an exorcism, but at least he was getting in the spirit.

Rella hesitated. She hadn't danced since she was a child and there would be celebrations at her father's palace. Back then, she quickly realized her lack of grace, often stumbling around the dance floor rather than truly dancing. Usually, she would dance with Elara, as boys rarely approached her. Her father said they were intimidated by her being the Governor's daughter, but she also did not believe herself to be a great beauty. Moreover, she sensed that boys were put off by her tendency to ask too many questions and her more argumentative nature.

Before she could muse any further, Lukas dragged her to her feet. With a friendly smile, he guided her towards the crackling fire, prompting her to mimic his rhythmic footwork. It was a pattern of moves that she just couldn't quite figure out, but she enjoyed trying to all the same.

As they danced, Rella realized she couldn't see Aaron. She spun her head round and caught sight of him sitting with the girl they had saved earlier. Kathe was reading a book, and Rella figured that was probably what had drawn Aaron's attention.

II

"I'm Kathe."

"Aaron," he said.

"You don't like to dance, Aaron?"

"Not really. And even if I did, my mind isn't really in the right place for it." Though Aaron's body was twenty-five, he still felt ten years younger in his head, and he was motivated by curiosity. "What are you reading?"

Kathe, who was probably about twelve years old, showed him the hieroglyphics on the pages of her book. "It's an ancient, dead language. I like the pictures, though."

"You don't understand the pictures?"

Kathe shook her head. "The elders say they are going to teach me one day. There aren't many who understand the language."

"I do."

"Really?" Kathe leaned forward and beamed bright. "How?"

"My mother is a Pure Blood. I thought all Pure Blood mothers taught their children to read and write."

"Maybe they do, but I lost my mother a long time ago."

"I'm sorry to hear that. What happened to her?"

"She traveled south into Eden when I was young. It was her duty to spy on the people there, and to see if we could come out of hiding. Omi Enforcers caught her. Other spies saw it happen."

"What's your mother's name?"

"Anett." Kathe's eyes brimmed with tears. "The Omi have probably murdered her."

"You don't know that for sure."

Kathe brushed the tears from her eyes. "I must be strong for her though and continue with my own duty."

"What duty is that?"

"All Pure Bloods have a duty to protect each other and to protect all of life." Kathe flipped to a page in her book and pointed to a symbol made of interlocking rings that created an eye-shaped oval. "I may not be able to read the symbols, but I know that this represents the grace of life."

Aaron nodded. "Indeed. It is the symbol of creation."

"It is?"

"It is meant to embody the Holy World."

"That's where my people are from. We came from there a thousand years ago," Kathe said. "It's why the Omi want to kill us."

"The villagers told me that you saw your people get attacked by the Ichu. It must have been terrifying."

Kathe's demeanor shifted and her voice filled with sorrow. "It was worse than anything you can imagine. The Ichu jumped my village like a pack of wild dogs. They gnawed at necks and crunched through bone. They howled the cries of death. But they were worse than wild dogs. They didn't kill because they were hungry or desperate. The Ichu don't need to eat, don't you understand? They're immortal. They ate my people just because they could."

"What do they want?" Aaron asked.

"The Ichu have been hiding in the shadows, awaiting the return of their Chief. Once he comes back, they will emerge and reclaim Arcadia. All they want is to destroy life. They are the bringers of death. Nothing more."

III

Rella was beginning to fall into the rhythm of the dance, and she laughed with Lukas. The elders surrounded the two of them and clapped in time with their steps. They were all smiling joyfully, though Rella couldn't tell if it was because they were impressed or amused by her efforts; she feared it was the latter but tried to pay it no mind.

Lukas leaned forward, pushed the hair away from over her eyes, and told her she was a good dancer.

"Really?" she asked. "I feel clumsy and as though I can barely follow the steps."

Just then, the music stopped and so did the people's partying, as one of the drummers yelled and pointed towards the tree line. There were sudden screams and the sound of boots on the ground. Dozens of Enforcers surrounded them.

Rella's heart sped as the people around her screamed. A woman and her children were dragged away by Enforcers, then locked inside wagons like cattle. The Pure Bloods tried to defend themselves as the Enforcers attempted to carry more away, but they were not natural fighters, and they had no weapons. The Enforcers beat men to the ground bloody and then tossed their limp bodies into the wagons. Standing next to the wagons was an old man in a grey tunic. He appeared to watch the carnage with indifference, his stare devoid of feeling. His badge told Rella that he was the one in charge of the Enforcers. He was likely Commander Straumme, Develon's Lord of Peace.

A girl's piercing scream filled the air. Rella looked to see Aaron lead Kathe through the swarm of bodies. An Enforcer stepped in their way. The girl had only Aaron to protect her. *Damn, she's doomed.*

Rella dashed over, drawing her sword. She stood between the Enforcer and the girl, telling Aaron to take her to safety. Taking hold of the girl's hand, Aaron whisked her away.

The Enforcer's eyes narrowed on her. He grinned and leapt at her with his sword. She swiftly evaded his attack, ducking under his blade, and slashed open his guts as she did so. Rella spun round and kicked him in the direction of the campfire. The man's legs collapsed beneath him, and he sat right on top of the flames. He screamed in horror in his last agonizing seconds as his grey tunic became alight.

"Rella!" Lukas yelled, and her peripheral vision caught a glint of light from the flames reflecting on a blade. She spun out of the way of the sword heading in her direction. Rella thrust her sword into her attacker's stomach.

Lukas grabbed her by the hand and pulled her over to the edge of the fire, where Aaron, Kathe, and some others had managed to escape to. "Let's go," he said.

The elders were rushing the children and adults onto horses. They gave one to Aaron and Kathe. There was no sign of Eric; that could only mean the Enforcers had captured him. Lukas mounted one of the horses and put out his hand. Rella took it, put her foot in the stirrup, and swung her leg over the horse. The horses stomped against the sand into the darkness. Rella glanced back over her shoulder to see the Enforcers escorting the elders into wagons.

Rella's instinct was to rush back and rescue them. There were dozens of soldiers though, and she didn't feel confident enough to take them all on. Not when the Pure Bloods didn't have weapons to help, and there were defenseless children. She had to think it through. They could trail the Enforcers, and then form a plan to rescue Eric and the others.

Once they were a safe distance away, the horse came to a stop, and Rella slid off the rump. Chaikou stood waiting for her, hands on hip.

"You did this!" he yelled. "Our people have been taken captive because of you!"

"What makes you think it was because of us?" Rella asked.

"We heard the Enforcers yelling that they were looking for the wild woman and for the monk. They were looking for *you*. They followed *your* trail. And *you* led them right to us!"

Rella felt her heart in her throat. The Pure Bloods had been captured, and it was all her fault. Now, she had to make it right.

Chapter Fourteen

Commander Straumme navigated the corridors of the Monastery, eventually ascending the stairs that led to Brother Guin's office. He was pleased to be meeting with Guin, instead of the Monastery's non-human abbot; Straumme had dealt enough with freaks and monsters. Still, he loathed the monks. They were physically weak, self-righteous, and acted superior to everyone else. The Omi needed more seasoned soldiers to strengthen it, not frail clergymen.

Brother Guin looked up sharply, greeted Straumme, and told him to take a seat. Straumme stayed standing, having no desire to stay long.

"After the arrest of Principal Sin, I'm surprised to see you, Commander," Guin said. "I heard that you and local Security failed to apprehend Brother Eric, and so General Karmeeleon decided to take the matter on himself."

"You should get better intel."

"Oh?"

"The monk met with a wild woman from Eden, and then they traveled into Tyrin together."

Guin waved his hand in the air. "I already know all of this. Get to your point in coming here, Commander."

Straumme said through gritted teeth, "The group joined a traveling community of Pure Bloods in the deserts of Tyrin. My men tracked them down and launched an attack. While the feral woman and a Monastery master managed to escape, we successfully apprehended Brother Eric and the majority of the Pure Bloods."

Brother Guin sat forward. "Pure Bloods? How many?"

"We captured twenty-four, and about a dozen of them got away."

Guin's eyes widened. "A community of thirty-six Pure Bloods? That can't be true! Where have they been hiding all this time?"

Straumme shrugged. "They won't say. Yet."

"Have you alerted General Karmeeleon?"

Straumme shook his head.

"Why not?"

"I would rather capture the wild woman and young master myself."

"How will the Pure Bloods help you do that?" Guin asked.

"The wild woman appears to have a connection with their community. The prisoners have revealed that she claims to have a Pure Blood friend. I suspect it might be the same girl that the Enforcers recently seized in Eden and are currently transporting to the Sanctuary."

"So, you believe they are headed to the Sanctuary?"

"I believe so."

"That would make sense. The object Brother Eric stole from the Monastery was a tablet, and he was adamant about delivering it himself to the Sanctuary."

"I also suspect the wild woman will attempt to rescue the Pure Bloods and Brother Eric, and so I plan to use them as bait," Straumme said. "Failing that, my Enforcers will ambush them at the Sanctuary."

"And since only monks, General Karmeeleon, and

Develon know of the Sanctuary's location, you have come to me for passage." Brother Guin smiled, understanding now what it was Straumme wanted from him. "What are you giving me in return?"

"I will give you the Pure Bloods that my Enforcers have captured. All twenty-four of them. You can deliver them yourself to the Sanctuary and offer them as a gift to Develon. My Enforcers will escort you all the way. As soon as the criminals make their move, my Enforcers will be ready for them. The criminals will be mine, but the Pure Bloods will be yours. Develon will be so pleased with your gift that he will make you a bishop, or at least an abbot. Can you picture it? The blood of twenty-four Pure Bloods spilt all at once. It will be the largest sacrifice to the Creator there has ever been."

Brother Guin smiled wickedly. "Lucky for you, I do want to be bishop or abbot. Not for selfish reasons, that would be prideful. I want the power to make the Monastery as it once was. When I first came here to become a Master of Medicine, women were strictly forbidden from entering the buildings. It was Develon's idea to install a nunnery, just as it was his idea to let women and non-humans become council members and soldiers. A monk should never have to look at the female form. It provides an opportunity for evil and temptation to compromise important work."

Straumme smiled. Finally, a monk he may actually like. He felt a sense of thrill at finding some support for his own convictions. Clearly, like him, Guin believed that the Omi had once enforced higher standards, and that the Omi had allowed a sickness to creep in under the rule of Develon. Perhaps, together, they could do something about this.

"Develon is too focused on finding the Holy World," Guin continued. "An important task, don't get me wrong, but there are other matters at hand. Despite the Omi's efforts, Arcadia is still plagued by sin and reformism. If I became bishop, I believe I could be the strict hand that Arcadia needs to enforce tradition."

Straumme stood with a smile. "Then I suppose I can trust you to lead my men to the Sanctuary?"

Brother Guin stood and tapped his elbow. "Absolutely."

Chapter Fifteen

I

Eric didn't understand the Omi's obsession with hunting and sacrificing Pure Bloods. Besides the fact it was immoral, it didn't seem likely that the Creator would value spilt blood. Men like Brother Guin simply received pleasure from feeling superior. That was why they felt the need to impose their beliefs upon others. It may have been a monk's duty to spread the Creator's words, but Eric didn't feel it was his or anyone else's place to force people into believing those words; people had to ultimately make up their own minds.

When Brother Guin arrived upon his primed horse, he introduced himself to the Pure Bloods as their captor and to the Enforcers as their acting commander. He was visibly outraged to see women among the ranks, and the first thing he did was relieve them of their duty. The entire time he addressed them, he stared at his feet as if making eye contact with a woman would cause him to melt.

Brother Guin's argument was that men were superior to women, and he was as conservative as a person could be, but Eric wondered if there was a simpler reason for Guin's uncomfortableness around women. Guin's pasty skin and thinning hair at such a young age made him strange-looking, and Brother Thomas had once told Eric that many men were defensive due to insecurities.

Brother Guin guided the convoy from horseback at the front; it was probably the proudest moment of the robed monk's life to be commanding and leading an army of men across the desert towards the Omi's Sanctuary. In his mind, Guin envisioned himself as the chosen savior, handpicked by the Creator to cleanse Arcadia of its sinners. The simple truth was Guin was no warrior, and he wouldn't even be able to exterminate a beehive without directing someone else from fifty feet away.

Eric traveled within one of the horse-drawn carriages, along with other prisoners. He felt so guilty it was hard to even look at his fellow detainees. The Enforcers had been tracking him and his friends, leading them right to the Pure Bloods. He told them to have faith that his friends would come to save them.

Brother Guin made the party stop every morning and evening for prayers, and he gathered all the Enforcers to listen to his hymns and preaches. At this rate, it would take them months to reach the Sanctuary and Guin's convoy couldn't have had more supplies than that to last them a week. After prayers, the prisoners were thrown stale bread to eat and bowls of water to share and drink from like dogs. They weren't allowed out of the carriages for anything; not even to relieve themselves.

On the second night, Enforcers took Eric from the carriage. They brought him to a fireplace where Brother Guin and a ring of Enforcers sat. A delicious-smelling stew bubbled within a cauldron atop the fireplace, causing Eric's belly to rumble. Eric's tablet lay at Guin's feet, as well as the blade that Rella had given him.

"I knew there was something strange about you," Guin

said. "No holy man should know how to use a sword. When Brother Thomas brought you to the Monastery, I knew it was a mistake to let you stay. First of all, you didn't even speak our tongue. You should have been left to die in the desert with the savages you came from. Luckily, through the Creator's wisdom, everything works out the way it's supposed to in the end. Now, you will be taken to the Sanctuary and executed along with the criminals you have sided with."

"A word of wisdom, Brother," Eric replied. "If you talk less, the people around you won't realize just how dim-witted you are. Or, at least, they won't recognize it quite so quickly."

Brother Guin scowled. "You're no brother of mine, and I'll hear no wisdom from you. You're only so confident because you think your friends are going to try some daring rescue attempt. It won't work though. If they're smart, they'll be on their way. My men are ready for them."

"Your men? Since when do humble monks command men?"

"Since the Creator granted us with the power to do what must be done to keep swine in line."

"I thought it was a sin to assume the Creator's will," Eric said.

"Excessive humility can also be seen as a transgression if it leads to disobedience. I am aware of the Creator's plans for me because of the gifts He has bestowed upon me and the path He has set me on. If the Creator did not intend for me to be a bishop, He would not have made me smarter than other men."

"If you're one of the Creator's smarter children, humanity is truly doomed."

"We'll see who's laughing when I'm recorded for the rest of time as a bishop and you're nothing more than a pile of ash."

"You'll be bishop when I shit gold."

Guin flushed crimson. "I didn't bring you from your cage to hear your insolence. You are a prisoner, and for now, you will be our server and cupbearer. Pour the men their stew, and make sure their cups are full. It's a long march to the Sanctuary; they need their strength."

Eric knelt and stirred the cauldron. When sure no one was looking, he rummaged through the bottles of herbal medicines and elixirs he kept in the inside pocket of his robe. One of the bottles contained the hallucinogen he had given Aaron, and another was intended to make men expel their stomachs —he had used it on Guin once before at the Monastery—that was the one he wanted. He covertly poured the contents into the stew and mixed it in.

"Hurry up!" Guin roared.

Eric scooped the stew into bowls and handed them out, being sure to serve Guin first. Guin snatched it from him and poured the stew greedily down his gullet right from the bowl. After Eric had served all the Enforcers, he sat back and waited. He knew that Rella and Aaron had to be waiting atop the sand dunes with the rest of the Pure Bloods, spying and waiting to make their move.

Eventually, Guin slumped forward and clasped his stomach. He turned to one of the Enforcers and muttered frailly, "I think one of the prisoners has cast a spell on our meal."

The Enforcer stared at him blankly. "Pure Bloods don't know magic. They're not Ichu."

Guin waved the air with one hand, still clutching his stomach with the other. "They are all the same—heathens, sinners. They know only the ways of evil and sorcery."

Pure Bloods can't cast spells, you fool, Eric thought. *They're just people with red hair*! He decided not to say anything for fear of drawing attention to himself.

The Enforcer shrugged his shoulders and kept eating. "Tastes fine to me."

Guin slapped the bowl from the hungry Enforcer's hand, spilling it over the ground. The man looked as though it took everything he had not to tackle the senior monk to the ground. "Are your brains made of dogshit?" Guin yelled. "I am telling you that this food is cursed. Stop eating, all of you! You do as I say!"

Eric eyed the circle of Enforcers cautiously from the outskirts of the fire circle. They all seemed too hungry to take anything Guin was saying seriously; they had been marching for days on rations and without a hot meal.

Guin stood and stomped the ground, enraged at being ignored. He wailed like a high-pitched infant not getting his way, "Listen to me: That food has been claimed by malevolent forces. I command each and every one of you to drop your bowls immediately."

For a moment, Eric thought there might be a mutiny and Guin's own men might do everyone a favor and take him out themselves. Before Guin could protest any further, his face twisted in pain, and he made a hasty departure from the group. He headed for the tree line, attempting to disrobe on his way, but not succeeding in time as he doubled over and disgorged from both ends. It was a sin to take pleasure in the misery of others, but Eric had to smile at Guin's predicament.

Just then, one of the Enforcers hunched forward and spewed over the campfire. Men stood and made efforts to distance themselves. Soon, they were all spilling their guts. The campground filled with a vile stench and suffering cries.

"This is an attack!" Guin shouted. "Call out the scouts!"

"There are no scouts," one of the guards said.

"Why in the depths of hell not?"

"All of the scouts were women, and you sent them away!"

Before he could say anything else, Guin threw up once more and then passed out in a puddle of his own making.

Eric made a run for his sword and tablet while everyone was distracted, and then he bolted for the wagons. There were still guards stationed by the carriages, but some of them had gone to check on their fallen comrades. He crept in the dark to one that was unguarded and tried the door—*locked*.

"Don't worry," he whispered to those inside. "I can use my sword to break through the wood. And my friends will be here soon. I'm sure of it."

There were mostly elders inside the cattle, but also Rikka, the boy they had saved from Peter's village.

"Take the boy back to his father," one of the prisoners said. "Don't worry about the rest of us."

Rikka managed to squeeze between the bars at the back of the wagon and Eric carried him to the ground.

"I have to save all of you," Eric said. "If you're taken to the Sanctuary, you'll be killed for sure."

"Even if we do manage to escape, how do you think we will outrun the Enforcers? They will come after us. We aren't going to take the chance that some of our people will be killed in the process."

Eric wanted to argue further, but there was the beating of footsteps behind him. He swiftly grabbed Rikka by the hand and they ran into the darkness.

Eric and Rikka ran through all the night. By morning, Eric was sure they had managed to escape from the Enforcers. The young boy asked where his people were and Eric told him that they would surely be looking now the sun was rising.

They had not been walking across the dunes for long in the daylight, however, when Eric suddenly froze, hearing the faint sound of hooves against the ground. The very land seemed to tremble in response, causing particles of sand to dance in the air around them.

Eric scanned the area. Soon, his gaze landed on a figure charging toward them on a sleek black horse. The rider was adorned in light brown armor, donning a hooded purple shawl, and a brown facemask.

Eric grabbed the small boy by the hand, who started to

cry, and stormed up a neighboring sandbank, the sand making the run twice as difficult. He glanced over his shoulder, and, to his dismay, they were not outrunning the bandit.

The bandit leaned forward and slapped the sides of his horse to command it go faster. Eric ushered the boy behind him and pointed his sword at the bandit. The bandit stopped short, glancing Eric up and down, his expression indicating he was more frustrated than afraid.

The bandit unsheathed a curved blade. "Step aside," he spat. "I don't want no bounty on me for killing a monk. I just want the boy."

The boy grabbed hold of Eric's legs and cowered behind him. "He's going to sell me to the Omi," the boy said.

"Just doing my duty as a loyal citizen." The bandit smiled, displaying a set of horribly stained teeth. "Pure Bloods are wanted by the Omi these days. If the Omi happens to pay a reward for them, that's merely a happy bonus. Don't be getting any ideas now though, you hear me? I spotted him first, and I'll fight you for him if you're thinking about getting that reward for yourself."

"I don't want the reward," Eric said. "But you're still not taking the child."

The bandit grunted and then charged his horse at him. Eric ushered the boy to the side, then leapt away, just missing a swing of the bandit's curved blade. Over the bandit's shoulder, Eric could finally see Aaron and the other Pure Bloods. He sighed with relief. There was no sign of Rella, though. Then he saw her: she was already running up the sand dunes to his rescue.

II

Before the bandit had a chance to charge his horse once more at Eric and the boy, Rella jumped at the side of the horse. The extra weight was enough to make the horse tip over, and it tumbled down the sand dune, Rella and the bandit rolling along with it.

At the bottom of the sandbank, the bandit landed atop Rella and pinned her to the ground. He cleverly sat down on top of her so she couldn't kick his vulnerable area, which she otherwise most definitely would've. Behind the bandit, Rella saw Eric and the boy make it down the dune just as Aaron and the other Pure Bloods ran to meet them.

As the bandit reached for his weapon, Eric suddenly stomped the bandit's hand into the sand. He cried in pain, and Rella wriggled her arm free. She picked up her blade and sunk it into his stomach, silencing his yelps as he collapsed on top of her. Rella twisted herself out from under the weight of his body, and Eric offered to pull her to her feet.

"It's fate," Eric said with a smile. "The Creator delivered you just in time."

Rella shook her head, not sure what to say, and she dashed over to Rikka.

The horse, unfortunately, broke its legs in the fall. Eric knelt beside it and muttered a few words under his breath. Was he uttering a curse or was he providing a short prayer? Rella couldn't tell. Eric was either simply an unorthodox monk or a deranged radical. She hadn't yet decided. He then cut the horse's throat with his blade. Rella winced.

"Are you all right?" she asked the small boy.

Chaikou, the boy's father, stepped between them. "You have done enough. We will take it from here. You and your friends should be off."

"But we need to help you free the rest of your people."

"We don't want your help," Lukas said. "You'll only make things worse. Our people take care of their own. We'll find a way to free our people."

"How can you be so sure?"

"I'm not," he replied. "But our people will live together, or we'll die together."

Chapter Sixteen

General Karmeeleon brushed against the tight walls of the Monastery as he made his way through the labyrinth of corridors towards the nunnery. His conversation with the novices had told him that Master Aaron was the one he was searching for, given that he was near the end of his noviceship and had recently disappeared from the Monastery without warning. The sinful runaway, however, had left behind a mother, who taught young girls at the Monastery.

Inside the nunnery's classroom, Karmeeleon found a grey-haired woman preparing for the first lesson of the day. Panic flared in her eyes as she spotted him in the doorway. He made his way inside without invitation and sat across from her desk. The woman had freckles beneath her eyes, and he knew the moment he smelled her that she was a Pure Blood.

"Is this to do with my son?" she asked.

"Why would you say that?"

"He's been missing for several days."

"I still don't see why you would draw a connection so quickly between his disappearance and my arrival. Do you know who I am?"

She nodded slowly. "Everyone here knows who you are."

"What do they say about me?"

"They say you are a monster, who betrayed his own species to help the Omi conquer Arcadia because he so desperately wanted to be accepted by humans."

"They are the Creator's chosen species," Karmeeleon said. "Who wouldn't want to be accepted by them?"

"When I first moved to the City of Eden with my family, Aaron so badly wanted to make friends. He went out to play with boys from our street. One of the boys had built a slingshot and the others thought it would be fun to hit birds with it in the forest. Aaron grabbed the slingshot off the boy and threw it into the river. He got a beating for that and became a pariah among the boys. I had never been prouder."

Karmeeleon clenched his fist beneath the table but tried not to show how much her words had pained him. "If you know who I am, you know that I only deal with the most serious of threats to the Omi. Do you have reason to suspect your son is a threat?"

"Aaron would never harm anyone."

"In fact, he has harmed quite a few people. That is why I am looking for him. He needs to be stopped."

A wave of sadness overcame her, and her voice cracked as she spoke, "Not my Aaron. You have made a mistake."

"The Omi don't make mistakes. Where did you think your son had gone when you heard he disappeared?"

"I thought he finally left to find a woman."

"A woman?"

She looked down, for a moment appearing as though she may defy him but then thought better of it. "Clare Ifran. He has been in love with her since he was a boy. I thought he might have gone to find her."

"The daughter of Walter Ifran? That man was a traitor, guilty of spreading heresy."

The woman lowered her head, and Karmeeleon tried to consider what this all meant. He had recently been in the highlands of Eden to capture a Pure Blood. There, he had discovered Alioth, an old enemy to the Omi in hiding. Karmeeleon had slaughtered Alioth's village as punishment for harboring him. It all had to be connected. Alioth had once created weapons for Queen Shanleigh's army, so it would explain how the fugitives had their blades if they had been in Alioth's village.

Karmeeleon turned his eyes back to the elder woman in front of him, who was close to tears. He should have arrested her and brought her back to the Sanctuary, but she was old and no threat to the Omi. Besides, he already had an unspoiled Pure Blood caught and ready to be sacrificed.

"I want you to do me a favor," he said.

She raised her head to look him in the eyes. "What is it?"

"When you teach the children about the Omi, tell them I am not a monster. After all, today I will let you live."

"What sin have I committed, General?" she asked.

"I know a Pure Blood when I see one."

She looked down at her feet. "Then I guess you know where I am if you ever need more blood to spill."

"Yes, I do."

Part II

Chapter Seventeen

CCXXXI (Present)

Nissa could not remember the last time she felt fear. Even clinging onto the mountainside above the clouds, she knew if she fell to the bottom that she would be unscathed. The climb was not dangerous, but it was difficult. The slope was rough and craggy, and finding a path required sure footing.

The wind howled relentlessly, but Nissa remained impervious to its biting cold. Dressed in sturdy black boots, to match her black, loose clothing, she had tied back her pastel-blue hair to keep it from being swept over her eyes by the gusts. The voices of her people echoed in the wind, their cheers resounding from below. Like her, they understood everything was about to change; by scaring the Pure Bloods into the Omi's territories, Nissa's people could no longer remain hidden. Their enemies would be ready for them, but Nissa was not afraid. Her people had been waiting centuries for a fight.

As she ascended further above the clouds, she wondered if any others had ever gone this far. If she were still human, the high altitude would have induced dizziness and breathlessness.

The sub-zero temperatures would have inflicted frostbite upon her skin. The dense clouds and treacherous wind made seeing almost impossible. Surely, no one could survive these conditions.

Yet, someone had.

Nissa came upon the unbelievable sight of human male faces carved into the mountainside. The noses of the men were at least twenty feet in length and fifteen feet in width. *Did the heretics build these structures? If so, why? And how?*

In front of the four faces, there was a flat piece of the mountain where she could stand. It was not flat by natural forces. Rather, some incredible technology had cut through the mountain at some point in time.

Turning away from the imposing faces, Nissa shifted her gaze toward Eden and the other territories of Arcadia, though the thick clouds obscured her vision. As the wind intensified, its powerful gusts pressed her against the monumental human carvings. This was precisely why she had embarked on this arduous climb: The wind was trying to tell her something, and she had ascended to hear it better.

Closing her eyes, Nissa inhaled deeply, letting the wind's essence fill her senses. Amidst its whispers, she discerned an unmistakable scent—the return of her master.

Her people would celebrate wildly when they heard the news. After centuries of waiting, the Chief Ichu had returned.

After descending the mountain, Nissa traveled south with a few comrades. Once they located the Chief, he would call the others. They stole some horses in Eden and traveled to Tyrin, a land of intense dry heat.

Eventually, they came to a large boulder in the middle of the desert, placed there as a marker. They dismounted and one of her comrades—Kannoe—moved the boulder with a few grunts. Hidden beneath it was a carved stone hatch, and Nissa meticulously examined the hieroglyphics inscribed on the entrance to confirm that they had arrived at the correct location. With Kannoe's assistance, she pushed the cover aside, revealing a dark hole illuminated by white stone rungs, which they used to descend into its depths.

When they reached an underground tunnel, Nissa lifted a torch from the wall and effortlessly conjured a flame with a flick of her hand. The illuminated path guided their way as the rest of the group followed her through the winding passageway.

It was a maze to reach their destination. Any wrong moves led to booby traps, intended to murder intruders. The others appeared lost, but Nissa strolled on. For years, she had dreamed of walking again down this corridor.

Along the way, carved markings on the walls illustrated the story of the Ichu and Omi's Great War. But, like the directions through the tunnel, Nissa knew the tale by heart.

Finally, as they reached the end of the passageway, they emerged from the tunnel, finding themselves in a crater sheltered by encircling mountain ridges. Within the crater, chambers were hewn into the walls, including one that had once belonged to their Chief. Ancient statues and columns lay shattered on the crater's floor, remains of the Ichu's headquarters from before the Ichu and Omi's Great War.

Nathan's chamber, however, remained almost completely intact. Columns and windows lay beside a doorway which led through the crater wall. An engraving of the Holy World hung above the entrance.

Nissa could sense her Chief's presence, and she wondered if the others could feel it too. She guessed they did, because, like her, they got down on their hands and knees, facing Nathan's doorway. They bowed their heads and awaited Nathan's entrance.

A shadow crept against the stone wall, heralding his

appearance. Emerging from the dark cavern, he gracefully stepped into the sunlight.

Nathan was pale-skinned, like all Ichu, and had bloodshot eyes, but he looked younger than Nissa remembered, with fewer wrinkles and firmer skin.

"It has taken many years for me to recover from my injuries," he said, speaking at last, and Nissa noted his voice sounded thin and penetrating, while it had once been husky and deep. "I am finally ready to lead our people into war once more against the Omi. However, this time we will not fail. Are you ready to follow me for a second time?"

"Yes, Chief Ichu," they all said in unison.

"Our people have fled to the outskirts of the continent to avoid detection by our enemies. Together, we will reunite them all. The Omi have allowed themselves to become weak. They will be no match for our army."

"What is your first command for us, Chief?" Nissa asked.

"Mamoru is currently being held prisoner within one of the Omi's prison camps. Release him. I have a special task for him. Soon, we will bring the Omi to their worthless knees and reclaim our lands."

Nissa and the others nervously rose to their feet. They bowed once more, then they left through the maze of tunnels they came through in order to complete their ask. However, as Nissa walked, an unsettling feeling gnawed at her core: This was not the master she remembered.

Chapter Eighteen

I

CCXXI (X Years Ago)

Lord Patrick was overcome with fury. Soon, he would return to Tyrin and tell his parents about his encounter with Clare of Eden, and they would be enraged. It would be greatly detrimental to their name for a merchant's daughter to have refused a proposal from a Governor's son. Naturally, Patrick's parents would blame him for the family's humiliation. They'd figure he mustn't have been charming enough or that he must have said something offensive.

He led his men across the lowlands of Eden on horseback, striking down any merchants on the way so they couldn't repeat what they might have witnessed in Clare's city. It would make no difference—Patrick had already told everyone he was going to marry Clare of Eden—but killing them made him feel less livid and pathetic. Patrick wished he could have killed the entire market for laughing at him. And Clare—he wanted to pin her down and make her love him. She had made him feel like when he was a boy, scolded by his father in front of others, unlike his mother who would only ever yell at him in private. The worst part had been everyone nudging each other and whispering as he exited the market. He had tried to act above it all by avoiding eye contact and keeping his head held high, but there was no hiding his reddened complexion or the sharp inhalations through his nostrils. He was a lord, and so how was it that a merchant's daughter could make him feel so small?

They spotted another lone merchant. Patrick unsheathed his sword. He was happy to kill someone. Anyone. As he got closer, he waved his sword into the air, but the man defended himself and kicked Patrick in the groin.

Patrick cradled over in pain. He clenched his teeth and knew he would make the man pay. When he was a child and felt angry or embarrassed, he would sometimes sneak into town and start a fire. It calmed him to watch the flames, and if the fire were big enough then it would draw the attention of those in town. He liked to stay and watch the crowd, feeling a buzz from their fear and horror. If he was lucky enough, someone would die in the flames, and he would feel an intoxicating surge of power course through him.

The leader of Patrick's men, Onrik, led the rest of the men over to the merchant. Onrik was unfriendly and not the bodyguard Patrick would have chosen, but his parents trusted his life with Onrik. He was short and bald, but broad and intimidating with a sizable growth on the left side of his neck. Onrik struck the merchant right in the face, busting his nose and flattening him to the ground. The rest of the men encircled the merchant to make sure he couldn't escape. Onrik presented him to his lord, knowing Patrick would want to be the one to deliver the kill.

Patrick removed his hat and riding gloves, handing them off to Onrik. He stood over the merchant. "You could have died quietly, but now I'm going to make sure it hurts."

The grey-bearded merchant was barefoot and destitute. His wagon was full of spices that he hadn't had much luck selling in Eden. He stared at Patrick with defiance in his eyes, then spat at Patrick's feet.

Patrick unsheathed his sword and dug it into the merchant's knee. It didn't go very deep despite his efforts, but it was enough to make the man yelp in pain, and so Patrick acted as though that was as deep as he meant to go.

He yanked back his sword and then hacked at the man's neck, attempting to cut the head clean off, but it was harder to do than he had realized, so it took a few attempts. Once the head was detached from the body, Patrick grunted for breath and kicked the body a few times for good measure.

Staring down at the body, Patrick spat and then noticed something in the dead man's grubby hand. Patrick remembered there had been rumors of Clare's father spreading heretic knowledge. It was one of the reasons his mother had not wanted him to go north and propose. She would have preferred him to marry a Governor's daughter than a merchant's, but Patrick was already a Governor's son and so had the privilege of being able to marry for beauty, rather than for power.

Patrick picked up the book and flipped through it. He had never bothered with learning to read, and he didn't recognize the words from those given out during services.

"What does it say, my lord?" one of his men asked.

"Shut your mouth until you're spoken to," Patrick snapped. He didn't want his men getting the wrong idea; they might think he couldn't read because he was stupid, not because he simply had no interest in the matter.

He tossed the book to Onrik, knowing he could read. "Is this what I think it is?"

Onrik took a look and nodded. "It's heresy."

"Do you think it could be from Clare's village?"

"It could be. You could show it to the Monastery and demand they search the Ifrans' residence for evidence."

Patrick felt a smile grow large on his face and told one of the men to ride ahead and tell his parents what he had discovered. Not only did he now hold the power to bring down Eden's Governor, but he would get revenge against Clare by having her parents arrested. If he could lead an attack upon the City of Eden for their treachery, he would also be able to teach people what happens when they laugh at him. All those who had wronged him would tremble in terror at his name.

Patrick and his men approached the palace within the capital of Tyrin. They walked past the rows of stone houses. Unlike the new and pristine homes within Eden's city, Tyrin's houses were in need of repair. Most of them belonged to artisans and traders, with their stores on the ground floor and their living quarters above. Patrick suspected most of them had more money than they let on. They probably avoided fixing their homes hastily to prevent Patrick's father from raising their taxes. Once he was Governor, no one would be able to pull the wool over his eyes, and he'd make all who had made fools of his family suffer.

His parents were there to meet him at the palace's door, and he noticed the disappointed scowls on both of their faces. His mother's lips curled into a slight smile once she spotted the book in his hand.

Patrick straightened his posture. "Dear parents, I have brought you evidence of treachery being committed in the lands of Eden. I suspect the Governor there has broken the laws of the Monastery."

"At least you did *something* right," his father sneered.

Patrick lowered his head, hiding his trembling lips.

"You did well, darling," his mother said.

"Thank you, Mama."

Patrick followed his parents inside so they could discuss the situation. As they entered the grand lounge, Patrick was surprised to find Brother Guin already sat there.

"What is he doing here?" Patrick disliked being in the presence of monks; he feared they could see into his soul and read all his transgressions. There was nothing he feared more than death, for then he would be judged by his maker.

"What do you think, you idiot?" his father roared. "He's here to examine the book you found."

"If the Monastery declares Walter Ifran as a traitor, it could help alleviate our embarrassment," his mother said more softly.

Guin stood. "Arcadia's peace is balanced by the laws of the Queen and of the Monastery. If the Queen's followers are choosing to forsake the latter, all will be truly lost."

"Eden has always been a cause of trouble," Father said.

"It's because they live so far from the Monastery and the rest of civilization," his mother added. "They run wild with their ideas and have no one to ground them."

"Indeed." Guin placed his palm in the air, indicating he wanted to do the talking. "I have further news: The Omi have returned."

Patrick's heart stopped, and, somehow, he knew that his world was never going to be the same again.

"What are you talking about?" Mother asked. "The Omi's followers never really disappeared. Everyone knows that."

"One of those followers rose as an aid of the Queen, and their numbers have multiplied in the south. Truthfully, the Queen's days are numbered. This aid—a non-human, named Develon—has a powerful army at his command, full of former war heroes from the days of the Omi. All they need is for someone to help them secure the north."

"You're asking me to betray my Queen?" Father asked.

"She won't be your Queen for much longer, and everyone

knows you've always truthfully been a loyalist of the Omi. This is your chance to help in their inevitable return and to reap great rewards."

"What is it you hope to gain from this situation, Brother?"

"If I help you conquer Eden for the Omi, I'm sure Develon will make me a bishop or at least the abbot of the Monastery."

Few people had seen the Monastery's current abbot. Patrick heard that he was a non-human, obsessed with the Holy World, and that he spent his days and nights in the archive rooms of the Monastery, hunting for clues over the Holy World's location, leaving the day-to-day running of the Monastery to his senior monks.

"We'll start by looking at the book you found and then search for more of them at Walter Ifran's home," Guin said. "Thus, turning the people against Eden's Governor and ensuring no one will fight for him. After all, if Walter Ifran has been spreading heresy, the Governor must have known."

"You can tell the Omi they have my loyalty. My son and I will lead my men to Eden as soon as we are given the order," Father said. He bowed and then left with Mother.

Guin turned to Patrick with a smile. "Is attacking Eden really something you want? I hear you want my cousin's hand in marriage more than anything."

"No, not more than anything."

"Then tell me, Lord Patrick, what is it you want?"

"I don't want to be afraid of anyone or anything. I want people to fear me instead and to know what happens if you cross me. And I never want to feel guilt or shame. I want to be strong all the time."

"Are these not feelings that make us human?"

Patrick frowned. "To be human is weak. It means you can be killed. I want to live forever."

"You sound like the Ichu. They too once searched for ways

to cheat death. You should speak to the monks in your city about what's been gathered about them."

"The Ichu were heathens," Patrick protested. "You dare compare them to me?"

"They were sinners, it's true, but they amassed great power. If we could learn the secrets to some of that power, it could be of great help in the war to come."

Patrick's eyes lit up. "What kind of power?"

"Power that will make you something more than human."

"How did the Ichu gain their power?"

Guin's thin lips bent upwards into a large smile. "The answers come not from our world, but from the heavens. The Chief Ichu collected cells from divine lifeforms and mixed their blood with blood from Arcadia." He reached into his pocket and retrieved a folded piece of paper, which he handed to Patrick.

It was a drawing of what Patrick could only describe as some sort of flying device.

"I caught Lady Rella concealing this."

"What is it?" Patrick asked.

Guin shrugged. "When you take her and her father prisoner, be sure to ask her. She won't want to tell you, so you must make her talk."

Patrick smiled at the idea of making his enemies pay, and at the thought of being remembered for leading the battle that reclaimed Eden for the Omi. He wondered if when people would tell the story, they'd know it was all because of a girl who hadn't known her place.

II

CCXXXI (Present)

After leaving the Pure Bloods, it was a long journey to the capital. Rella had been taken aback by the myriad of unexpected differences since leaving the highlands of Eden. The accents of the people she encountered grew smoother and smoother, the once fierce winds now calming with each passing day, and the air becoming drier and drier. But most striking of all was the relentless, intensifying heat that seemed to permeate everything around her. It was as if she could even smell the scorching heat in the air.

During their travels, they practiced with their swords most nights. Alioth had taught Rella many techniques, which she could now apply to coaching Aaron and Eric. Aaron's poor coordination meant he wasn't a natural fighter, though he was gradually showing some signs of improvement. Eric, however, had come far from when they had faced Security; Rella no longer feared him cutting off his own limbs when he swung the blade.

Hunting for food and gathering water hadn't been any problem. They had mostly tried to avoid other people, in order to not repeat another incident like the ones at Kal's village and with the Pure Bloods.

A gigantic wall surrounded the city, obscuring sight of any buildings. Rella knew this, though, to be the location of the capital, as the capital was the only place within Tyrin that would be large and rich enough to fund a wall protecting such a mass of land.

A massive entrance had been carved into the thick wall, leading into a dark tunnel. Curiously, there were no guards present, so they cautiously ventured inside. The wall surrounding the city was incredibly thick. It took some time to walk through the tunnel, but finally there was light in sight. A portcullis blocked the rest of the passage, lit only by a single torch. A guard sat at the other side.

Unlike the Omi Enforcers or Security they had encountered before, the guards in Tyrin's capital were personally recruited by the Governor. This particular guard, attired in simple leather armor and laced boots, seemed less menacing compared to the Omi. As they approached, he rose from his creaky wooden chair. "Greetings. I am Aelius, the leader of the capital's guards. What brings you to our city?"

"We wish to enter," Rella replied, stepping forward.

"Then you must join the competition."

"What competition?"

"Our Governor offers everyone the opportunity to enter the capital. However, they must first prove their worth in his arena."

Rella thought about this and then turned to the others, looking to see their view.

"He mentioned an arena and proving ourselves. What does he mean?" Aaron asked.

"It will be a fight to the death. Presumably, it's their method of managing overcrowding within the city."

"Not only that," Aelius said. "It serves as a means of bringing joy to the lives of those residing in the capital."

"In what way?"

"A fight to the death provides entertainment. Our Governor is smart enough to see that entertainment is a way of finding pure joy in life. So, he invites every resident in the capital to watch the battles in his arena. Therefore, if you agree to participate in the competition, you must also swear that you will strive to entertain. The Governor wants a good show. If you succeed, you will gain a comfortable lifestyle for the rest of your days within the capital's grounds. There is an ample supply of exotic foods and drinks, all paid for by the taxes of Tyrin's villages. And you can enjoy watching future battles in the arena. You will never again have to face the daily struggles of beating a living out on the soil, so the competition is well worth the risk. However, agreeing to take part in the competition isn't something that should be taken lightly. Sometimes, we get fools who think they can fight, only to change their minds during the competition and wind up begging for mercy in the arena. They don't receive any."

"What about the monk?" Rella asked.

Aelius shrugged. "Unless he has an invitation from the Governor or Omi, he will have to fight just the same as everyone else."

Eric stepped forward. "We'll fight."

Rella grabbed his shoulder and pulled him back. "What are you talking about?'

"The Creator has gotten us this far. He won't abandon us now."

"I don't remember the Creator being there when we were attacked by bandits, cannibalistic villagers, or Omi Security. I remember us having to fight them all on our own. We'll be alone too in this arena, and I don't know if we'll all survive."

"Eric's right," Aaron said. "We've been through too much to turn back now."

"Aaron, if we enter this competition, you'll almost certainly die."

"At least I'll die fighting to reunite with Clare, rather than alone in the desert."

There was no convincing them. Rella turned to Aelius and shrugged. After all, it was Aaron and Eric she was worried about, not herself.

"Will we each face a random opponent?" Rella asked.

"Your opponents await you already," Aelius replied with a grin.

"Then we will fight."

Aelius opened the gate and let them in. He frisked them and told them they could keep their swords but confiscated the taser guns they had held onto from their confrontation with Security. He then led them to a chamber in the passageway, where ten competitors waited. Aelius told them that they would be spending the night there, reminding the others that if they killed each other during the night no one would be given citizenship. The first battle would begin in the morning.

Observing the other participants, Rella noticed a range of expressions. Some appeared frail and desperate, clad in tattered garments, armed with meager spears, and bearing terrified expressions. Others seemed far more prepared, adorned in sturdy armor, wearing confident smiles, and wielding an assortment of weapons such as swords, knives, bows, and arrows. One individual even brandished a thick wooden club, adorned with a long, sharp nail.

Amidst the competitors, a lone woman stood apart from the rest. Clad in a vibrant purple shawl, she had short black hair and a dark complexion. Meanwhile, the man wielding the ball club passed by her, directing his attention towards Rella.

He grabbed her by the arm, pulling her close enough to smell his terrible breath. "What's a little thing like you doing in a competition like this?"

"Let me go, or I'll end you tonight, instead of in the arena," Rella spat.

Aaron then yanked him off from behind. The man turned and bashed Aaron in the gut with his club. Aaron crumpled and fell to the man's feet. Eric and Rella rushed to his aid and pulled him to his feet. The man gave an angry grunt and wandered off, probably to harass someone else.

"Thank you, but I don't need you to defend me," Rella said.

"Just as well or you wouldn't make it very far," Aaron replied.

They made their way over to a small table in the room. Another man at the table offered them a drink from his large bottle of rum. Only Aaron accepted. He gulped greedily from the bottle until he was numb. The man, silver-haired and dressed in brown fabric, introduced himself as Kade, and asked where they had come from. Rella explained where her village was, and he seemed reasonably impressed with how far they had walked. He told them that he had been preparing for the arena for years, desperate for a better life.

"How did the competition even start?" Rella asked him.

"It's been around since the new Governor came to power," Kade explained. "He opened the doors of the capital, allowing people from all over Tyrin to become citizens. But he put in place a system which would lessen the immigration numbers to an amount that the capital could manage."

"A hedonistic monstrosity," Aaron commented with contempt, before swigging more rum.

"It's an offer of paradise for those who can survive the competition," the man retorted.

"What kind of Governor would put such a system in place?" Rella wondered.

"Stories say that Governor Radmir's father had been very strict with him. He believed in making Radmir into a man like himself, one that would be respected by his people. Upon his father's passing, Radmir's sister, Ariel, was in line to assume the Governorship. However, Radmir orchestrated her marriage to the son of the Governor in Eden, a wealthier territory, thereby seizing the throne for himself. Now, he rules Tyrin with his wife. His main goal is to bring smiles and laughter to all of his subjects within the capital, or so he says."

"Does the Omi not care that one of their territories is being ruled by a madman?" Eric asked.

"Of course not," Kade replied. "The Omi only cares about taxes being paid and laws being maintained. So long as this is done, they do not care who the Governors are and what they do."

Rella listened to him, sickened by how a citizenry could support a lifestyle completely dedicated to entertainment and watching people die for their amusement. She had been fascinated to see the different approaches various settlements took to dealing with the laws of the Omi. She had yet to hear of a place that did so successfully, but perhaps, somewhere a place had.

However, she couldn't think about that right now. She had to focus on surviving the arena tomorrow. They had been given no food, advice for the battle, details on the arena, or even any special weapons.

There was a loud thud as Aaron's chair toppled over and he fell onto the stone floor.

"I think he's had too much to drink," Kade pointed out. "Perhaps, he should rest. If he drinks any more, he'll have no chance of survival on the morrow."

Rella thanked him and lifted Aaron to his feet, dragging him to a corner where he could rest in peace. However, whether Aaron was hungover or well-rested, Rella doubted it would make any difference in the arena.

III

Having accepted a little too much alcohol from the friendly stranger, Rella pulled Aaron over to the corner of the room. Aaron figured if this was going to be his last night alive, he might as well drink it away. With his brain dulled by alcohol and bitterness, he was unable to continue pretending he possessed any strength.

The dank chamber echoed with the curses and revels of the grizzled warriors Aaron would face in the arena. Rella plopped him down on a pile of hay, intended to serve as bedding for the competitors, but no one else seemed to want to sleep.

Rella sat down beside him. "You really are hopeless, Aaron."

Aaron nodded in agreement. His head spun, making him

nauseous. He saw a stack of hay to his side he could use as a pillow and wondered if his head would land on it if he toppled over to the side. Aaron wanted to lie down and lose consciousness, ideally in that order. He needed the day—and maybe even life—to just be over; he needed his pain to end.

First, he searched through his pocket for the only comfort he had left in this mystifying world. After rummaging to no avail, Rella delved into the pocket for him, and retrieved his rock. She showed it to him, and he nodded pitifully, taking it from her.

"What is it?" she asked.

Aaron rubbed its smooth surface without reply, too embarrassed.

She helped him lie down by settling his head upon the stack of hay. Then, she removed his shoes. He furrowed his brows at her.

"Don't worry, I'm not going to undress you." She sat back down, and after a pause said with a smile, "We're going to be fine tomorrow, Aaron."

"I know that you will be, but I don't even know what I'm doing here."

"You're fighting for Clare," she reminded him, still with that optimistic smile.

"How is it you don't have someone to fight for?" he asked her, noticing for the first time just how pretty she was.

"I'm fighting for Elara."

"Do you love Elara?" he asked.

"Like a sister."

"Then you didn't answer my question."

"Boys my age are yet to know who they really are."

"So, what kind of man do you like?" he asked.

"A man who is driven by a noble cause and will fight for it."

"Does such a man exist?"

"You do."

They exchanged glances, like opponents over a chess game.

"But I'm hopeless," he reminded her.

“I have hope for you."

"Only because you don't know me."

"That's what you think, but you're not as enigmatic as you think you are."

At that, he had to smile. He felt a small rekindle of the light inside him.

"To answer your question more directly," she said, "I think I may have been in love once."

"You think?"

"Love has always been an alien dream to me. It has always been so empty in my world. But I met someone, and I think I felt it. It's complicated."

"It always is. Tell me about him."

"He's a Governor for the Omi. The Governor that Kade spoke of, actually."

"Who's Kade?"

"The man who gave you the rum," she said with a look of disdain.

"Ah, yes, good man."

"Richard rules Eden now, along with the sister of Tyrin's Governor."

"How did you meet Richard?" he asked.

"In a robbery."

"Ah, he saved you from thieves."

"Actually, I was the thief."

Aaron furrowed his brows in confusion.

"I stole jewelry from him and the woman he is betrothed to marry."

"Sounds like it'll work out," he remarked.

She smirked at his sarcasm and then continued with her story. "After I stole the jewelry, I figured they'd quickly move on to another town. What's a few pieces of jewelry to the

Omi's Governors? There was a ring there though, special to Richard. He tracked me down and had me take him to the peddler I had sold the jewelry to. At first, we hated each other. He was Omi, and I was a thief."

"So, what happened?"

"We opened each other's eyes to one another's worlds. He had no idea how badly people had it outside the capital cities. Growing up as the Governor's son within Eden, he only saw how the Omi had banned weapons and prevented any outbreak of war. On our journey, walking on foot to the peddler's village, Richard was forced to see the cramped, dank hovels where most of the populace live, see how hard they work, and how gaunt they are. I think he came to understand why I stole from him. He told me he didn't really love Ariel but was being forced into the marriage by his father.

"I wanted to tell him how my father was the Governor of Eden before the Omi, but it didn't feel right to do so. I still wasn't sure if I could trust a Governor's son, even if he seemed genuinely good. After retrieving his ring, Richard let me go. He promised to be different from the other Governors and rule Eden caringly. Only after he left, did I begin thinking of him in a way I had never thought about a man before."

"Why did Develon make Richard's father the Governor of Eden, and not Patrick's father?"

"Patrick's father had flaked before," Rella replied. "Develon appointed only those he truly believed were committed to the Omi's cause."

Aaron pointed to her silver, wing-shaped necklace. "Did you steal that, too?"

She shook her head. "It was my mother's." Rella glanced down at the rock in his palms. "Please tell me about it."

"My grandfather gave it to me before we came to the City of Eden. During the rebellion, I was so afraid. My father was away fighting, and my mother was a Pure Blood who would be sacrificed to the Creator if the Omi ever found us. There was so much I couldn't control. My grandfather told me, if things became too much, by rubbing the rock I could remind myself I still had control over something. It's silly, really."

"No, your grandfather sounds like a good man."

"He was the best. Once, a boy in our village wanted to fight me just out of nowhere. I was so afraid of people after that. My grandfather sat me down and asked what I could have done to stir such a behavior. I thought back and remembered, I had been sharing some treats with friends but left the boy out. My grandfather asked me to think about how that would have made him feel, and suddenly I felt less afraid of people. I wasn't afraid of the boy anymore, because I understood him, or at least empathized with him."

Rella smiled and lay down next to him. Aaron thought she looked more relaxed than she had during their whole journey.

"You're quite different with me than you are with Eric," he said.

"Eric stresses me out. You have a calming way about you. Maybe it's because you remind me of the child I was when my father was the Governor. I yearn so badly to be that girl again. She was ignorant but hopeful."

"You're still hopeful."

"Only because I try so hard to be. Back then, it was easy. The day before my father died, he told me that the Omi would try and convince me that life is ugly. I couldn't believe them, he said. Instead, I had to remember life is beautiful."

"In fact, it is precisely because life can be ugly that its beauty shines through."

"You mean that to appreciate one, we have to first experience the other?" she asked.

Aaron nodded. "Food wouldn't be satisfying if we didn't know what it felt like to be hungry. And we wouldn't long for love if we didn't know what it was like to be alone."

"That's true," she said. "You know, when we were children, I was envious of Clare. She never cared about others' opinions and always followed her own path. Meanwhile, I was consumed with the desire to please my parents and fear of looking foolish. All I wanted was to be as true to myself as Clare was."

It was hard to imagine Rella being self-conscious, and he still couldn't get used to her talking about them being children as if it was so far in the past. "I know what you mean about Clare. Most of us stay in line and keep our heads down, but Clare always spoke her mind fearlessly. That's one of the things I admire about her too."

Rella shifted onto her side, her gaze fixed intently on his. "We may die in the morning."

Aaron knew what she wanted, but he wasn't able to offer her that. His heart still belonged to Clare. "I'm sorry," he simply said.

Rella smiled, as though it was the response she expected. She lay down and squeezed his hand. They nestled closer to each other on the hay, seeking solace in each other's touch, until they drifted off to sleep, on what would likely be Aaron's final night.

Chapter Nineteen

The lizard's fondness for young human girls had made transferring the prisoner particularly difficult. He had to restrain himself. Through the grace of the Creator, he had found the strength to avoid giving in to such temptations.

His job and purpose in life was to end the lives of those who sinned and soiled the territories of Arcadia. He couldn't afford to be a hypocrite. The greatness of the Omi was it required everyone to live righteously, and he knew he was a part of creating a virtuous world. It was their test to make Arcadia as pure as the Holy World. Once the test was passed, the Holy World would reveal itself to the righteous.

Leaving the prisoner with the guards outside, Karmeeleon entered the Chamber of Life, located beneath Develon's palace. The circular chamber was constructed of stone, illuminated by torches mounted on golden brackets, their flickering flames casting a mesmerizing glow upon the beige marble floor. Positioned at the heart of the room, a solid gold sphere floated just above the ground, symbolizing the Holy World. Mysterious symbols were engraved on the marble walls, detailing ancient scriptures from the lost world, which few on

Arcadia, other than Develon, could understand. Grand columns lined the periphery of the chamber, with a vigilant palace guard stationed before each one.

Develon was praying silently, tracing the hieroglyphics with his finger. Karmeeleon's footsteps echoed as he entered, yet Develon disclosed no interest.

Karmeeleon waited for Develon to finish. At last, the Omi's Head turned to face him, the golden mask hiding his face as always, his red robe swirling around him.

The general bowed. "Your Highness."

Develon stared through him, as though he wasn't there. "Have you brought me the girl?"

"Yes, Your Highness." He rose and called for his guards to bring in the red-haired girl. She trembled and tears leaked from her eyes, but she had been gagged to stop her blubbering.

Develon's piercing, bright blue eyes glimmered from behind the mask as he approached the girl. "Yes," he said, drawing closer to her. "She possesses pure blood; I can sense it."

The Pure Bloods descended from those who had left the Holy World a thousand years ago, right at the beginning of the Great War between the Ichu and Omi. Most of them had stuck together, only mating with each other, meaning their blood hadn't been spoiled too much. They once formed cults across Arcadia, trying to find ways of returning to the heavens, but the Omi's reign had scared them into hiding. It was, therefore, difficult to capture one for Develon's purposes.

The Omi's Head sacrificed those of pure blood within the Chamber of Life, hoping that their lives would bless the Holy World, and that it would reveal itself to him in exchange for his offerings. All sacrifices so far had yet to bring about such a revelation. At the edge of the chamber, there was an elevated marble table, used by Develon for stabbing his victim with his golden dagger, an artifact from the Holy World.

"Brother Guin is on his way with a whole herd of these creatures," Develon said. "And how goes your pursuit of the monk and his companions?"

"I have intel that they are heading to Tyrin's capital, and I have instructed the Governor there to inform me immediately when they arrive. Their fate is sealed, Your Highness. You need not concern yourself any longer."

"I shall determine for myself what merits my attention, General." Develon's voice was as soft and impassionate as always, but Karmeeleon didn't need to hear an angry tone in order to know when the master was upset.

"Yes, Your Highness, I apologize. The sole ambition of my life is to serve the Omi. I meant no disrespect."

"There is nothing more important than stopping what was prophesied—the warriors with the blades."

"They are not warriors, Your Highness, but merely a rogue monk, feral girl, and fainthearted architect. They pose no threat to the might of your kingdom."

Ignoring that comment, Develon said, "The young woman wielding the blades, she hails from Eden, correct?"

"Yes, Your Highness. It is possible she is a survivor from Culloden, a village recently destroyed."

"That's *this* girl's village," Develon said, pointing at the red-haired girl.

Karmeeleon nodded and removed the gag from around the girl's mouth. The girl took several deep breaths, tears dripping down her face.

Develon lowered his back to look at the girl in the eyes. "What is your name?"

"Please, my father is gravely ill, and he needs my care," she pleaded between sobs.

"Answer the Omi's Head!" Karmeeleon roared at her.

She trembled and raised her head to look at the master in the eyes. "My name's Elara."

"Elara, you have been brought here for a momentous

honor. You must offer yourself to the Holy World. By doing so, it will reveal itself to the people of Arcadia, bestowing its blessings upon all, including your father. However, before that, I believe you can be of even greater assistance to the Omi. There is a young woman, a brunette, believed to be from your village. She is causing considerable trouble for the Omi, and you might have the ability to help apprehend her. Was there a young brunette woman in your village who had a sword? A very beautiful sword."

"You will never find her," Elara spat out. "She's too smart."

"Traitor!" Karmeeleon yelled, striking the girl over the back of the head.

"Do you not wish to be reunited with your father?" Develon asked her.

"My father is probably dead already," she cried.

"Keep this girl alive for now," Develon ordered, looking at the guards. They immediately put the gag back over her mouth, knowing the master was finished with her.

"Your Highness, the security will be able to make her talk," Karmeeleon suggested.

"That is not currently necessary," Develon replied. "You have assured me that the situation is under control, and the criminals will meet their demise upon reaching the capital of Tyrin. Or was I mistaken in placing my trust in your promise, General?"

"No, Your Highness. The criminals will face their reckoning in the capital." The general bowed respectfully before exiting the chamber, accompanied by the guards who dragged the captive girl along.

An Enforcer stood outside, waiting for him.

"What is it?" Karmeeleon asked.

"General, the criminals that you're pursuing have been spotted in the capital."

"What?" His blood boiled at having not been informed immediately about their arrival.

Karmeeleon hurriedly made his way down the corridor. He would keep his promise to Develon, and deal with the fugitives at the capital before they had the chance to escape. Otherwise, his blood would be the next to be spilt by the master.

Chapter Twenty

I

A guard opened the chamber and led them all down a stone corridor, where the thirteen competitors were separated. Rella stood at her gateway, sword in hand, hearing the cheering crowd outside. All thirteen of them had been assigned to a different gate, meaning all of them would be fighting each other. She had thought Aaron, Eric, and she would fight in different battles, each facing only one competitor. However, that was not the case; there would be only one survivor.

The gateway opened, revealing the arena. It was a large square pit in the ground, made of black marble, located in an enormous, windowless building. Thousands of cheering spectators sat above the arena. The room was lit by hundreds of oil lamps, dotted all across the building.

Rella stepped inside. Beneath her feet was about an inch of water. The clear liquid cascaded down all four walls of the arena, flowing steadily towards a perfectly squared, deep hole situated at the center of the stadium, where it drained away.

The other contestants entered the arena. Rella saw her friends grasping their weapons; Aaron was only three gates away, but Eric stood at the opposite side of the battlefield. How would she cope with fighting them both? She decided to focus only on the other ten competitors. After the rest of the competition was defeated, she'd have to deal with Aaron and Eric, if they were even still alive.

Located in his own private booth, a man rested on a throne, perched above one of the arena's walls, clearly Governor Radmir. A woman sat beside him, who Rella assumed was his wife. She wore a hooded shawl and was staring down at her feet, as if she'd rather be facing anything other than the arena. Rella couldn't get a good look at her, but it was clear she was absolutely miserable.

Rella had expected the Governor to look like a cruel man, being the kind of person who could allow such a horrible tradition in the capital. He had also ignored all of his subjects within the rest of Tyrin, leaving them to starve and be terrorized by people like Cyllene, the warrior who had murdered Peter's village. The look of the Governor, however, was a surprising one. Rella had never seen anyone as flashy as him. He had bright blue hair and purple makeup smeared all over his face. He wore a sparkly blue robe. Two women dressed in bright colors and makeup fanned him from both sides with gigantic feathers. Rella realized then how hot it was inside the arena. There was no fresh air to cool them. The place stank of sweat and blood.

The cheering stopped abruptly as the Governor stood. His words echoed, as he announced to the crowd, "These thirteen competitors have graciously offered to grant us a show of entertainment. It is a grand battle, which allows a chance at prosperity and joy for every single resident of Arcadia. These competitors are not just fighting for their lives, but for the luxurious lifestyle that we all enjoy. They have sworn to give us a good show. Thus, it is too late for them to refuse to participate. If they surrender during battle, no mercy will be shown. Those who fail will fall for our amusement, and their lifeless bodies shall be carried to our sewers."

To demonstrate, the Governor shoved one of his servants into the pit. The woman fell, screaming, carrying the large feather she had been using to fan the Governor. She slammed into the arena's marble flooring, breaking and jutting her bones. The crowd resumed their cheering. The water coursing through the arena bore her lifeless body towards the center, tainted crimson by her spilled blood, until she vanished into the depths of the gaping hole.

"I wish you all good fighting as you strive to entertain us!" Governor Radmir shouted over the crowd's applause. "Let the competition begin!"

As Radmir sat down, his wife looked up for the first time, and Rella realized it was Clare.

II

Even with a hooded shawl around her hair, Rella knew there was no doubt that Radmir's wife was Clare. She wondered if Aaron too had spotted her. There was no time though to consider this; the competition had already started.

The competitors stared at each other, waiting for someone to make the first move. The heavy man who'd harassed Rella the previous night was the first to rush in. He held up his ball club and slammed it into the chest of his nearest competition. A puny man in ragged clothing collapsed to his knees, and the heavy man yanked back his weapon from his prey's chest. A flow of water carried the body into the pit, vanishing into darkness. The heavy man roared to the crowd, holding up his club.

A small throwing knife stabbed him in the back. The man turned to face his killer—the other female contestant. She had thrown off her shawl, revealing thick armor covering her entire body. The woman had come prepared for battle. She threw a couple more throwing knives into the man's chest to finish him off, and then turned and unsheathed a heavy sword as another man ran towards her. She slashed him in half.

A man blocked Rella's view. He held an armed bow in his hand. It was aimed right at her. She had been too focused on watching what was going on around her; she hadn't noticed him run towards her. She ducked. The arrow shot above her.

Rella jumped back to her feet and pointed her sword at the man. He went to grab another arrow. Before he could do anything with it, Rella pierced her sword through his chest. She spun around to scan the arena. The place was a bloodbath. With nearly a third of the participants already dead, it looked like it was going to be a short competition.

She looked for Aaron and Eric. Eric was holding his own in combat. However, Aaron seemed to be in a precarious situation, with two formidable men looming over him.

Rella ran across the water towards him. With the two men focused on Aaron, it enabled her to stab one of them in the back. Aaron smiled with gratitude.

They turned to face the remaining man. He was dressed in clothing made of poor fabric, but he held a sword in his hand and had two daggers tucked into his belt, leaving Rella unsure as to how prepared he was for the fight.

"If you fight us both," Aaron said, "you will surely fail. If you surrender, maybe you can survive this. You could go into the hole, still alive. Maybe it's not that deep."

"Or maybe I'll fall to my death."

"Maybe. But at least you'd have a chance."

Aaron's attempt at compassion stirred a twinge of guilt within Rella. She had just killed two men without a second thought. It was a fight to the death situation, after all.

Aaron asked, "Is a chance of entering the capital really worth dying over?"

"You clearly know nothing!" the man yelled.

"Then help me understand."

"I lived in a poor village, in starvation, with no choice. But, now, I have a choice. There's a chance I can live rather than just survive."

Rella figured that the man was most likely right, and that Aaron probably never had experienced the depths of desperation or starvation. But, as sympathetic as Rella was, it was either them or him. Therefore, the man could never become a citizen of Tyrin's capital. She hoped he would follow Aaron's advice, so they wouldn't have to hurt him.

He didn't.

The man leapt at Aaron with his sword. Reacting swiftly, Aaron raised his own blade to block the attack. The man pulled back his weapon and then struck once more, this time colliding with Rella's sword as she instinctively raised it to shield Aaron. The man sidestepped in an attempt to target Rella's vulnerable side. Aaron jabbed his sword forth, and the man fell to the ground. Dead.

The water carried the man's body to the hole like the others. Rella looked at Aaron, realizing this was his first kill. They didn't have time to reflect on it.

The other woman was busy fighting another man, while Eric faced Kade, the silver-haired man who'd shared his rum.

Kade wore a polished armor that glistened in the light. He held an impressive sword in one hand and a metal shield in the other.

Eric thrust his sword forward, only to have it clash against Kade's shield. In response, Kade swung his sword, prompting Eric to swiftly evade the attack. As Aaron and Rella hurried to join Eric's side, Kade took a step back, undoubtedly recognizing that his chances of survival had significantly diminished.

Aaron stepped forward. "Please, surrender."

"You heard the Governor. There is no surrender, boy."

Aaron looked up towards the Governor and Rella saw

recognition dawn upon his face as he spotted the woman next to him. "Clare!" he yelled.

Clare stood from her seat and stared down, but she didn't speak.

Rella grabbed Aaron by the shoulder. "You have to concentrate on the fight. We will find a way to Clare. At least now you know where she is."

Aaron nodded. "Now I have to survive."

They turned their attention back to Kade, who suddenly leapt forward. Rella kicked the shield flying from his grasp. As he stumbled, she deftly slashed her sword against his, causing his weapon to clatter onto the ground before being swept away by the current. Left defenseless, Kade sank to his knees, knowing the battle was over.

Aaron stepped towards him. "Will you surrender now?"

"I refuse to die a coward."

Aaron brought his sword closer to Kade's neck. The blade shook in his trembling hand. "Please, just surrender."

"I will not."

Aaron raised the sword into the air and the man closed his eyes, preparing for the final blow. As Aaron lowered the sword, he flipped it to its opposite side and hit Kade on the head with the handle, knocking him unconscious. The water carried him off.

The three looked around the arena. The only competitor remaining was the woman. She stood at the other end, sword in hand, looking as cold as before.

The crowd's cheers got louder. The audience stood up with excitement. The Governor, however, sat displeased, seeming unamused by the team-up.

The woman called over, "Three-on-one is a little unfair, but I can still take you all! My name is Erna—"

Bang!

The sound echoed throughout the enclosed pit. The three of them covered their ears, as Erna dropped to the ground.

They turned their heads to the source of the gunshot. The Governor stood, pointing a small, still smoking, cannon-gun. He lowered the gun, declaring, "Team-ups within the competition are most unorthodox. But, ladies and gentlemen, we were expecting this."

The audience looked just as surprised as the three of them were.

Governor Radmir continued. "These three particular troublemakers are wanted fugitives, hunted by the Omi. Their arrival was forewarned to me by General Karmeeleon. The general wished for me to inform him once they arrived, but in Tyrin's capital, we have our own way of dealing with things. The competition is a treasured tradition within our city, but I suspected these three would try and outsmart it. So, I had something else lying in wait for them. I have brought our territory's finest warrior. If the three of them can defeat her, they shall all be granted citizenship, but we all know this is impossible. Our greatest warrior has never been defeated."

The Governor sat back on his throne, a smug smile plastered over his face.

One of the gates slowly creaked open. Out stepped a dark-skinned woman with bright green eyes, her frizzy dark hair parted down the middle, wearing navy leather armor and laced navy-blue boots.

Rella realized immediately, she was the warrior that Peter had spoken of—Cyllene.

Chapter Twenty-One

Cyllene was the city's champion, undefeated in the arena. She had also built quite the reputation outside the capital as the destroyer of villages, burning homes to the ground and always leaving only one survivor to spread terror by her mere name. Yet now, she faced three amateurs in the arena. General Karmeeleon had warned Radmir that they were on their way, and the general would be greatly displeased about not being informed of their arrival. The Governor remained resolute in handling these criminals according to the city's customs and traditions. After all, the three would be no match for Cyllene, champion of the city.

Cyllene didn't understand the big deal over the three fugitives. They didn't appear particularly menacing. One of them was only a girl, another a monk, and the man with the dark hair looked as though he was about to wet himself.

"You are the Champions?" she sneered. "You are not worthy of fighting me."

The young brunette woman approached her, sword in hand. "What makes you think you're a worthier fighter than any of us?"

"I am a warrior!" Cyllene pounded her chest with a fist.

"You, on the other hand, are nothing more than a novelty, here as a show." She stepped forward, closing the distance between them. "I have brought warriors far superior to you to their knees."

The blond monk leapt forward, bearing his sword towards her. Cyllene plunged her boot into his stomach, knocking him to the ground.

She turned her attention to the girl and pounced. The brunette blocked her attack, forcing Cyllene to back away. It was a strategy she had learned long ago: attack and retreat.

But the brunette did not allow her to regain her footing, instead lunging forward. Cyllene leaned backwards, narrowly evading the girl's swinging sword as it sailed over her head. She ran under the girl's outstretched arm and got back into position. Cyllene blocked another thrust of the girl's sword, only to be hit in the ribs by the sword's pommel.

Cyllene groaned and grabbed her side, but she was grasped from behind. She felt the cool steel of a sword at her throat. It was the dark-haired man. She had not noticed him sneak up behind her; she wasn't used to fighting three opponents at once.

Cyllene leaned backwards to get away from the blade of the man's weapon, until the back of her head rested against his shoulder. She could hear the rapid beating of his heart, feeling his fear. "My head is yours, warrior. Do with it what you will."

"Finish her, Aaron!" the brunette girl yelled.

The dark-haired man stood still, having no words for her, his heart continuing to pound, and his labored breath continuing to exhale heavily from his lungs. He stood a moment longer, then removed his sword from her neck, and pleaded, "You cannot defeat the three of us. Please, surrender."

She immediately swung her sword, but the man raised his to meet hers. The clash of their weapons echoed in the stadium. Cyllene kicked his chest, causing him to stagger backwards and fall into the water.

She could hear the splashing of water behind her and spun around to block the girl's attack. Cyllene raised her sword over her head and brought it down with force, but the girl managed to block it in time.

The impact reverberated through Cyllene's entire arm, momentarily jarring her. She shuffled backwards, maintaining some distance. Cyllene wanted to keep her opponents close, but she had to follow her instructions: attack and retreat.

The brunette, however, would not allow her to rest. She lunged towards Cyllene, swiping her sword at her knees. Cyllene raised her leg to step over the weapon. As she did, the hilt of the blond man's sword slammed into her jaw. Cyllene flew through the air, landing with a bitter thud on the marble flooring, splashing the water around her. Lying there, battered and broken, Cyllene felt the metallic taste of blood fill her mouth. Turning her head, she expelled a crimson-laced spit into the flowing water, watching as it mingled and was carried away, disappearing into the depths below.

When she looked up, all three of her opponents stood above her, their swords pointed at her neck. The cheering of the crowd reached a peak, the spectators standing, applauding, and chanting.

Cyllene felt destroyed when she realized what they were yelling. They were calling for her death, ordering the competitors to finish her off. Her title meant nothing to them. After years of assuming she had gained support from the public in the arena, she realized that not she, but death was the people's champion.

She scanned the eyes of her opponents standing over her, feeling their anger, coldness, and indifference towards her survival. However, the dark-haired man's eyes were also filled with compassion. *What did the brunette call him? Oh yes, Aaron.* She looked up into Aaron's eyes and told him she surrendered.

Aaron lowered his sword. Two guards ran into the arena, grabbed Cyllene by her arms, and dragged her to the side. She stared at her victors, whom she had severely underestimated. The three looked just as surprised over the outcome of the battle as she was.

A bow and quiver of arrows that lay at the girl's feet had failed to get carried away by the water. Cyllene noticed the brunette eying them. Another competitor must have left them behind, the quiver filling with water until it became too heavy to be swept away.

Governor Radmir stood from his throne, glaring. The victors had made a mockery of his tradition. General Karmeeleon was going to punish him severely for not dealing with them as instructed, but his citizens would lose all respect for him if he didn't declare them the winners and grant them entry into the city as promised. He stared off into the distance, searching for a way around this. Once he realized there wasn't, he turned his attention back to the victors, but not soon enough.

Before Radmir or his security could do anything, the brunette woman loaded an arrow into the bow and released the string. The arrow hit him in the chest. The audience gasped as the Governor collapsed, falling over the side of the balcony to the cold, hard floor below, before being washed away into the arena's hole.

The brunette stepped forward. "The Omi allowed this madman to rule over your city! Now, the Omi will come here and punish you all for disobeying them! But you don't have to let the Omi dictate your life! This is your chance to take your city back!"

Silent concentration turned into loud chatter. It wasn't long before the arena's stands were filled with arguing and violence.

Cyllene smiled. The brunette wasn't the innocent girl she had mistaken her for; she was cold and ruthless, starting something that would ensure murder on a vast scale. Aaron, the one who had shown her mercy, stared out at the violence breaking out, appearing deeply shocked and saddened.

Cyllene's smile soon faded, however, as the guards holding her took her towards the arena's pit. She squirmed to get free, but it was no use, and they tossed her down the hole into darkness.

Chapter Twenty-Two

I

CCXXI (X Years Ago)

Aaron sat by the river, waiting on Clare, rehearsing what he was going to say. Finally, he was going to announce his love for her. His heart raced and his palms shook at the thought of being rejected by her. The various ways she might turn him down flashed through his head. She was his entire world, and he didn't want to risk doing anything that might scare her off. Since meeting her, he bubbled inside with completely new emotions. The mere sight of her filled him with joy. She was the only thing ever on his mind.

He felt sure she liked him too, but the odds made it hard to believe. After all, she was the most beautiful girl he had ever seen. For her to like him too would be like catching a falling star.

Aaron stood at the sound of shouts. The air grew thick with smoke, billowing from the vicinity of the Governor's palace. Standing on his toes, he strained to catch a glimpse of the unfolding chaos, witnessing a frantic rush of people hurrying to extinguish the flames. Terrified at the thought of Clare being in danger, he dashed towards the city walls.

As Aaron got closer to the walls, he froze at the sound of hooves drumming against the ground from behind. In the distance, he could make out hundreds of horses making their way through the valley towards the city gates. They were waving red flags, symbolizing loyalty to the Omi. Then he realized the City of Eden was under attack and the fire was a diversion. The lookouts had likely left their positions to deal with the fire and no one would be able to hear the approaching army over all the commotion. Aaron realized it was up to him to alert the others or the entire city would be conquered.

Aaron made his way through the streets, clouded with smoke and full of people racing towards the palace, carrying buckets or whatever they could use to carry water and throw over the flames. He slammed open his front door. "The city's under attack!"

Of course, his father wasn't helping put out the fire but was resting in the living room with a jug of beer. "What are you talking about?"

"The fire is a distraction! There's hundreds of horses approaching the gates!"

His father made it to his feet. "Hundreds?"

Aaron nodded.

Robert muttered a curse under his breath as he went for his armor and sword. Aaron's mother came out of the kitchen, holding jugs and pots to help put out the fire, and asked what was going on.

"Aaron says we're under attack," Robert replied. "I have to grab Elijah and warn the others."

"I'll come too, Father," Aaron said as his father ran upstairs to grab his younger brother.

"Wait here," Claudia ordered.

"What is it, Mother?"

"I don't want you to fight with your father and brother, Aaron."

"Why not?"

"Because you'll be killed."

"Still, I must."

"No, I forbid it. I'm going to take you to the monks, and they will protect you. The abbey is the one safe place in the city during an attack."

"Why would the monks protect me?" he asked.

"Walter has already spoken to them about sending you to the Monastery to become a master. We will show them your notebook and designs, then they will know you are worth saving."

"I'm no more worth saving than anyone else in this city," he protested.

"Aaron, I am your mother, and this is my order."

He looked down at his feet. "I don't want to leave Clare."

Before Claudia could reply, Robert returned downstairs with Elijah, both donned in armor and holding swords. "Let's go," Robert said. "We have to warn the Governor and tell him to get ready for an attack."

The four headed towards the palace, smoke and tears blurring Aaron's vision. To his horror, Aaron realized that it was Walter's library that was on fire. People were busy trying to put out the flames, and Aaron's family went to warn them about the Omi's soldiers.

Aaron coughed, inhaling a lungful of smoke. He rubbed his eyes and glanced around for signs of Clare or her family, but they were nowhere to be seen. Robert had rallied together a few dozen men by now, and they stood ready to defend their city from the Omi's army. Aaron slipped past them, despite his mother's cries, and raced to the front door of Walter's house in search of Clare.

To his relief, Clare was standing outside her house. Her

eyes beamed upon spotting him. "Aaron, I'm so happy to see you."

"You are?"

"Yes."

"Why?"

"Because I love you."

A wave of warmth washed over him, dispelling his earlier anxieties and the chaos that surrounded them. "You do?"

"Mm-hmm."

"I love you, too." He grabbed hold of her and brought her close. "What happened?"

"Lord Patrick came to see me. While his men were outside, we smelled smoke. The library was on fire. Then, Patrick's men came and arrested my parents as traitors to the Monastery."

"The fire was just a diversion," Aaron told her. "The Omi's army is attacking the city. Patrick's father must be helping them. We have to leave."

"I can't leave my parents."

"Please come with me."

"If I meet with Patrick, I know I can convince him to show my parents mercy. Even if I have to marry him."

"No, you can't!"

"I love you Aaron, but I won't let my parents die. I'll do whatever I must to save them."

Aaron realized she was right, and he stared off regretfully. His dreams had come true—she loved him back—yet they wouldn't be together. *How can this be happening?*

Clare reached in and kissed him, then pulled away. "I'm going to find Patrick now. Get somewhere safe with your family."

As Clare dashed off, Aaron went back to find his parents. The incredible sound of cries and of horses galloping made Aaron realize it was too late to warn anyone else—the Omi's army was already here.

He got back to where he had left his family and saw Patrick's men slaughtering citizens. Lord Patrick stayed back, surrounded by armed men for his protection, allowing his soldiers to do most of the work. A gang of soldiers dashed at Aaron's father and brother. They were outnumbered and quickly wounded and sent to their knees. Patrick stepped forward once the men were no longer a threat. Just like that, Aaron saw his brother and father cut down in front of him, the final blows delivered by Patrick himself.

A surge of anguish washed over him as the devastating reality sank in—he was defenseless and his mother was nowhere in sight. Tears streamed down his face as Aaron sprinted in the direction of the abbey. His only glimmer of hope was the possibility of finding his mother there, seeking solace and safety amidst the chaos that enveloped the city.

II

CCXXXI (Present)

Aaron and his companions found themselves amidst chaos as people scattered from the capital in fear. Riots and violence had broken out. While the women and children had escaped to seek refuge, most of the men had joined the unrest. Rella had been the cause of the turmoil, murdering Governor Radmir.

Aaron glanced around to find Clare, but she had left her seat and had disappeared. He felt restless now that he was so close, yet so far. They were in the same city, but he was surrounded by rioters, and she was likely fleeing for her life. Though she had been the Governor's wife, Aaron felt sure she had been forced into it somehow; the fight to the death competition was not the kind of thing she would ever have condoned.

At the back of his mind, though, there was a nagging fear that maybe she had changed, that she was no longer a person he would recognize.

He turned his attention back to the arena and asked Rella, "Are you sure that was a wise move?"

Rella explained to him that she had planted the seeds for things to get better, giving people the freedom to start again. While she appreciated Aaron's compassion, he wasn't able to make hard decisions or to be ruthless when necessary.

Eric remained unusually quiet during their conversation, neither siding with Rella's decision nor displaying judgment; he seemed completely indifferent.

The three of them were trapped in the arena. Rella pointed to one of the open gates. "This way." They all started running.

A group of guards quickly blocked their path, led by Aelius.

"The capital's in ruins!" Aelius roared. "Because of you!"

With his sword unsheathed, Aelius lunged at them, his men trailing behind. However, Rella swung her sword and blocked his advance.

Behind them, more men emerged from the gate, not guards, but soiled men dressed in leather armor. They leapt at the guards, clubbing them with sticks and swords. Aelius turned to face them, but too late. One of the escaped fighters plunged his swords into Aelius' stomach and then tossed his lifeless body towards Aaron.

Aaron stumbled, landing in the water on the floor of the arena. He tried to stand up, feeling himself drift away, but the weight of Aelius' body kept him down. He heard Eric and Rella call him, but before he knew it, he was falling through the central pit of the arena.

He landed in fast-flowing water, trapped in a large pipe. The coldness of the water stung like pins and needles all over his body. He felt himself struggle to breathe as the current dragged him along, pulling him under. Aaron tried to fight against it, but it was too strong. He was being brought towards a large orb of light, where the pipe ended.

There was an immense noise. As Aaron grew closer, he saw that the water poured into a vast lake. He was flung through the pipe and dropped through a blanket of mist below. Once under the mist, he plunged into the water.

That was the last thing he remembered before darkness.

When he woke up, Aaron was on land, washed up at the edge of the lake. Beside him was the warrior from the arena—Cyllene. Perched on a stone, she squeezed her soaking hair. He realized how he got to shore—she had dragged him out.

He coughed up water and her eyes turned to him.

"You saved me?" he asked. "Why?"

"You saved my life in the arena," she replied. "Now, my debt is repaid."

"Thank you."

"Don't thank people. It makes you look weak. You're not from here, are you?"

He shook his head.

"Well, I suggest you go back to wherever you came from. You don't belong here. If you treat people like you did me in the arena, you won't last two minutes."

"If that's what you've been taught, then I feel very sorry for you."

Her eyes darted through him. "Don't. I've been taught how to survive in this world." She marched back towards the capital.

"You're going back?" Aaron asked. "Why?"

"To gain control of this riot. The guards ignored me earlier, but they will listen once they discover I'm a member of Security."

"You're Security? You don't seem like the Security I've met," Aaron commented, though all he really knew was that they wore red uniforms.

"What would you know?" she asked, almost defensively, still marching.

"Wait!" He dashed after her. "My friends are still inside the capital. Let me go inside with you, and maybe we can help stop the riot."

"Your friend caused the riot in the first place!"

"Which is why we should help end it."

"How did you even fall into the hole?" she asked.

"There was an attack in the arena between guards and some sort of warriors."

"The warriors are the ones gunning for the championship title. People may have released them to help crush the riots, but it's unlikely to work."

"Odd, you'd think bloodthirsty warriors would make excellent peacemakers."

She didn't seem to understand the sarcasm.

"Let me help you," he said.

"How can you help me? You're weak."

"I defeated you in the arena," he reminded her.

"Only because I was outnumbered. If it were just the two of us, you wouldn't stand a chance."

As if to disprove her statement, he unsheathed his sword and charged at her. Swiftly, she spun around, seized his arm, and tripped him to the ground.

He looked up at her from the ground. "You have so much to learn, it's embarrassing," she said. "But you do have more nerve than I thought. Maybe you're not a jellyfish, after all."

"So, I can go in with you?" he asked.

"Get off your ass and let's go," she said, marching off. "Just don't get in my way when I slaughter these rioters."

He got up and followed her. "Wait. Slaughter? By taking control of the riot, do you mean kill the rioters?"

"Exactly. What did you expect?"

"I don't know—something that isn't insane. There must be another way to end the riots without resorting to killing innocent people."

"I don't kill innocents," she argued. "I only kill sinners."

"Right... Still, there has to be another way."

At the passageway through the city's wall, a guard stood at the exit, preventing people from leaving. A woman was arguing with him, trying to get past, but he shouted at her to stay back.

"The city's in turmoil," Aaron said. "Why are they stopping people from leaving?"

"I don't know," Cyllene replied, appearing equally displeased. Her glare landed on the guard, and she called over to him, "Hey! Let these people leave. I'm Security, now do as I command!"

The guard glanced her over. "You don't look like Security to me. Besides, I have orders from General Karmeeleon to stop anyone from leaving."

"Please, I have children!" the woman cried.

A little girl grasped her leg, and a small, teary boy stood behind her. Cyllene noticed them too, then pulled out her sword and dug it into the guard's chest.

The mother hurriedly ran from the city, with the girl taking her hand, and the boy close behind them.

"I'm glad you helped them," Aaron commented, watching them leave.

"They should have been able to help themselves," Cyllene replied.

Cyllene wiped the blood from her sword on the guard's shirt and told Aaron to keep going. They stepped through the dark passageway, and Cyllene sheathed her sword.

Aaron glanced towards the guard's body and then turned back to her. "If that guard didn't believe you were Security, what makes you think anyone else will listen to you?" This made her stop in her tracks. "Don't you have a uniform?"

"I do," she replied. "But it's at home."

"Is your home far?" Aaron asked. "Maybe we should get it first."

"Home isn't far." She turned back and he followed her out of the passageway.

"Where is it?"

"Karmeeleon's palace."

Chapter Twenty-Three

I

CCXXI (X Years Ago)

At first, Rella thought the smell of smoke was coming from the kitchen. However, when she glanced out the window, she saw that smoke was rising from Walter Ifran's home next door. She looked closer and saw that riders were approaching the palace, some waving the Omi's red banners and others wearing armor from Tyrin. Their gigantic horses charged into men, women, and children, trampling them. The riders swung swords and used them to cut down anyone in their path. Midst the chaos, Rella's gaze locked onto Lord Patrick of Tyrin, his eyes burning with fury. She watched in horror as he mercilessly swung his sword, ruthlessly ending the lives of Robert, the wool merchant, and one of his sons.

"Father," she turned and called.

Her father came into the room and studied the horrifying sight.

"Are we under attack?" she asked.

"Quickly, I must hide you," he said.

"What about you?"

"I cannot abandon my people."

"They're my people too," she declared sternly, and before he could argue, she dashed from her room and headed downstairs.

"Rella, wait!" her father roared after her, but she ignored his calls and stepped towards the front doors. There were screams coming from outside.

A couple dozen of Father's men now stood at the entrance, ready to defend the palace. Beyond them, the Omi's army was setting fire to everything. The entire city was going up in flames. Some of Father's men had collapsed the bridge to the palace, but it was no good as too many of Patrick's men had already crossed. If anything, it would do more harm than good, preventing the citizens of Eden from coming to help.

Father appeared and stood by her side. An army of riders galloped towards them. The guards defending the palace would have no chance—they were about to be squashed like bugs. Patrick and his father—Governor of Tyrin—were leading the attack. To Rella's shock, they were accompanied by Brother Guin and a gigantic green lizard in green armor. Rella couldn't believe her eyes. Was this creature a non-human?

Father looked around and appeared to know it was over. The bleeding bodies of his people lay scattered around them. The guards in front of the palace were ready to die for their Governor. However, Rella's father stepped between them and the approaching army, raising his hand and telling them to stand down.

Patrick's father brought his horse to a stop and told his own men to cease. "Governor of Eden, do you surrender?"

"If you leave everyone else in this city unharmed, including my daughter, then I surrender."

Patrick looked displeased that there wouldn't be more

bloodshed, but his father smiled and his men cheered in victory.

Brother Guin leapt from his horse. "The Governor of Eden is a traitor against the Monastery. As a representative of the Creator, I can confidently declare His approval of this seizure."

The green lizard said, "You should all know that Queen Shanleigh is dead, and the Omi will soon reclaim all the territories of Arcadia. As the Omi's new general, I hereby declare Eden to be under rule of the Omi. A new Governor will soon be appointed."

This sent a shockwave of whispers through the crowd.

Brother Guin stepped towards Rella with a smug smile and sneered, "This is what happens to traitors, girl. Now that you are no longer a Governor's daughter, you will have to learn your place."

It took everything Rella had to not throw herself at the monk and begin thumping him.

The general pointed to her father. "Arrest this traitor. He will await execution by the Omi."

Rella cried and ran to her father, but Brother Guin held her back and the general's guards carried her father away.

||

CCXXXI (Present)

"Where are you going?" Rella called to Eric. "We have to find Aaron!"

Eric ignored her, yet she continued to follow him. Avoiding the crowds and riots, he marched to the outskirts of the city as though he was on a mission and knew exactly where he was going.

Eventually, they came to a large, wooden warehouse. Rella, who instinctively stayed back while Eric knocked, immediately heard the undoing of locks on the other side. The speed of the response unnerved her and without conscious thought she reached for her weapon in anticipation. It was as if they were expected.

The door opened, revealing a stubby non-human with a thin layer of grey fur over his body and a long trunk protruding from his face.

"Hello, Stout, I'm here for access to the tunnels," Eric said.

"What tunnels?" Rella asked.

"The tunnels to the Sanctuary."

"What about Aaron?"

"Aaron will have to survive on his own for now. We came here to get access to the Sanctuary and to save Elara. The Omi will be arriving soon to deal with this carnage, and then our chance to enter the tunnels undetected and save Elara will be gone. It has to be this way."

Rella nodded reluctantly.

"You have to pay for access first," Stout replied. "Give me the necklace."

"What necklace?" Rella asked.

"Stout collects artifacts from Eden," Eric explained.

Now Rella knew why Eric hadn't told her everything. She grabbed the necklace around her neck, the one her father had given her as a child. The small non-human eyed it yearningly, the silver wing-shaped necklace glistening in the light.

"You want me to give up my necklace?" she asked.

"Please," Eric said. "It's the only way."

"Was this always your plan?"

"Since I met you, yes."

"How did you plan on entering if I hadn't joined you?"

"The Creator would have shown me another way."

Somehow, Rella didn't quite believe him. She wondered if

she had always been part of his plan. And if that was true, did he also know about the competition they would need to win before entering Tyrin's capital?

Regardless, they had gone too far to turn back now. The only thing that drove Rella onwards was the hope she may see Elara again. She could no longer afford to hold onto her past. She gave Stout her necklace.

He clutched it happily, and then opened the door fully. Standing behind him was a pair of eyes that Rella recognized immediately. Fierce, red eyes. She hadn't seen those eyes since the day Omi arrived at the City of Eden. They belonged to the monster who attacked her home and killed her father—General Karmeeleon.

"Run!" Rella screamed. She and Eric both turned and dashed.

The giant lizard got on all fours and hurried towards them, flooring the crowds that were in his way. He removed a sharpened throwing ring from his belt and flung it at Eric's leg, tripping him over. Rella stopped to help him up, but Karmeeleon was now too close.

She felt frozen, being so close to the monster who had taken everything from her, murdering her father, destroying her home, and forcing her to leave it behind as a child. There was so much she wanted to say to him, in order for him to understand the volume of what he had done.

But this wasn't the time.

She pulled his throwing ring from Eric's leg and hurled it at Karmeeleon's arm. The bladed edge of the weapon dug into his flesh, breaking through his scaly exterior, and he let out a sharp screech. Maimed, the general lost his footing and fell backwards.

Rella pulled Eric to his feet. Another throwing ring fired into her shoulder. She turned to see two of Karmeeleon's personal guards, dressed in green armor and facemasks, exit the warehouse. One tossed another ring, this time hitting Rella's lower leg, and she fell.

The guards caught up to them and pulled Rella to her feet. General Karmeeleon stood and he ordered his guards to arrest them both.

It was all over.

Chapter Twenty-Four

I

Clare hustled through the riots in Tyrin's capital, holding a shawl over her face as she ran so no one would recognize her as the Governor's wife. While she had tried to use her position for good as much as possible, setting up a shelter for orphans in the capital, she had not been able to prevent Radmir from living out many of his sick fantasies, including the competition. The world would be a better place without him.

When she and her family had fled from Eden, she had married Radmir to keep them safe. The last ten years had been mostly misery, but she had channeled her energy into her orphanage and that had kept her sane. The shelter housed children who had lost their parents either in the savage arena battles or through other tragic circumstances. She had hired women from the capital as teachers to help prepare the children for life in Tyrin, providing them with skills in counting, business, and farming. Clare didn't know much about farming, but she understood how to count, read, and write. Occasionally, she even told them stories she remembered from her father's library. Of course, she had to be careful what she said, in case the teachers reported her to the Omi as a spreader of heresy.

While she no longer had her father's book collection at her disposal, during her time at the capital, Clare had taken advantage of her access to knowledge by talking to many of the large number of people who resided there. Remembering the stories she used to read with Aaron by the river, she had asked many about the origins of the Ichu and Omi and since then had learned a great deal. A thousand years ago, Princess Ava fled from the Holy World to Arcadia with a group of Pure Bloods and a warrior to protect them. There, they met Nathan and his race of Ichu. Desperate to learn the secrets of the Holy World, Nathan attempted to kidnap Princess Ava. The warrior—also Ava's lover, named Daniel—fought Nathan to protect her. He gained the help of a religious sect on Arcadia in his attempt to defeat the Ichu, thus beginning the Great War between the Omi and Ichu that lasted for many centuries.

It had been a shock to her system to see Aaron in the arena and she still could not make sense of what she was feeling. He was the only man she had ever loved, and that had been back when he was a boy. She wondered if it was a coincidence that he was in the capital or if he was here to find her. Clare wouldn't describe herself as being the most sentimental of people, but she had thought about him on the odd occasion when she allowed the past to creep into her thoughts.

Clare had to get the orphans to safety while the riots went on, then she would look for Aaron. Maybe once she was standing in front of him, she would know what she was feeling.

As she rounded the street corner towards the orphanage, however, she caught sight of two guards. They were not the city's guards, but General Karmeeleon's own, meaning he was somewhere in the city. Clare turned away, but there were guards approaching from that direction, too. One of them grabbed her by the shoulder.

"Lady Clare," he said. "You need to come with us. The general wants to see you."

II

Aaron followed Cyllene to Karmeeleon's palace, a grander-looking version of the one Rella's father had owned when Aaron was a boy. However, it also boasted intricate carvings of gargoyles and religious symbols, reminiscent of the Monastery.

He waited outside while she entered to collect her Security uniform. When she reemerged, she not only donned the blood-colored outfit, but had washed the blood and grime from her skin and hair.

"Do I look the part now?" she asked.

"You *look* it," Aaron replied, yet something about her still didn't quite align with the Security personnel he had encountered before. Though Cyllene was clad from her toes to her neck in red, Aaron could see in her eyes that there was a person there, unlike the Security Rella fought, who had seemed more mechanical than human, as if they had been stripped of their emotions.

"But what? I don't *feel* like it? What do you even know? Do you want me to knock you down again? Maybe when your ass hits the sand, you'll feel differently."

"That's it. Right there. You just got angry. I didn't think Security got angry. They just seem to do what they're told."

The anger drained from Cyllene's face, replaced by a tinge of annoyance. "Well, I'm not a slave to the Omi, like most Security are. I wear this outfit to be a daughter Karmeeleon can be proud of. Now, we need to go. We're going to gather more Security for additional assistance. Leave your sword here; otherwise, they'll kill you on sight."

"Won't they kill me anyway?"

"Not if they think you're with me."

This only slightly alleviated Aaron's apprehension, yet he followed Cyllene, nonetheless, as it was the only way he could see to help Eric and Rella.

They approached a towering stone structure, adorned with three interconnected turrets, located just outside the capital city.

"What is this place?" Aaron asked.

"It's a bathhouse and a haven of relaxation for the Omi's Security," Cyllene replied. "There are many of them scattered across Arcadia, but this one houses Zylina, the Lady of Peace and Captain of the Omi's Security. She can grant us a Security squad to deal with the riots in the capital."

"Is she likely to help us?"

Cyllene's face twisted in disgust at even speaking about the Omi's captain. "Zylina is the most loathsome creature to ever be a member of the Omi, but she's a coward and will do as I say. After all, anyone knows if they displease me, they displease Karmeeleon."

"If she's such a coward, how did she become the Security's captain?"

"She'll do anything that Karmeeleon says and stabbed all of her competition in the back, figuratively and literally. Now, she stands as the first woman to hold one of the Omi's four lordships, alongside General Karmeeleon, Principal Sin, and Commander Straumme. It's a mockery. Zylina only wanted to get to the top so she wouldn't have to do any work and could exert her tyrannical rule. She's cruel, selfish, lazy, and corrupt; everything that is wrong with the Omi."

"If you think the Omi is so wrong, why do you work for them?" he asked.

"They are not all wrong. The Omi was created to rid Arcadia of evil and to protect good souls from sin. It has become corrupt because of a few rotten eggs, like Zylina. I intend to change the system from the inside."

"That doesn't seem like something Karmeeleon would approve."

"My objections to the imperfections within the Omi angered him, and that's precisely why he sent me away to become stronger. He had me burn down villages, ones he said deserved it, so no one could say that I was weak. Karmeeleon has a thing for making fires; he likes to pretend he's serving the Creator's will, sending sinners to their eternal damnation. He's not so righteous himself, however."

"Is he another rotten egg?"

"Not like Zylina. Karmeeleon is harsh to keep soldiers in line, while Zylina is cruel just because she can be; she doesn't care about optimizing the Omi's strength. If Security fail her, she sends them to one of the Omi's torture camps, where they are were kept alive for decades to be tortured day to night until their bodies can take no more. It is only meant for the worst of criminals and is a despicable fate for a member of Security."

They entered the tower, and came to a grand bathhouse at the heart, made of marble. The central area boasted exquisite pillars and a painted ceiling that arched above a serene pool, portraying the legends of the Holy World. The artwork depicted the first sinless man and woman, as well as ancient warriors who were said to have vanquished the corrupt when humanity succumbed to sin.

Two servants added flowery and sweet aromatizing scents to the water, where steam danced in the air, creating an atmosphere that was both tranquil and inviting.

The doors to the bathhouse opened. A woman strolled inside, who, unlike the rest of Security, was sheathed from head to toe in white, perhaps showing that she no longer had to get blood on her hands. Her blonde hair was pulled tightly back over her head, and the only bit of color to her milky skin was her rosy cheeks.

Approaching the marble tub, she was about to disrobe when her gaze fell upon Cyllene and Aaron standing in the room. She scrutinized Cyllene's Security uniform and frowned. "That attire is reserved for authorized Security members only."

"My training is now complete, Zylina," Cyllene responded, meeting the woman's gaze unflinchingly.

"You will not be initiated until you have proven your strength."

"My father said I had to fight well at the capital to prove my strength, and I fought so well that I became their champion."

Zylina gave a bored wave of dismissal. "Your father may be General Karmeeleon, but I will decide for myself who becomes a member of my Security."

"You answer to the general!" Cyllene shouted, still smiling. "You may get away with bossing around other Security members, but not me."

A flicker of unease passed over Zylina's face, though it quickly vanished, replaced by her composed and cold demeanor, as if attempting to project fearlessness. She pointed to Aaron. "Who's this?"

"He's just my servant," Cyllene replied quickly. "Pay him no mind."

Aaron tried not to look offended.

"Security members are trained from childhood," Zylina went on. "Your father may think that fighting in some primitive competition gives you the right to bypass all that training, but that doesn't mean I have to agree."

"We don't have time for petty arguments. While you're enjoying a bath, the capital is experiencing a revolution."

"I am well aware."

"And you're doing nothing?"

"Tyrin's capital can sort the fight themselves. Develon does not care who runs his territories, just so long as the territories are contained."

"News will spread. Other places will revolt. This requires our attention immediately, and I want to lead a squad to sort it now."

A smug smirk played on Zylina's lips. "And under what authority do you plan to do so?"

"Do you dare risk displeasing my father?"

"Your father is a great general, but you are a mere warrior, and you will answer to me." She turned her attention back to the pool.

Cyllene twisted Zylina back around, firmly gripping her by the sides of her head. She swiftly brought her knee up, delivering a powerful strike directly to Zylina's face, bursting her nose. Cyllene then forcefully pushed Zylina's head down into the tub of water.

The other Security in the room stood frozen, probably too afraid to intervene in case Cyllene reported them to her father. As Cyllene held Zylina beneath the water's surface, time seemed to stretch on. For nearly a minute, Zylina thrashed and struggled desperately, fighting to break free. Aaron thought she was going to drown her. Finally, Cyllene pulled her out of the water, and Zylina let out a watery cough.

"We will go to the capital to sort this mess," Cyllene ordered, now addressing all the Security members in the room.

Zylina nodded, taking a deep, raspy inhale to steady herself.

Cyllene took the lead as they embarked on their journey towards Tyrin's capital, accompanied by a squad of Security. The other Security members were clearly only following Cyllene out of fear of her father, but so long as she kept control over Zylina, the others would follow.

They passed the large lake into which water sprayed from

the pipe on the mountainside, where Cyllene had found Aaron earlier. The lake served as the sewer exit for the capital, where the bodies from the arena were deposited. Currently, there were scavengers looting some of the bodies.

Pillars of black smoke rose into the air. The fire was contained by the enormous stone walls surrounding the city, as the entire capital burned. The air was rent with screams.

"It's clear that we cannot handle the revolution in the capital on our own," Zylina said. "The city is engulfed in flames. There is nothing for us to do here."

Aaron and Cyllene stood frozen, listening to the cries for help as an entire city perished in flames.

"You brought us here for nothing." Zylina smirked, then kicked Cyllene's legs from under her. Two Security members held Aaron back as Cyllene fell and Zylina ordered the squad to keep her down. The Security members kicked and beat her, while Zylina watched, her grin growing larger and larger.

Cyllene grunted in pain when the squad backed off, leaving her bloody lying on the grass.

Zylina sauntered over and said, "Leave her for the rioters."

The last thing Cyllene would have seen was Zylina towering above her before a white boot slammed down on her face. Seconds after, one of the Security members hit Aaron across the back of the head, and he fell silent, too.

Chapter Twenty-Five

I

CCXXI (X Years Ago)

Patrick had to get answers concerning the drawing given to him by the monk. Now that the Omi had decided against making his father a Governor, it was necessary for Patrick to find an alternative route to power. Worse than that, he hadn't even been able to enact revenge on Clare. Once she realized he didn't have the power to set her parents free, she had fled his reach. All the misery he had endured was entirely her fault. Every waking second, he envisioned ways to torture her and to make her pay.

He had already demanded records on the Ichu from the Monastery, discovering the invocation for immortality. In order to have any chance, though, he needed to replicate what the Chief Ichu had done exactly, and that meant finding cells from heavenly lifeforms.

He went to the prison cell where the traitor's daughter was being kept until her father's execution. To his glee, she looked terrified upon seeing him; her widened eyes and agape mouth were like gold to him.

Patrick showed her the drawing given to him by Brother Guin. "If you lie to me even once, I will cut your arm off. Do you understand?"

She nodded.

"You drew this, didn't you?"

Again, she nodded.

"What is it?"

"I saw it crash from the sky, but I don't know what it is."

"Where?"

"In the hills, overlooking the lowlands. There is an old stone building there."

Patrick smiled at her obedience, and he left the cell in search of the fallen object. The Omi would face the consequences for failing to reward his family. They would never have secured Eden without the help of him and his father. Once he attained divine power, he would remind them of it.

||

CCXXXI (Present)

The warehouse burned.

Karmeeleon had punished the grey non-human for illegally providing access to the city's tunnels by torching the building to the ground with the non-human inside.

He wiped away the blood from the wound on his arm, the only price he had to pay for his long-awaited run-in with the warriors he sought. Not only had he laid eyes upon two of them, he had them in his clutches. Talitha had been right. They didn't appear like much, but they were clearly not to be underestimated. Like Develon, Karmeeleon was aware of the prophecy. Now that he'd seen the blades for himself,

Karmeeleon knew they were the very ones he feared them to be.

He clutched the winged necklace in his hand, something that the errant non-human had accepted as payment from the criminals. It belonged to the family of Eden's previous Governor. Eden had been a personal victory of the general. So, if a member of the Governor's family had escaped his wrath back then, only to come back and cause trouble now, Develon might blame him for this whole mess.

It had to be the daughter. Karmeeleon had killed the Governor himself and burned the palace to the ground. He had decided to show mercy in front of the people by letting the daughter live, though he had always assumed she would have soon perished alone in the forest.

Develon would already be furious with him for allowing the warriors to cause such havoc on Arcadia. If that hadn't already sealed his fate, this latest revelation surely would. He had to catch them *all* before Develon found out.

Karmeeleon made his way beneath the city, to where the arena competitors were held. Luckily, his reputation proceeded him, and none of the rioters were stupid enough to get in his way. He hoped that his daughter, Cyllene, had forgiven him for having sent her to this awful place. Surely, she had come to realize he had done it to make her strong.

Ever since he adopted her as a child, rescuing her from the destruction caused by the war between the Omi and Queen Shanleigh's army, she had been the center of his world. His overwhelming desire to shield her from harm and keep her pure had inadvertently weakened her. Recognizing this, he had made the difficult decision to send her here, hoping it would help her find her strength.

There was another reason he sent her to Tyrin's capital. From when he first set eyes on her, as a lost, little girl, she had filled him with temptation. Karmeeleon had devoted his life to following the words of the Creator and to avoiding sin. When it came to Cyllene, however, she was his weakness, and he often had slips. He hoped some distance between them would settle his urges.

Perhaps she would realize her feelings for him and then they could love each other without sin. Cyllene was of a suitable age now so the Creator would have no objections to their relationship if they both consented to a nuptial.

When he arrived in the holding cells for the competitors, he found them empty. Cyllene was gone.

He ordered the guards to place the prisoners inside a cell—the blond monk and the brunette huntress. The master from the Monastery was nowhere to be found. From the other two prisoners, however, he would find out where the third was. He had to find them all before alerting Develon, for it was the only way he would be forgiven. Luckily, he had acquired some leverage—Radmir's wife, Clare, whom the young master was searching for, according to his mother.

His guards brought Lady Clare to the cells and restrained her as she writhed to get free.

He told his guards to wait outside with Lady Clare and entered the warrior's chambers. The blond sat at the edge of the cell, appearing just as nonchalant as he did when he was arrested. The brunette stood behind the bars, staring into him with burning fury in her eyes.

Karmeeleon held up the necklace. "Where did you get this?"

"It's mine," the brunette spat out.

"Don't lie to me," he warned.

"I'm not."

"So, that would make you the daughter of Eden's traitor?"

"My father was the *Governor* of Eden!'

"How did you survive alone in the forest?"

"I wasn't alone."

"Yes, Alioth took you in and gave you his swords,"

Karmeeleon said, deciphering. How had he not put it together sooner?

She stared back at him, confused as to how he knew so much.

"My men and I discovered the ex-Queen's weapon builder hiding in the highlands while we were there looking for a Pure Blood. I ordered his death personally, as well as that of the town that harbored him. He sent you on this whole revenge mission, didn't he? Well, it was pointless. You're getting involved in something you don't even understand."

The brunette seethed behind gritted teeth. "I understand perfectly well that the Omi deprives people of food and freedom."

"It requires sacrifice in order for the Omi to keep the world pure."

"Is that what you've deluded yourself into believing?" she replied. "So, my father's death was a sacrifice? That doesn't seem very fair."

"If he had never opposed the Omi to begin with, he wouldn't have had to die."

"And what exactly does Develon sacrifice?"

"Develon has paved the way for all righteous men to reach salvation. The world *will* be purged of its temptations and sins."

"I hate to break it to you," she said, "but you're not a righteous man. You're a big, evil lizard."

"Enough!" he roared. "Now you're going to tell me where your other traveling companion is. If you do, I'll let you see your friend—the Pure Blood."

"What makes you think I'd betray one friend to see another?" Rella asked.

Karmeeleon decided to tempt Rella with a larger carrot. "What if I gave you the chance to save two friends, instead of only one?"

"What are you talking about?"

Karmeeleon opened the doors and pulled Clare inside. The brunette's eyes widened in shock.

"Rella!" Clare said. "What are you doing here?"

"I'm with Aaron," she replied. "He's looking for you!"

"If you tell me where Aaron is, I'll let Lady Clare go," Karmeeleon said. "That seems like an offer Aaron would accept if he was here to do so. As for Brother Eric, he is not your friend. He's the whole reason we caught you. We came looking for Brother Eric after he stole a tablet belonging to the Omi. How much has he really told you?"

The big, evil lizard left them to talk alone, taking Clare with him. Rella turned to Eric. "Time to come clean."

"It's like I said, I was sent to collect you and to deliver the tablet to the Sanctuary by a messenger from the Creator."

"Tell me more about this messenger."

Eric shrugged. "His name was Marko."

"Marko?"

"You've heard of him?"

"Alioth told me stories about someone called Marko. Not sure if it's the same man. He was Queen Shanleigh's right-hand man and the director of her army. He trained the warriors who defeated the Omi's First Empire and assisted Queen Shanleigh in her rebellion. After Queen Shanleigh's defeat, he disappeared."

"The man I met was too old and frail to fight now."

Rella's eyes lingered on him for a few seconds. "How come I feel like you're still not being honest with me?"

Eric sighed. "I'll tell you something you don't know."

"Go on."

"I was never actually given as a gift to the Monastery by my parents. That's a story I took from a young novice."

Rella crossed her brows. "Then how did you really come to be a monk?"

"Ten years ago, Brother Thomas found me in the desert after I crashed. He brought me in and taught me the way of the monks, including their language."

"Crashed?"

"From the sky." Eric nodded. "I come from a land of heretics."

"The heretics were all killed by the Omi."

"In this world, yes." Eric locked eyes with Rella and inhaled. "But I'm not from this world."

Chapter Twenty-Six

When Aaron woke up, Cyllene was still lying bloody on the ground. He helped her up and supported her as they walked back to Karmeeleon's palace.

"I don't understand," Cyllene said weakly, as he placed her on a chair in Karmeeleon's dining room. "Why are women and children being stopped from leaving if the capital is on fire? The Omi are committed to ending sin, not the lives of innocents."

"Maybe it's time to consider that Karmeeleon may have lied to you about some things concerning the Omi."

Cyllene turned red; anger seemed to rise like fire inside her. "You're right. I have something to show you."

"What?"

"A sword, that is just like yours. It was given to me as a girl."

"Let me see."

"First, let me tell you how I got it..."

~

Life in Tyrin was a simple one, made up of farming communities, centered around the harvest and festivals held in homage to the gods. However, prior to the rise of the Omi, the people enjoyed the freedom of not having to pay taxes and didn't have their religion dictated.

The first time Cyllene heard of the Omi was when news arrived that the capital of Tyrin had been conquered. Her father, the village's minister, was in the middle of one of his services. The entire village gathered around, and he recited one of the ancient stories about the Holy World. After hearing of the news, Cyllene clung to her father's robes and asked why the Omi wanted to hurt them.

"It doesn't matter. So long as we have faith in the Creator, he will protect us," her father replied.

Soon, the Omi came to the surrounding villages to conquer them. Cyllene's village sent men to join the battle that held the Omi back. However, before long, the Omi broke through the lines and proceeded to slaughter the villages that had sent men to fight them, not sparing the women, children, or elderly; they were to serve as a warning.

One night, Cyllene's father woke her up and told her she had to leave with her brother, Tyrell. He gave her a pack and told her that he had been wrong about the Omi: "Not even the Creator can save our village from the Omi now. They are taking over everywhere. There is no hiding from the wrath of General Karmeeleon and Commander Straumme. You and your brother must leave, Cyllene. Tyrell needs you to protect him."

"Why can't you come, too?" she asked.

"Too much of a crowd will attract attention. Besides, as minister, the Creator would want me to stay and comfort our people. Go to the capital. The Omi have conquered the capital city, but at least the war there is over. Maybe someone will be willing to show compassion to a couple of children. I pray that the Creator will watch over you."

Her brother was only four years old at the time. She was double his age, and so she led the way, taking him by the hand, as they climbed the neighboring mountains.

By the time they were at the top, their entire village was engulfed in a blaze. Black smoke rose into the air, clouding all else, except for the bright glare of the flames.

Cyllene told Tyrell not to look. He was too young to understand what the Omi were or that their village was in danger. He seemed more confused than frightened, wondering why he had been dragged from his bed.

They camped in the mountains that night. Using what her father had packed, Cyllene laid out blankets for her and her brother. She didn't make a fire for fear that the light would draw the attention of the Omi, and so they huddled together for warmth under the stars.

"Can you tell me a story like Father does?" Tyrell asked her.

Before settling in their village, their father had served as a preacher for the Creator, spreading his word to settlements across the continent. Even after the birth of Cyllene and Tyrell, he still made occasional trips, leaving them in the care of the village. He always had many stories to tell about the foreign places he'd visited, in addition to knowing each of the Creator's tales.

Cyllene wasn't so gifted at telling stories, but to get her brother to sleep, she thought back to one her father had told her. During one of his preaching journeys, their father encountered both Death and an assassin.

Clad in obsidian armor and armed with a tall, mighty sword, Death traveled the lands of Arcadia, seeking souls to claim. Unyielding, Death felled all who crossed his path, be it young newlyweds, innocent children, or mothers cradling newborns.

On the shores of a tranquil lake, a young fisherman prepared his boat when Death emerged from the shadows.

Unsheathing his sword, Death prepared to strike down the young fisherman.

"Halt," a stern voice demanded, as an assassin stood before Death, her own blade poised at his neck. She warned the young fisherman to flee.

"Do you intend to slay me?" Death inquired.

"I should," the assassin retorted. "You have extinguished the lives of innocents, and their grieving families have commissioned me to end yours."

"Then, do it already," Death replied calmly.

The assassin hesitated. "I would, but on my journey to find you, other families paid me to spare you."

"Why?" Death asked.

"You have relieved the suffering of the afflicted, lessened the burden on villages, and purged the wicked."

"Then what will you do?" Death questioned.

"I don't know," the assassin replied. So, they continued to stand there.

"Maybe I can help," the young fisherman said.

Both Death and the assassin turned to the young fisherman startled, having not realized he was still standing there.

"How can you help, fisherman?" Death asked.

"Why didn't you run?" the assassin said.

The young man explained that he was catching fish to help feed a local village, but that he wasn't a fisherman by trade. "I am a preacher. Through me, the Creator shares his wisdom, and he has some words for you two."

"Well, what are they?" Death demanded.

The young preacher explained that Death should keep on killing, but he wasn't to strike down everyone he meets: "The Creator encourages you to assess each soul's deeds, intentions, hopes, and dreams before deciding their fate. Focus on those whose suffering you can end and spare the lives of the young and healthy, including my children, Cyllene and Tyrell. You have already taken enough from me by claiming my wife after the birth of my son. However, the Creator understands that strict adherence to rules might not always be feasible. There will be difficult decisions where you must be both merciful and merciless."

The assassin agreed to accept half payment from each of her employers, and Death continued his journey through the lands of Arcadia, sparing some and claiming others, guided by the Creator's wisdom and the preacher's words.

"So, you see," Cyllene told her brother once she was finished. "Death can never harm us. Father made him promise."

Tyrell had fallen asleep. Cyllene clasped onto her blanket and tried to clear her head, but it didn't happen. She kept thinking of her father and how he was alone in his final moments as he perished in burning flames. Now, she had to protect Tyrell. It was going to be difficult finding refuge in the capital. The citizens would be focused on recovering from the attack and rebuilding their own lives.

A sudden light broke the darkness. She gasped. There, only a couple of hundred feet away, was a fire burning along the edge of the mountain.

It could be the Omi, coming after them. Or it could be other survivors.

Careful not to wake Tyrell, Cyllene slipped out from under the blanket and crept over to the fire.

A middle-aged man sat alone with his back to her. He wore white robes and had greying, curly hair. He rubbed his palms above the flames. "Don't be afraid," he said, without turning to face her. "Come join me, child. The fire is warm, and the night is cold."

She gasped in fright, frozen to the spot.

"Come, Cyllene," he added further. "I have a gift for you and your brother. I mean you no harm."

Cyllene shuffled over to the flames and looked the man in the face. He had a full beard and tired eyes. A gold tablet rested beside him, and a ragged bag was perched over his shoulder. "How do you know who I am?"

"I don't know much about who you are, actually. But I know very well who you will become. Please, sit down."

She sat down beside the fire, enjoying its warmth. "Who are you?"

"Name's Marko, trainer of the Queen's army."

"The Queen's army! They're here? Have they come to save us?"

Marko maintained his sullen look. "I'm afraid not, my child. The Omi have faced Queen Shanleigh and her army, and these old bones are all that still stand."

"So, the war's over? The Omi have won?"

"They haven't conquered everywhere. Not yet."

"But they will?"

"Oh, yes. Nothing can stop them now."

She turned her eyes to the flames. How many other souls would perish like her father's, alone in scorching blazes?

"Cheer up, child," Marko said, a slight smile appearing on his face. "Now is not the time to abandon all hope. We need that now more than ever."

"Hope for what? The war is over." Cyllene frowned.

"Hope that things will get better." He reached into his shoulder bag with a smile. "I have a gift for you."

"You're giving me a present?" she asked. "You don't even know me."

"The gift is from the Creator, Himself, the Lord of the Holy World." Marko pulled from his bag something that was wrapped in cloth. Unveiling it, he revealed a sword. It was fancy looking, with a ruby embedded in the golden branch, but still just a sword.

"A sword?"

"Not just any sword. A blade that belonged to the Queen's army. It's made of metal from the Holy World and was constructed by a very close friend of mine. Metal from the Holy World cannot break."

"But why are you giving it to me?"

"Before training Queen Shanleigh's army, I handpicked the members myself," Marko said. "You see, I foresaw their futures and knew they would be the ones to defeat the Omi. Now, Queen Shanleigh's army has been defeated, and I must be led to their replacements. These are the warriors that will defeat the Omi's Second Empire. This is why I have been led to you."

"To me?" Cyllene raised an eyebrow.

"Yes. I'm placing this sword in your care. One day you will know what to do with it. You're destined for great things."

"Alone?"

"No, there will be others."

"Who?"

"I don't know. I haven't chosen them yet. I do know that they will most likely be orphans, like you. All of them will be alone. They'll be lost and desperate. Searching for purpose, meaning, and love. The things that make us human. But, like you, they'll never find them. That's why their destiny, like yours, will be something greater."

"I'm not alone," she said. "I have my brother."

"For now." Marko placed the sword beside her and turned away.

"Wait!" she yelled. "You're leaving?"

"Yes, I must. You must walk your journey alone, Cyllene, for it's that journey that will make you into the warrior Arcadia needs. I see great pain in your future and for that I am sorry. Darkness will try to pollute your mind. But your soul and heart are pure. So long as you try to keep them this way, the light will prevail. Take care, my child." He stepped into the shadows.

"What am I supposed to do now?"

"Go to the capital. There, you will find refuge. Make sure

to look after your sword and tell no one of it. One day, you will need it." He was then gone, completely swallowed by the darkness.

Cyllene returned to her brother, but she got no sleep that night.

After a full day of walking the next day, they made it to the capital. The wall surrounding the city was the most impressive structure Cyllene had ever seen. She never dreamed that mere men could construct something so tall and thick.

Inside the walls, the destruction from the Omi's invasion was evident. People struggled to rebuild their homes and replant their gardens. Red flags and banners hung everywhere, indicating that the Omi now controlled the city. The streets were littered with guards. Posters, announcing the new tax laws and how much the citizens had to pay, were nailed to walls.

Cyllene and Tyrell were turned away from every door they went to, despite pleading for shelter and food.

"We have enough to worry about without more mouths to feed," was the usual response they got before a door was then slammed in their face.

Cyllene could see that Tyrell was getting upset. She, too, was feeling rather hopeless. They hadn't eaten since before they left their village, and both of their stomachs ached.

There was a small stall selling hunted animals. She and Tyrell eyed the meat like wolves spotting their prey. When the seller wasn't looking, Cyllene reached for a piece. However, her arm was immediately grabbed.

Cyllene gulped as she studied the heavily armed guard.

"And what do you think you're doing, you little rat?" He pulled her tighter to him.

She turned around. Another guard had her brother. "What do you say we take them to the Governor? See how he feels about a bunch of snot-nosed brats stealing food from his people."

Governor Valen had been placed in charge of Tyrin by the Omi. He was aged, his long grey hair tied tightly in a ponytail. Dressed in a black robe, he sat in his throne room, his expression cold and serious as Cyllene and her brother were dragged before him.

His two children, Ariel and Radmir, sat on smaller thrones beside him. Radmir had been styled to look identical to his father. The only difference between them was that Radmir's face looked blatantly miserable. Ariel, on the other hand, donned a vibrant pink dress, her hair and makeup expertly arranged to accentuate her radiance.

"Sin is no longer tolerated in Tyrin," Valen said. "And thievery is a sin. What do you think we should do with thieves, child?"

"Execute them!" Ariel yelled.

"Not you," Valen told her sternly, causing Ariel to lower her head.

"I'm not sure, Father." Radmir's voice was barely audible in the large hall. He kept looking at his feet.

"You're not sure? A Governor must be sure, boy. Otherwise, why should anyone listen to you?"

"Yes, father." He nodded his head slowly and tried to look stern.

"Your sister is right, boy," Valen spat. "We must execute criminals. Otherwise, our citizens won't take our authority seriously and their evil will spread. Honestly, how did I end up with a son as stupid as you?"

Radmir sulked in his chair. His lower lip trembled.

"Chop off their heads," Valen ordered the guards. "Display them on the city's walls for all to see."

The guards drew their swords. Tyrell hid behind Cyllene. The three guards in the room encircled them. Cyllene unsheathed her own blade for the first time in her life and told her brother to stay close.

"Children who can fight! What is this savagery?" Valen said. "It's good the Omi has come to cleanse this land. Get on with it and kill them already."

Cyllene had never fought before in her life, but she was willing to give it a go to defend her brother. Just then, the doors opened, and a large lizard entered the throne room. He walked on two legs, like a human, and was dressed in green armor.

Governor Valen stood, his face marked with surprise. "General Karmeeleon, this is an unexpected honor."

Karmeeleon's face was impassive. "I'm here to ensure Tyrin's capital is now fully enforcing all laws of the Omi."

"Indeed, my lord. We were just about to deal with a couple of criminals." Valen pointed to Cyllene and Tyrell.

The general's gaze fixated on Cyllene, his attention drawn to the sword gripped tightly in her hand. His eyes held an intensity that sent a shiver down her spine.

"What is their crime?" the general enquired.

"Stealing meat, my lord."

"Clear the room," Karmeeleon ordered. "I want to be alone with the girl."

"My lord?" Valen asked, furrowing his brows.

"Are you deaf? Clear the room!"

The guards took Tyrell, and followed the Governor out the door, along with his children. The doors were closed behind them, leaving Cyllene alone with the general.

"Where did you get that blade?" he asked.

Cyllene didn't want to tell him, but his fierce, red eyes burned like a brand through her.

"I'm not supposed to say," she replied.

"Who said you're not?"

"The old man."

"What old man?"

"The one with the white robes. He said his name was Marko."

"And did Marko tell you what you're supposed to do with that blade?"

She paused, knowing Marko wouldn't want her to say. But Marko wasn't here now, and he couldn't protect them. All she cared about was protecting her brother. "He said that one day I'd be a warrior, but he was wrong. I'm not a fighter."

Karmeeleon's smile was chilling. "Of course, you're not. You're just a little girl. A very beautiful, special, little girl. Did Marko say you were special?"

She nodded.

The general stepped closer. "And that you are. What's your name, special, little girl?"

"Cyllene," she said timidly.

"Cyllene," he repeated in an unsettling whisper, sounding more like a curse than a gesture of politeness.

The stare of his red eyes terrified her, but she couldn't identify why. He looked at her like how she had looked at the meat earlier.

"You want to protect your brother, but he's destined to meet the fate that all criminals must. As are you. You understand this, right?"

She nodded.

"But, maybe, you and I can come to an understanding." He reached out with his scaly arm and stroked her cheek. "The guards here will do whatever I command because I am the second most powerful man in the world. Do you understand this as well?"

"Are you a man?" she enquired.

His stare turned angry. "Of course, I am a man." He grabbed her tight, and his stare was fixed and unyielding. "You do as I command, and no harm will come to you or your brother. Understand?"

"What do you want me to do?" she asked.

"Exactly as I instruct."

Cyllene didn't understand what happened between them that day, but she knew it hurt, and it made her feel unclean.

After they were finished, Karmeeleon took her and Tyrell to his palace, just outside the city. They were given their own rooms in one of his towers, though Karmeeleon would come and join her most nights.

After nearly ten years of living under his roof, she came to think it was normal, though she still didn't enjoy it. She longed for the nights when he was away, usually at the Omi's Sanctuary within Anubai, reporting to Develon. Only a couple of times did he ever take her to Anubai with him.

But on the other hand, she and her brother had been brought up in a palace, never wanting for anything, eating the finest food in Tyrin. Perhaps, the uncomfortableness she endured during her nights with Karmeeleon was a small price to pay for the salvation of her and her brother.

Karmeeleon had opened her eyes to the Omi also. While her father's intentions had been noble, to spread virtue across Arcadia through words of the Creator, there would always be those forever corrupted by sin. The Omi were aware of this and were set on ridding the lands of evil. A thousand years ago, the Omi had begun as nothing more than a small religious sect. But they had grown a great number of followers during the rise of the Ichu. The Ichu had been set on nothing but the end of humankind. The Omi had saved the entire world.

Not only had she and Tyrell been given the life of royalty, but they were destined to join the Omi's Security when they came of age. To protect the Omi's kingdom and maintain order and virtue, by putting out the sparks of evil, was the greatest privilege that there was. Karmeeleon already had

Cyllene's Security uniform made, and she couldn't wait for the day when she would sport it.

Even when everyone thought the Omi had been destroyed, the Security training camps continued to function underground. Typically, those who aspired to join the Security underwent grueling and rigorous training from a young age. However, Karmeeleon made the decision to spare Cyllene and Tyrell from such arduous preparations. Despite the uncomfortableness she felt during their nights together, he cared for them both.

Tyrell, however, held a rebellious spirit and was far less excited to one day be a member of Omi's Security. He said that Karmeeleon had brainwashed her, and that the Omi weren't really the virtuous saviors of Arcadia that Karmeeleon made them out to be. He said they were corrupt and evil.

Cyllene never told Tyrell of what went on between her and Karmeeleon, who told her to keep it their secret. Besides, she didn't want to give Tyrell further cause to hate Karmeeleon, like he already claimed to.

Tyrell had a habit of sneaking out of the palace at night, but Cyllene made sure to keep it a secret from Karmeeleon to avoid getting her brother into trouble. Karmeeleon believed that Tyrell's rebellious behavior was just a phase that all teenagers went through, assuring Cyllene that it would eventually pass. However, Cyllene couldn't recall going through a similar phase herself. One night, her curiosity got the better of her, and she decided to follow her brother.

She shadowed him to the capital, where he went underground, to a large, empty chamber above the sewers. A mass of people was gathered there. They looked like the bottom of society and shouted in agreement at a man who said terrible things about the Omi. He called them tyrants and spoke about bringing them to their knees. Everyone in the crowd seemed to love this statement, and they all raised their fists into the air.

Cyllene spotted her brother and dashed over to him.

Pulling him aside, she yelled, "What are you doing here with these maniacs?"

"They're going to bring down the Omi, Cyllene," he replied.

"What? That's madness!"

"People are starving outside the capital, Cyllene, unable to pay their taxes. They are executed for not following the religion Develon tells them to follow. These people only want to be free."

"But father says—"

"That giant lizard is not our father! Our father was killed by the Omi!'

"Karmeeleon gave us a home."

"He's a liar, Cyllene. He tells us that the heretics were savages, and that human beings knew nothing before the Omi conquered Arcadia. He says that there's nothing to learn other than the Creator's texts. But I know people who have made amazing discoveries—tunnels, containing tracks, and houses with copper chains and glass hanging from the ceilings. The Omi are liars. More than that, they're murderers. Things are only going to get worse once the Governor's son takes over. Radmir is going to turn this very room into a fighting arena, where the poor and desperate will fight and die for his amusement. He will close off the gates to the capital, denying the rest of Arcadia's citizens any chance of prosperity."

"These sinners have polluted your mind, brother," she cried, pulling him by the arm. "Come with me, please, and we will pray for you to get better."

He knocked her arm away. "No, Cyllene. It is your mind that has been tainted by that terrible lizard. Tomorrow, just before Radmir assumes the position of Governor, we shall launch an assault and reclaim the city for the people."

"You can't!"

"Stay off the streets, Cyllene." He turned back to the crowd and continued shouting with the others.

As Cyllene went back to the city above ground, she cried for her brother's lost soul. She thought about telling the guards about what was happening below, but she didn't want to get her brother killed.

"You look lost," a voice called. "Like two children alone in the mountains."

It was a beggar at the side of the street, an elderly man with a long, white beard, dressed in a tattered white robe.

"Do I know you?" she asked him.

"Have I aged so badly that you don't recognize me, my child?"

"I think you're mistaking me for someone else."

"Have you been looking after my sword?"

Now she remembered him. He was the old fool who told her she'd be a warrior someday and bring down the Omi. "You should leave before I tell my father about you. He doesn't take kindly to traitors."

"Your father?" he asked with a puzzled expression. "That's strange."

"What is?"

"You don't look like a lizard."

She frowned. "My father, General Karmeeleon, is a great man."

"He can call himself a man as much as he likes, but his skin will always have scales and his tail will still slither after him. Have you really forgotten your true father, Cyllene?"

"General Karmeeleon is my father now," she argued. "He has given me a home and shown me the light. But I remember my old father every day. He was a preacher, who met with Death, and told him to never harm me or Tyrell. I owe him our lives, as well as my new father."

"Cyllene, you must come to realize that your father's tale was nothing more than a story. No man can bargain with death. And no one man can decide who lives or dies. It was your own strength that got you and your brother to the capital when you were children. You owe no man your life."

"Leave me alone, or I'll alert the authorities." She turned away.

"I once said your heart was pure," he called after her. "Though your mind has become soiled, I hope that is still true about your heart. Tomorrow, when your brother attacks during Governor Radmir's celebration, it will be put to the test. You must choose between your brother or the words Karmeeleon has filled your mind with. Bring your blade tomorrow. You'll need it."

~

The next day, Cyllene did bring her blade, like the old man suggested.

She stood among the crowd, listening to Governor Radmir. He looked so different from when she met him as a child. No longer did he look like a sad little boy, forced to live in his father's shadow. Dressed in a bright purple robe that matched the color of his dyed hair, and with blue makeup plastered over his face, he beamed with joy.

Her brother had been right—Governor Radmir was closing off the gates, except to those who wished to fight for citizenship in his new battle arena. The arena would also host a separate series of competitions where victors would fight to be the ultimate champion. With his older sister being married off to the Governor of Eden's son, there was no one to stop Radmir from claiming command and bringing his depraved fantasies to life. He believed in making his citizens smile and was prepared for everyone else to die to make that happen.

At first, Cyllene saw no sign of her brother or his errant gang of protestors, but then someone hurled a rock towards Governor Radmir, striking him squarely on the head.

His guards immediately shielded him, taking him inside.

Men and women wielding sharpened sticks dashed at the guards. Cyllene recognized them from the assembly the night before. Among them was her brother.

Tyrell impaled his stick into the chest of a guard. The other protestors did the same, taking down several other men. The guards unsheathed their swords and fought back, cutting down the activists with ease.

One of them hacked Tyrell's stick in half, and another grabbed and pinned him to the ground. He kicked Tyrell in the ribs. Her brother grunted in pain. The guard lifted his sword into the air, ready to slam down and chop off her brother's head.

"Stop!" Cyllene yelled, stepping forward.

"Keep back, girl," the guard spat.

"What are *you* going to do?" the other added.

She drew her own sword. "I'm the daughter of General Karmeeleon."

They stared at her.

Her father wasn't a person to displease. Ultimately, the guards decided to just arrest Tyrell and he was sent to the cells beneath the city. The rest of the protestors were all slain by the guards, their heads then placed on pikes across the wall.

Karmeeleon was furious at her showing pity towards Tyrell, who he claimed was now a traitor, nothing more, and that she was never again to call him her brother. More than anything, however, her father seemed most concerned over her having used her blade in public.

He tried melting her blade down in the fire, but the flames did nothing. They didn't even blacken it.

"Metal from the Holy World cannot be destroyed," she told him, remembering the old man's words.

"Then we shall just make sure it can never again be used," Karmeeleon replied, and he hid it beneath the stone flooring of his bedroom.

He took Cyllene to nearby villages he said were full of sin.

There, she saw prostitution, drinking, gambling, and thievery. They were all acts of evil by the laws of the Omi, and so the villagers had to be punished.

She and Karmeeleon burned them to the ground. Karmeeleon instructed her to always leave one survivor, who was to go and spread her name, telling other communities to avoid falling into sin, or they'd meet a similar fate.

Her father hoped this would show she wasn't a traitor, like her brother, that she was committed to the Omi and would serve as part of Security. He decided, however, it wasn't enough. Security's Captain was already unhappy with her bypassing the usual training Security members underwent and now there was sufficient argument to claim Cyllene couldn't be trusted with the honor of serving. So, to make her "strong", Karmeeleon entered her into Radmir's fighting arena.

Karmeeleon trained her before sending her away, telling her to become Arcadia's new ultimate champion or die trying.

The day Cyllene won the championship, she had faced true competition, not like Aaron and his friends in the arena, or Zylina, who had attacked her from behind like a coward. The noise of the crowd had been deafening, their roaring demand for blood overpowering all else, even the thumping of her own heart.

She stood at the other side of the gate, waiting to enter the arena, clad in nothing more than a cloth modestly around her waist and a skimpy metal breastplate. She'd have to become champion before receiving the luxury of proper armor. Until then, she was just something pretty to be gazed upon and to entertain. Unlike her male competitors, she had to earn the right to be taken seriously as a fighter.

Her skin was coated in blood and grime, and her hair was almost indistinguishable from the dirt, the result of hours spent inside the stadium earlier that day. She had fought her way up through the ranks, and now, there remained only one final obstacle.

At last, a guard released her restraints. The chains around her ankles fell to the ground, offering sudden relief from the pain. She refused to glance down at the marks left by the chains; acknowledging her pain would be a sign of weakness. Instead, she fixed her gaze forward as the gate began to rise.

The cheers got even louder, but over them, she heard the Governor's voice; "We have seen Cyllene fight and kill unworthy opponents. Now, we shall see her face our champion!"

As if on cue, a long metal rod prodded at the center of her back, urging her forward. She shuffled into the arena, shielding her eyes from the blinding lights, sizing up her opponent. The towering figure stood with a muscular frame. He gave her a hard look as she came forward. Cyllene read the arrogance clearly in his eyes. *You're dead*, they said, *I am not like the others*.

The champion lowered his silver mask over his face. He was much more prepared than she was. Hard armor covered his body, and he had been given leather boots to help add strength to his kicks. Before Cyllene could unsheathe her sword or get her position, the man lunged towards her with a frightening roar.

Cyllene avoided the swing of his sword, rolling away. Using the force of the missed attack, the man pivoted around and charged again, but missed her once more. He was quick, quicker than any other opponent she had faced, but she was strong. He elbowed her in the ribs as she ducked under his blade. She grunted in pain but recovered immediately.

Retreating a few steps, Cyllene retrieved her sword, swiftly spinning off her front leg, and delivered a powerful kick to the man's temple with the back of her bare heel. He toppled to the ground. Cyllene gave him no time to collect himself. As she stood over him, legs on either side of his body, she lowered her sword to stab him as he lay on the floor.

The man rolled to the side to avoid the blow. The impact reverberated through her arms, sending a sharp jolt of pain. Seizing the opportunity, the man propelled himself back onto his feet and unleashed a forceful kick to Cyllene's stomach, causing her to stagger backwards.

He lunged forward, ready to finish it all. But Cyllene rolled back, standing on her hands, before coming down to her feet. She raised her sword to shield herself from his attack. She tried to slash his side when he was distracted, but the man beat her to it.

The following moments blurred together in a whirlwind of chaos. Cyllene emitted a sharp cry of anguish as she felt the searing pain of the slash across her side. In quick succession, the man's boot collided with her gut, followed by a brutal punch to her nose. She crumpled to the ground, her grip on the sword loosening, blood streaming down her face and onto her chest. The man chuckled hysterically as she squirmed helplessly on the ground.

Summoning every ounce of determination, Cyllene scrambled to her feet, but she was still without her weapon. She faced the man and shrieked. As he ran towards her, she flipped backwards in the air, her foot hitting the man's chin during the turn over. As he fell onto the ground with a hard thud, Cyllene picked up her weapon.

Unfortunately, the flip caused the wound in her side to open more. Blood coursed down her hip and leg. She spat blood from her mouth, strolling towards the man, her head held high.

He attempted a blow, but she caught his hand and forced his sword to point into the air. She kneed him in the gut, lifted her own sword, and plunged its sharp tip into his stomach. The man's eyes changed, as he looked at the wound, doubling over and holding it with his free hand. At that moment, he knew he was beaten. He looked into Cyllene's eyes. She gave an exhausted exhale, took her sword, and finished him off.

His lifeless body collapsed on the ground. Only then did Cyllene once again notice the roar of the crowd around her, as well as the smell of blood and filth. The audience cheered her on as Governor Radmir announced that Tyrin had a new champion.

Winning the championship title made her feel proud, a feeling rarely experienced in her life. She was sore, dirty, and bloody from the fight, of course, but still had her life. Moise, the former leader of the guards before Aelius, led her back to her cell. Each step on the hard, uneven stone floor exacerbated the pain in her already aching feet and legs. Moise noticed her injuries and asked how her side was.

"It's only a flesh wound. I'll live," she responded.

Moise congratulated her on her victory, and then informed her that as champion, there were perks she could take advantage of, including new fighting armor, boots, a helmet, and a sword to use in future battles against those who would challenge her title.

Moise's wife approached them. "You cannot possibly be considering taking her to the warrior's chamber." She gestured towards Cyllene as she spoke.

"She's a warrior," Moise argued. "Where else would she stay?"

"Moise, it's a den of savagery down there. If she is sent there, she will be..." His wife's voice trailed off, the thought too sickening to voice. "I refuse to entertain the idea. She will come with us. We can find a place for her among the servants, but she must be cleaned up first."

Moise turned his attention back to Cyllene. "You will sleep in the servants' quarters of our home, then you will spend your day with the warriors. Understand?"

Cyllene told him that she understood, though she didn't really; compassion was an alien concept to her.

Moise asked her a lot of questions about how she had become a warrior, including if she came to the capital because she dreamed of becoming a champion and bringing honor to her name.

"My father brought me here. He says I have to learn inner strength," Cyllene replied.

Moise looked at her with an expression she didn't recognize at the time, but what she now understood to have been pity. He must have realized that she had been given little choice in coming to fight at the capital, so he offered to train her during the days; "You won't learn much, fighting the other competitors. I could train you instead."

When their first training session rolled around, she dressed in her best, most appropriate attire. She dressed in a navy corset fastened to a petalled skirt, complemented by silver armor adorning her chest and shoulders. Leather gauntlets covered her arms, extending to protect her elbows, while dark leather boots and silver knee pads completed her ensemble.

He tossed a sword in her direction, which she swiftly caught. "You must use your speed against their strength," Moise said, immediately swiping his own sword through the air. She retreated backwards just in time. "Attack and retreat. Let him wear himself out."

He roared at her to attack him. Cyllene lunged at him, trying to drive her sword into his stomach. However, Moise effortlessly deflected her strike with his shield and swiftly brought his sword down upon hers, knocking it from her grip. It clattered on the cobblestones. He refused to let her pick it up, instead kicking her legs, knocking her to the ground.

With the point of his sword pressed against her throat, Moise asked, "Do you surrender?"

Cyllene's brow furrowed in confusion at the notion. Instead, she responded by delivering a swift kick to his forearm, causing his grip to falter and the sword to soar through the air before landing on the ground.

With Moise distracted, she stretched her foot behind him, swiftly yanking his legs out from under him, and pulled him to the ground beside her.

As they both lay there, bathed in the warmth of the sun, Cyllene turned her gaze towards Moise. "I don't surrender," she said.

Rising to her feet, Cyllene extended her hand towards Moise, who chuckled to himself. Retrieving both swords, she threw one to Moise, poised and ready to fight again.

Moise charged at her, employing his shield to block her strike. He forced his shield forward, hitting her in the face. Cyllene found herself lying on the hot stones once more. She brought her leg up to kick him, but this time he was ready and grabbed her ankle.

"Attack and retreat!" he yelled, pushing her leg back to the ground. This time it was Moise who extended his arm and helped her up. Clasping her shoulder, he remarked, "You are doing well, Cyllene."

"But retreating? Running away?" Frustrated by the concept, she threw her sword to the ground in contempt, stirring up a cloud of dust around her feet.

Moise swung his sword at her, and she deftly ducked beneath the blade. "You couldn't block that strike, but you easily evaded it. It takes more energy to swing and miss than it does to swing and hit," he explained.

Cyllene sighed but said nothing. Sleep came fast for her that night, dreamless and peaceful. She paid no mind to the resting servants around her. She rose early and ate with them, but instead of going about household chores, she made her way into the courtyard, where she would wait for Moise every day.

That day, she was grateful for the cleansing rain that refreshed her skin. Normally, she would only be offered a wash after a brutal and bloody fight. As the raindrops fell upon her, moistening her body, Cyllene felt a sense of renewal. Moise emerged from the house and made his way towards her, seeming less pleased to be out in the rain.

"Today, Moise, do not hold back on me. I can handle it," she called. Moise had gone easy on her the previous day, and she was about as thankful for it as Moise was for the rain.

As Moise turned back towards his house, seemingly checking that they were alone, Cyllene realized she had unintentionally addressed him by name, which was highly inappropriate for a guard, let alone their leader. She hadn't meant to, but it had just slipped out. He said nothing about it and turned back to her, chuckling. "Are you sure? I never hit a little girl before."

Cyllene smiled at his condescending tease, and they sparred with each other. She kicked his legs from under him with a huff. Moise landed on the wet cobblestones with a thud. Cyllene stood, still smiling. "Think of me not as a girl, but as a warrior. And attack me with some bloody purpose, you jellyfish!" she roared, causing Moise to laugh. It was a term he had coined on her first day of training, whenever she had held back during an attack, accusing her of acting spineless.

She kicked Moise in the hip, encouraging him to get up. He stood and gazed at the sky, running his fingers through his wet hair to push it back from his forehead. "Let's take a break," he suggested.

"Why?"

"I could use a break from the rain. Let's find shelter and sit for a while."

He led her away, and they settled down on some chairs under a protective roof. Cyllene gathered her wet hair and draped it over her back, wiping the water from her face. When she looked up, she noticed Moise staring at her.

"You told me your father brought you here," he said. "How long does he plan on making you stay?"

"I don't know. Until he thinks I'm ready."

"I can't see what he's waiting for. I've never seen such a fine warrior."

"Thank you, Moise."

They both seemed oblivious to the fact that she had called him by his first name again.

"Does the fighting ever weigh on you? Do you find it troubling afterward?" he asked.

"I'm destined to be a fighter. When I fight, I make my opponents pay for their sins. My father believes it is the will of the Creator that they meet their end."

Moise appeared confused, but before he had time to question her further, a guard came running over. He addressed Moise with a statue stance. "Sir, the girl is being requested in the entrance chamber. She has a visitor."

The music had resonated through the stone walls from the fighter's chamber as Cyllene made her way to the entrance chamber. She heard them screaming and laughing and wondered if they didn't know they were destined for death.

She walked alone, her visitor requesting complete privacy. Once she reached the portcullis at the end of the tunnel, General Karmeeleon stood, waiting at the other side. He greeted her in his usual elegant, aristocratic tone, "Hello, Cyllene. You are doing well."

"Thank you," she replied, her voice much quieter than usual.

"Now, do you see the sin of those around you?"

"I do."

"And do you still believe they are deserving of redemption?"

"I don't."

"You must make them pay for their sins. Cleanse this land by eliminating those who tarnish it. Only by doing so can you bring honor to the Creator."

She nodded in understanding.

"The guards' leader has sin in his heart," he told her.

She looked up, her eyes full of worry, and shook her head. "Moise? No, it can't be."

His fierce, red eyes glared into her soul. She lowered her head, powerless before him. "You dare question me, girl?"

"Of course not. It's just… he's very good to me."

The general's expression twisted with disdain. "Only because he thinks you're pretty, and because he wants you."

"Maybe he's just nice."

General Karmeeleon's anger flared, his voice dripping with scorn. "Don't be so naïve, you stupid girl. I've seen the lust in his eyes when he looks at you. He dreams of committing adultery against his wife. He must pay for his sins. Do you understand, Cyllene?"

She nodded.

"You must draw his blood, Cyllene."

"Yes, Father," she replied.

Moise was the only person to ever show her kindness, giving her shelter and teaching her to fight. How could she kill him? She wanted to believe that he did things for her out of the goodness of his heart or because he respected her as a person, not because he desired her flesh.

On the way back from her visit with Karmeeleon, she saw one of the fighters being escorted from their chambers by Moise and a couple of other guards.

"So, this is the girl I've heard so much about?" the fighter said with a throaty laugh.

"Tyrin's champion has been put in the arena many times and always came out victorious. Let's see how you do," one of the guards said, dragging the man to the arena.

"She's nothing but a gimmick," the fighter scoffed, planting his feet firmly on the ground. "A girl is no champion of Tyrin."

Cyllene's blood boiled. She brought up her foot and kicked him between his legs with all her strength. He collapsed to his knees in pain. Cyllene delivered a series of knee strikes to his face until she heard the sickening crack of bone. The man collapsed onto his back, blood seeping through his fingers as he clutched his face.

"You broke my nose," he cried.

"A little taste of what's to come," she said.

The guards dragged the bleeding man away to the arena.

Moise stayed behind. "Why do you let him get to you?"

"He doesn't think I belong here because I'm a girl. So, I showed him otherwise."

"You should save your teachings for the arena. That man isn't worth your anger. You're a fine warrior, Cyllene. You should be comfortable with that. You may not be as strong as your male competitors, but you are faster and smarter. You see into their soul."

"I see into their soul?" she asked.

"Yes, I've seen it. You watch how your opponents move and spot every twitch of a muscle before they strike."

"Their eyes reveal all."

"You're the sharpest, most skilled warrior I've ever known, man or woman." Moise smiled in a way that made her heart flutter and her soul brighten.

She couldn't fully grasp the emotions swirling within her, but one thing was certain: Moise made her feel good. His presence, his belief in her abilities, sparked something she had never experienced before.

After about a week, Cyllene was called for another visit from General Karmeeleon at the city's entrance chamber. As she approached the portcullis, he wasted no time in questioning her, "Why haven't you eliminated him yet?"

"I still see no sin in his eyes," she replied meekly.

"Liar!" he bellowed. "You must see his desire for you! Perhaps you do see it and you like it."

"No!"

"You wish to tempt him from his wife, is that it?"

"I would never!"

"You're a sinful siren!"

"Please, Father, you know you made me pure. I strive only to cleanse the Creator's lands, as you command."

"Good," he stated. "In that case, eliminating the wicked leader of the guards should pose no problem for you. Otherwise, the Creator may demand retribution for Tyrell's transgressions."

Cyllene felt a chill in the air. "Tyrell? What does he have to do with this?"

"He is a traitor to the Omi and the Creator. Since his pitiful rebellion with his comrades, he has been rotting away in the city's dungeon. However, if you anger the Creator by disobeying, He may demand a harsher punishment for your brother. Do you understand?"

She lowered her head. "Yes, Father. I will not disappoint."

"Good. Kill the leader of the guards, and do it without delay. If you fail to do so by day's end, your brother will be executed, and I will present you with his skull when I next visit."

Cyllene turned to leave.

"Another matter, Cyllene," he called out. "Prepare yourself for some newcomers in the arena."

She faced him. "Newcomers?"

"Three warriors, wanted by the Omi, are making their way here. I've instructed Governor Radmir to inform me immediately when they arrive."

"Why are you telling me this?" she asked.

"Because, if you see them, you'll notice they have blades just like yours."

The other sword owners, she remembered, were the ones the old man had told her about as a child, who also were destined to be great warriors and end the Omi.

"If you encounter them, pay no attention to their blades. Remember, they are not your allies, regardless of what the foolish old man once told you. They are enemies of the Omi, and thus, your enemies. You are one of us. You will never be one of them."

Cyllene turned to leave once again.

"One more thing," he called after her. "I love you.

Hearing that made her feel sick, but she couldn't quite place why. Perhaps it was because he'd whisper it in her ear whenever he spent the night in her bed.

A guard waited for her outside Moise's home. He told her to go to the stables next door and so she did. When she opened the doors, she found that the hay and horses had all been cleared out. The inside had been completely renewed, with new walls and flooring constructed. All of the pens had been detached, and new furniture took their place. There was a large bed, a table for eating, and even a small bathroom.

Moise stood in the center of the building and stretched out his arms to show off the place.

"What is this?" she asked.

"It's yours."

"Mine?"

"Yes, I've been working on it for some weeks now. It isn't much, I know. But you're not a servant so you shouldn't be living with them. This place belongs to you. You're a champion and you should be treated as one. I will have one of our servants attend to your every need."

Her heart began to beat fast in that way Moise so often made it do. "But where will your horses go?"

He shrugged. "I have no need for horses."

"It's too much," she said.

"No, it isn't. It isn't enough, but it's all I have to give you."

Cyllene didn't know what to say and so they both just stood there.

"Do you like it?" he finally asked.

"It's beautiful."

"It also means we can have some privacy. Well, only if you allow me to visit you, of course. This place is yours."

"Why would we need privacy?" she asked.

"It's all right." He stepped forward. "I know we both enjoy spending time together."

She thought about this, then said, "Yes, I enjoy our time together when you train me, sir."

His expression turned slightly offended, and he spoke with gentle firmness, "You never call me that, even though you should. And I let you call me by my name because I'm not just your trainer; I'm your friend. I enjoy not just fighting with you but talking to you and listening to you. And more than anything else in the world, I enjoy seeing you smile. It doesn't happen often, but I feel so happy when it does. I don't know what has happened in your past that was so terrible that it led you here, but nothing gives me greater pleasure than knowing I've made your world a little brighter. Because I love you, Cyllene. And I know you love me."

Before she knew it, he was standing right in front of her. He grabbed her by the waist and pulled her into him, kissing her on the lips.

Her heart raced. Flashes of General Karmeeleon in bed with her echoed in her head. This was different—it warmed her soul and she felt connected to Moise in a way she never had before. However, at the same time, it made her feel sick.

She reached for her dagger and plunged it into his stomach. She stared into his eyes. At first, they were full of life and passion, but then they turned to pain. Cyllene pulled it from his body. Moise collapsed to the floor with an agonized grunt. Blood spread under her boots and more dripped from the dagger in her hand.

She dropped her weapon to the floor and cried. It was the first time she ever remembered crying.

Karmeeleon had been right about Moise. His heart had been full of lust for her; he was a sinner. But that wasn't why she plunged the dagger. She did that out of panic. The thought of a man ever touching her like Karmeeleon did made her stomach churn and her body sweat, even if she loved him. Moise had been right; she did love him. Did that make her a sinner, too?

The guard outside must have heard her dagger drop. Just then, the stable's door burst open. He seized her and took her back to a cell underground, where the other competitors for the arena waited.

There, she fought endless battles, while waiting for the warriors with the blades, only to fail at defeating them in the arena. Now, she was allied with one of them.

She left Aaron in the dining room, now he knew her whole story, to retrieve her sword from under Karmeeleon's bedroom floor. Beneath the loose stones of Karmeeleon's bedroom floor, she found something else, along with her sword: a skull.

She didn't have to think about it. She knew it belonged to her brother. By the looks of it, he had been killed some time ago, probably when he was first arrested.

She had killed Moise for nothing. For the second time in her life, she cried.

Aaron and her brother had been right; for too long she had blindly followed Karmeeleon's orders, without question. She felt sick to her stomach as flashes of stabbing Moise snapped in her head, as well as the villages she had burned.

With her blade in hand, Cyllene and Aaron marched together through the capital towards the cells. Next time she saw Karmeeleon, she would confront him about all the wrong he had done to her. Then, she would kill him.

Chapter Twenty-Seven

Nissa had relied on her heightened senses to lead her to an Omi torture camp, meaning the Ichu that Nathan had sent her to find what was inside.

Sensing great energy emissions was a talent Nissa had mastered, along with harnessing and using those energies. Becoming an Ichu not only rid her of weak human emotions and provided immunity from disease and illness, but it made her able to manipulate the elements—fire, air, and water. She could create flames with the flick of a wrist, lift people off their feet with the mere showing of her palm, or cause seas to part. While all Ichu, not just Nathan, had the ability to learn these powers, only she had mastered them, thanks to Nathan's tutelage.

The Omi's torture camp was in the heart of Arcadia's vast desert, hiding from the population the horrors of what went on there. Getting inside was easy; no one was expecting someone to try and break into the prison, only out. Nissa knocked out the two guards stationed outside. She unlocked the bolted door. As Kannoe and her other comrades kept watch outside, she snuck inside to free the ancient warlord who resided somewhere within.

Pinpointing the exact cell would be too difficult, and so would getting any of the guards to talk. Workers of the Omi were trained from an early age to withstand torture. Getting a prisoner to talk might be easier.

In one of the first cells she passed, Nissa saw a non-human in Omi robes being tortured. The grey-faced male was laid out on a wooden table, his arms and legs being pulled by ropes in opposite directions, unleashing agonizing screams.

Nissa raised her palm and blew the door off its hinges. The man turning the wheel spotted Nissa and ran for her. She waved her hand and broke the torturer's neck.

"What kind of witchcraft is this?" the prisoner asked. Nissa stepped to the table. The trembling non-human's face was blistered and peeling, the raw color of someone who had been recently burned. The prisoner's eyes rested on Nissa. He gritted his teeth. "Do your worst, witch."

"I'm not here to hurt you," Nissa replied.

"Then what do you want?"

"Information."

A bitter scoff escaped the prisoner's lips. "I won't tell you anything. Just kill me."

Nissa considered this, and then said, "I can, if you would like, end your suffering. But first, I need some information."

"I will never help your kind. The Ichu can never be allowed to grow again. You're evil spawns of the devil."

"Is that what they teach you?"

The prisoner frowned. "Just kill me."

Nissa noticed that he didn't ask to be set free, meaning he was well beyond that. All he prayed for was an end to his agony. "I can, but first, like I said, I need some information."

"I won't betray the Omi."

"It looks like they've already betrayed you," Nissa said, glancing at the torture equipment.

"I earned my fate," the prisoner replied sadly, "by being a failure. I was the Principal of the Omi's Council, in charge of maintaining order and ensuring the safety of the Omi's people. Instead, I allowed evil to grow undetected. You can't make me talk."

"What's your name?" Nissa asked.

The prisoner furrowed his brows.

"It isn't important information that I want. It's very simple. If you provide me with this minor piece of information, I will grant you a swift end to your suffering. No more torture or agony—just the release of death."

The prisoner's lips trembled. "Please, kill me."

"I will. I'm not looking for any details about your superiors, and you're not going to cause the downfall of the Omi. I just want to know the whereabouts of one prisoner."

The prisoner considered this, a tear trickling down his cheek. "Just one prisoner?"

"Just one," Nissa replied gently. "What's your name?"

"Sin," the prisoner replied. "If I tell you the whereabouts of only one prisoner, you'll promise to kill me?"

"I promise, Sin."

Sin nodded, still sobbing. "Who are you searching for?"

"An Ichu named Mamoru. He is being held captive here."

He took a deep breath. "His cell is on the lowest level at the end of the corridor. Now, please, kill me."

Nissa thanked the prisoner, then, true to her word, ended his life quickly, snapping his neck. She made her way to the lowest level and killed the guards there, throwing their bodies against the stone walls with the energy in the air of the room. In the cell at the end of the corridor, she found Mamoru, huddled in the corner.

He was a brownish insect-like non-human, a hard shell covering his body and two antennas on his head. Two yellow-skinned arms and legs protruded from his body, unprotected by his shell. Tattered brown fabric draped from his shoulders, a far cry from the majestic figure Nissa remembered—once adorned in gleaming armor and a resplendent golden cape.

Mamoru had once given orders in battle and served as a high-ranking leader in Nathan's army. He had planned the Ichu's last attack against the Omi, during which most of the Ichu were killed, including, or so everyone had believed, Nathan.

It took him a moment to recognize her. "Nissa?"

"I'm here to release you," she replied.

"I don't deserve rescue. It's my fault that our Chief is dead. My failure was beyond contempt, and I deserve this agony. Leave me."

"Nathan didn't die in battle."

Mamoru stood. "That can't be true!"

"It is, and I'm here to bring you to him."

Like her, Mamoru was ready to serve the Chief again. He followed her out of his cell. Nissa, however, hoped Mamoru could also assist in another way. Given his close relationship with Nathan, she longed for Mamoru to set aside her doubts and assure her that the man currently occupying Nathan's former chambers was indeed their esteemed leader. It seemed preposterous to consider the notion that anyone could successfully impersonate Nathan or replicate his extraordinary powers. Yet, she didn't know how else to explain how different he was.

Chapter Twenty-Eight

Growing up in Tyrin's desert, Karmeeleon's village was the only place his species could be found.

The neighboring village contained humans, the master race of Arcadia. He used to watch them every day from the bushes, beside a dirt path, which the human children used for walking to school. They filled him with such wonder, mainly because they were better than him.

Karmeeleon was not allowed to speak to the humans or even be seen by them. The mere presence of his abominable species would be enough to corrupt them. At least, that's what he had been taught. His species was a mistake by the Creator. They were lucky the humans even let them live.

As Karmeeleon gazed at the passing human children, he yearned to meet them, to join in their play. He couldn't comprehend how one species could be deemed more deserving of the Creator's love than another. He held onto the hope that what he had been taught was mistaken, that the humans weren't the only pure ones. The thought of being destined to be a sinner crushed him.

Karmeeleon wanted more than anything to be accepted by them. To be perfect like them.

The usual children walked by, dark-skinned boys and girls with varying hairstyles. He noticed how pretty some of the girls were, but immediately tossed that thought from his head. Lust was a sin. An unforgivable sin in the eyes of the Creator. At least, that's what he had been told. Karmeeleon didn't quite believe everything he was taught, questioning whether the Creator was truly as severe as his species claimed. Perhaps they were so desperate to please the Creator that they went to the extreme.

Once the children passed, he dashed back to his village, feeling the scorching sun on his back and the heat from the sand under his feet. It was almost time for service. The crossbow over his shoulder, which he always carried for protection, bounced off his back as he ran.

It was always unpleasant to return to his village. The entire place had a dreadful smell and was infested with rodents. The tiny rodents lived inside their homes and nibbled at the children's feet during the nights.

Outside the church, there was a table laid with freshly cut meats. He came to a halt, his gaze fixated on the tempting spread. The aching pain in his stomach returned. He was so hungry, having not eaten in two days. Food was scarce. He wanted the food mostly for his little brother, Caloo. He was so small and needed the energy. Karmeeleon gave into temptation and swiped a piece of meat while no one was looking, and then ran inside the flimsily built church.

Inside, the other younglings of the village were already engaged in prayer. As Karmeeleon entered, all heads turned to gaze at him. The village's teacher, who also served as the minister, shouted at him for being late.

Karmeeleon nodded in response and took his seat beside his brother. Caloo looked weak, his reptilian skin clinging to bony frames. He handed his brother the piece of meat, and Caloo then chewed it immediately.

The teacher preached about the Holy World, telling them

how the Creator had sealed off the world due to Arcadia's sins. The lost world would only reveal itself again once people reached salvation.

The story halted, as the teacher's glare turned to Karmeeleon. "Stand, Karmeeleon!" he roared.

Karmeeleon did so, confused as to why he was being called out, when it was Caloo who was eating during service.

"Did you steal that food for your brother?"

Karmeeleon saw no reason to lie. "Caloo was starving."

"Come here!"

Karmeeleon walked to the front of the church.

"Your brother is pure and would not steal, no matter how hungry he was. But, you, Karmeeleon, are corrupted. Now, confess!"

"I stole."

"Ask the Creator for forgiveness."

"If Caloo is pure, why would the Creator want him to starve?"

The teacher spun Karmeeleon round and whipped him on the back with his stick. The teacher roared with every strike, "Repent, Karmeeleon! Repent! Repent!"

The other children mostly glanced away from the terrible sight, but some eyed him with contempt, clearly believing he deserved his punishment. Worse than the whipping though was the look on his little brother's face—one of shame.

After that, Karmeeleon tried to abide by the rules of his village. He made sure to walk on two limbs, like the humans did. Whenever the younglings failed at this, the teacher would beat them with his stick, screaming, "We do not crawl! We walk! We are not animals!"

He tried to look out for Caloo without stealing. His brother grew independent and strong, but still needed protection against the struggling world. Karmeeleon wished he could give his brother the life of a human.

Karmeeleon walked from the dirty river, carrying buckets

in both hands, when he heard marching from the road. He ducked into a bush and watched. It was Omi Enforcers, dragging a cart of children behind them, kidnapped from the neighboring villages and chosen to be trained as Omi Security. Some of the little girls were ones he used to watch walk to school.

The squad headed to Karmeeleon's village. They barged in, seizing the children and forcing them into a line. The squad leader assessed the captives, selecting those who appeared the strongest. They were thrown into the cart, along with the other captives.

Caloo was in the middle of the row. As the squad leader grew closer to him, Karmeeleon's heart beat more rapidly, like it was about to break from his chest. His little brother shook and stared at his feet, not daring to look at the man in the eyes. The squad's leader raised his hand and pointed. Caloo screamed as two Enforcers grabbed him and pulled him to the cart. Karmeeleon fired an arrow from his crossbow, piercing one of the Enforcers in the chest. The other released his grip on Caloo.

Everyone turned to him. Karmeeleon quickly loaded another bolt and pointed right at the squad leader. The other Enforcers raised their weapons.

"You can't kill us all," the leader said.

"Just you," Karmeeleon replied simply. "Let my brother go, please."

The squad's leader glanced over to Caloo with a smile. "Fine… if you take his place."

Karmeeleon didn't even have to think it over. He lowered his weapon and nodded. Two Enforcers grabbed him and tossed him into the cart, while Caloo screamed for them to stop, but the teacher held him back.

The cart pulled off, and he realized he had finally been given what he always wanted—to be among humans.

He waved goodbye to his crying brother, knowing he'd

probably never see him again. Then, he spotted the cold eyes of his teacher. They were full of judgment. Only then did it hit Karmeeleon what he had just done—he had committed murder. He could feel his teacher telling him that the Creator would never forgive him.

Karmeeleon spent the rest of his days trying to prove the teacher of his old village wrong. As part of the Omi, he had dedicated his life to purging evil, as the Creator would want.

Now back in Tyrin, two of the sword owners were still locked in the cell. The prophecy stated that whoever yielded those swords would bring down the Omi. Even if it seemed impossible that a few mere warriors could bring down the Omi's entire reign, history showed that it could happen.

The echoes of riots reverberated above them, as the city roared with unrest. Karmeeleon turned to one of the guards. "Haven't you resolved the situation yet?" he asked, seeking updates on the ongoing turmoil.

But the guard brought worse news. "My lord, three Ichu have been spotted in the city."

"Impossible!"

"My lord, at first, I didn't believe it either. But I saw them with my own eyes."

"How can you be so sure?"

"Because one of them was a human. Her skin was so pale. She was like a walking corpse. Only Ichu could have skin that white. What are we going to do, my lord?"

"We'll burn this entire city to the ground, with both the Ichu and prisoners inside."

"What about the third warrior? Don't we need the prisoners to locate him?"

"No. Escort Lady Clare to the Omi's Sanctuary and keep her there with the imprisoned Pure Bloods. She is all we need to lure the third warrior into our clutches."

The guards left with Clare, despite her protests.

Karmeeleon pulled out his small flamethrower and blasted at the walls of the room. They were soon ablaze. Flames spread across the door to the warrior's chamber, where the prisoners were locked in their cells.

Chapter Twenty-Nine

Eric refused to accept this as the end.

The door to the cells was on fire and it quickly spread across the room. Locked in their cell, Eric and Rella were helpless to do anything but await their fate.

But Eric had waited too long to find his calling. He had put all his faith into delivering the gold tablet, believing this was his time. It hadn't been easy to find Aaron and Rella and convince them to come with him to the capital, but he had managed it. Because he trusted they, like him, were destined for greatness.

Rella cowered at the edge of the room, but Eric stepped closer to the flames.

"What are you doing?" Rella called. "Get back!"

Eric was close enough to the fire he could feel it scorching his face. He closed his eyes, smiled, and waited. Something had to come along and save them. He had to believe they were too important to die like this. Everything that had happened so far led them down a certain path. That path didn't end burning in flames.

He was right.

Just then, the door was kicked open. On the other side

stood Aaron and Cyllene, the warrior from the arena. Clutched in Cyllene's hand was a silver blade adorned with a crimson ruby set within a golden branch, just like Eric's, Aaron's, and Rella's—identical in every way.

Cyllene handed Aaron a key and he dashed inside, unlocking their cell doors.

"Come on!" he shouted, as if they needed any encouragement. They followed him and Cyllene out of the warrior's chambers.

"What is she doing here?" Rella questioned, her gaze fixed on Cyllene. "And where did she get that sword?"

"It's mine," Cyllene replied. "It was given to me when I was a child."

"Liar! You must have stolen it. Alioth would never give away one of his blades to the likes of you."

"Stay back from her," Aaron warned. He stepped between the two women.

"An old man gave me the sword," Cyllene said.

Rella eyed Aaron. "You have already saved this woman's life once. Why do you feel the need to step in again?"

"Because I believe her."

"She slaughtered people in an arena for a mere title. And do you remember what Peter told us about her? She destroyed villages, murdering children. She deserves to die!"

"We are not executioners. If we take it upon ourselves to decide who lives and dies, we're no better than the Omi."

"We'll talk about this later," Eric said, gesturing at the flames that were all around them. "First, we need to make it back to the tunnels."

"What tunnels?" Aaron asked.

"The tunnels that lead to the Omi's underground city of Anubai."

"Is that where we'll find the Sanctuary and Elara?" Rella questioned.

Eric nodded.

"I think Cyllene should come, too," Aaron said.

As they scanned the area for Cyllene, Eric realized she had managed to slip away unnoticed. "Where did she go?" He turned to the others, and they joined in searching. "We don't have time to wait. Let's go." Eric led the way to the exit. They followed him from the warriors' chambers to the surface.

Upon emerging above ground, a scene of utter devastation greeted them. The capital was now mostly deserted, though some still fought over who should rule a ruined city. The once-thriving wooden homes, market stalls, and stables now lay engulfed in flames.

They ran in the direction of the warehouse, but three beings blocked their path. One had green skin and a plump body, like a giant toad, dressed in khaki robes. The other male had yellowish arms and legs protruding from a brownish shell. The woman with them was draped in a black shawl and had ghostly white skin. She looked like a walking corpse.

"Ichu," Aaron uttered, his voice filled with dread.

Eric turned to him. "Ichu? Are you sure?"

"Only becoming an Ichu makes a human's skin go that pale." Aaron pointed to the woman. "Kathe, the little girl, described them to me while you both were dancing with the Pure Bloods."

"But how can they be back? I thought they had been extinct for centuries."

The pale woman's eyes studied them. "Get the swords, Mamoru," she told the brownish non-human. Then, she and the other Ichu disappeared down a passage.

The brownish non-human held up a wooden club with prismatic teeth fixed in the sides. He ran, quickly closing the gap between them, roaring like a demented demon thirsty for blood. Eric shuddered, knowing that was all the creature hungered for.

They unsheathed their blades. Mamoru slammed his weapon against Rella's sword. The weight knocked her to her knees. She cried out in pain as her wrist bent back and she dropped her blade.

Eric hacked his sword into Mamoru's back, but it barely cracked the creature's thick shell. Mamoru spun around and kicked him to the ground.

The creature swung his weapon at Aaron, who darted out of its way. Their weapons clashed. Mamoru's club pierced through Aaron's leg, eliciting a sharp cry of anguish. Mamoru pulled out his weapon and turned just in time to block an attack from Rella.

Eric jumped to his feet and sprung at Mamoru with his weapon. The creature blocked his attack, and then deflected another blow from Rella. Eric chipped at his shell while Mamoru's back was turned. The creature whirled around to deflect the next attack, managing to successfully block attacks from both Eric and Rella with his wooden mace.

This creature was a surviving member of the Ichu race, intent on nothing but destruction, and hadn't aged in centuries, but it had probably been many years since he was in a decent fight. There had to be a way to defeat him. Eric had waited too long to find his purpose to have it taken away now.

Eric went for Mamoru's leg, breaking through the flesh. Blood spurted from his wound, but the creature felt no pain and continued fighting, making sure to protect his head and leave only his shelled body exposed.

Aaron hobbled over from behind. He slammed down his sword against the creature's arm. Mamoru's limb dropped to the ground, his weapon still in hand. Still, the Ichu didn't react, despite the surge of blood. The wound healed, skin cells multiplying rapidly over the gash.

The creature pounced atop Rella, knocking her to the floor. He was like a rabid dog they couldn't put down, and Rella struggled to keep him back as his teeth went for her neck.

Eric ran at him, holding a blackened stone recovered from

one of the collapsed houses. He smashed it against the back of his skull, caving it in, and bringing the creature's attacks to an abrupt halt. Rella shoved off his motionless body and jumped to her feet.

It was a good thing the Ichu were mostly extinct, Eric thought, because he wouldn't want to face many of those.

They stepped over the unconscious Ichu and continued to the warehouse. Once there, they realized it had been burned to the ground, but Eric dug through the ash to find the entrance to the tunnels.

"You go ahead," Rella said. "I'll catch up with you."

"Catch up?" Eric asked. "What are you talking about? We're about to go save Elara. That's everything you wanted!"

"Seeing that lizard who killed my father brought back some things. I need to confront him while I still have the chance."

"Are you mad?"

Rella arched a brow. "Aaron is searching for Clare, someone he loves. I'm searching for ways to save Elara and to avenge my father. The ones I love. What are you searching for, Eric?"

"The exact same as you and Aaron—meaning to my life. That meaning is in front of us, not behind. Killing Karmeeleon won't bring your father back."

"I guess we'll never understand each other."

"You never gave it a chance. You thought you knew me from the moment you saw I was a monk," Eric said.

Rella didn't dispute it.

"Karmeeleon's palace is on the outskirts of the city," Aaron said to her. "I went there with Cyllene. She killed the guards at the entrance of the city so you should be able to slip out easily enough."

Rella thanked Aaron and left, while he followed Eric into the tunnel.

"When we get to the Sanctuary, Aaron," Eric said, "I'm

confident you will get some answers over what happened to Clare. Karmeeleon brought her to see us while he had us prisoners. Then, you can uncover your true calling. The three of us have been chosen for greatness. I can feel it."

"All I want is to find Clare. No one is chosen for greatness. Great people choose to do great things, and that's not me. We're here because you led us here, Eric, not because we were meant to be."

"I suppose time will reveal which one of us is right," Eric muttered, perhaps more to himself than Aaron, as he disappeared into the tunnel.

Chapter Thirty

Her eyes.

That's what had first drawn Karmeeleon to the girl. Those bright green marbles had radiated and pulled at his soul. He had wanted her since he first saw her, but only now did he realize that it had all been a test.

Within the grounds of his large palace, Karmeeleon stood in the marble chamber of his personal praying house, kneeling before the shrine of the Holy World. He lowered his head. The devil had been tempting him and he, like a fool, had wolfed the forbidden fruit from his coaxing hand.

He was Arcadia's general, the Lord of Peace, and the leader of the Omi's army, dedicated to sweeping away the evil. The girl's curse quelled his faithful virtue by tormenting him with thoughts of lust. He would not, could not, allow this wicked witch to rule supreme over his righteous soul any longer.

When he got to his palace after leaving the capital, the first thing he noticed was Cyllene had taken back her sword from under his bedroom floor. If anyone saw her with it, Cyllene and Karmeeleon would both be doomed.

The first moment he laid eyes on her holding that sword, he should have killed her. He had been foolish to think he could make her an ally of the Omi in spite of the prophecy. The prophecy was the work of the devil and those who yielded the blades were his chosen agents, destined to destroy all that was good with the Omi's reign. How could he have ever thought he could tame an agent of evil? Or to make one love him?

If Develon ever found out that Karmeeleon's adopted daughter was destined to end the Omi and Karmeeleon had known about it, his punishment would be beyond imagination. It was time to do what he should have done years ago—slay the siren.

On the other hand, he missed the warmth of her body more than anything in the world. The scent of her hair, the touch of her skin, the sound of her voice, and the sight of those captivating eyes were the very things he lived for.

He had felt this conflicted before. The day he returned to his village, another test had been placed before him by the Creator.

He was no longer the child taken by the Omi. His return was met with a spread of whispers throughout the village. The church was the same as when he left it, but it had a new minister and teacher—his brother, Caloo.

They locked eyes and embraced each other lovingly.

"It's good to see you again, brother," Caloo said, and he led Karmeeleon into the village's church.

"I was very proud, Caloo, when I heard you had taken over the church." They both sat down. Karmeeleon felt like a child again, sitting across from his smiling brother.

"Why has it taken so long for you to return home? Thanks to Queen Shanleigh and her army, the times of the Omi are over."

"The Omi's reign may be over, but the Omi are not."

Caloo shook his head. "Karmeeleon, the Queen has brought peace to Arcadia. You need no longer be a slave to the Omi."

"The Queen did not give me free will, just so she could tell me what to do with it. I chose to follow the Omi, brother."

"Why?"

"Right now, across the river, your neighboring village is building weapons that will then be used to kill. Without fear, there is chaos and sin that spreads like a terrible disease. People need to be told how to live their lives in accordance with the will of the Creator. Can't you see, Caloo? I am doing this for the salvation of all our souls."

Caloo looked at him as though Karmeeleon was a confused little child. "You no longer need to deceive yourself, brother. I understand that the Omi made you do terrible things, and I'm sure you felt a need to justify those acts. But you don't have to hide from your guilt any longer. You can reach salvation through confession and repentance. Our village is always looking for preachers and for those willing to go and help the needy in the starving villages."

Karmeeleon stood. "You think the Omi are something of the past, but they are not."

He marched to the exit, and Caloo rose and called after him, "Let me help you, brother, please! Before it is too late and your guilt consumes you!"

Outside, a squad of Enforcers had already surrounded the village. They stood, waiting for Karmeeleon to give the order. Children had run to their parents' arms, and the villagers looked on with worry in their eyes.

"What is the meaning of this?" Caloo asked.

"The Queen is no more," Karmeeleon declared, causing the village to erupt into a collective murmur of disbelief. "Her advisor, Develon, has seized the throne, and his armies are currently conquering the territories of Arcadia. Through his wisdom, the Omi will rise again."

Caloo's eyes betrayed a sense of betrayal. "How could you do this?"

"I'm saving Arcadia from sin!" Karmeeleon roared. "I am following the words of the Creator, purging the world of those who corrupt. The Creator said in his texts that all those who sin must receive eternal damnation."

"The Creator will not forgive these means."

"Do you remember the day the Omi took me, little brother? It was the first day I ever killed a man, and I did it to save your life. Will the Creator forgive me for that? Now, I told you, the Queen is dead and the Omi are the new rulers. You must surrender this village to us."

The villagers grabbed their weapons. They were weak and hungry looking, but they clutched their flimsy bows and spears with determined eyes.

"Tell your people to stand down," Karmeeleon ordered.

"I cannot."

"You'd rather this entire village be slaughtered than give in to me?"

"We will not give into evil. So long as we don't, our souls are safe."

"Then the blood of our village is on your hands!" Karmeeleon turned to his men and gave them the wave.

The villagers fired their arrows and chucked their spears, but they did little against the armor of the Enforcers. The Omi soldiers charged forth and pierced their swords through every villager.

Karmeeleon took out his own blade and pointed it at his horror-stricken brother. "You made me do this."

"I made you do nothing, Karmeeleon. We make our own choices."

"What choice do I have? To admit I'm damned? I have to save my soul!" He plunged his sword forth, driving the blade into Caloo's chest. Karmeeleon stared into his dying brother's eyes and begged for forgiveness.

Karmeeleon became the very last of his species that day, but they were a repulsive kind anyway. He would forever be a part of the human race for now on, the master species of Arcadia and those chosen by the Creator.

Karmeeleon stood and eyed the golden globe sculpture on his chapel's wall, pleading for the Creator to show him another way. Examining his reflection in the polished surface, he saw the same desperation in his eyes that had plagued him since his youth, yearning to attain the same perfection he saw in the human children.

A hesitant knock on his chamber door interrupted his thoughts.

"Come in," he called.

Captain Zylina entered, looking too terrified to speak. A wave of disgust surged through his stomach at the sight of her, knowing the uniform of Security members were made from the skin of his own species.

"What is it?" he asked.

"My lord, those with the blades have escaped the capital."

"They were locked in cells as I set the room on fire! How is that possible?"

"Apparently, they had help from your daughter."

His blood boiled. "What?"

"Guards said she slaughtered those defending the exits and then she was spotted going to the warrior's chamber. Soon after, the prisoners were found to be freed."

"And what of the Ichu?"

"Two of them left the city. We believe they were looking for you and left when they discovered you were no longer there."

"Get out!" he roared. "Find Cyllene and bring her to me. I want my daughter, and I want her now!"

Zylina bowed her head and then left the chapel.

He shook with rage and then stomped on the tiled flooring. He would untangle his soul from this evil and make Cyllene pay for her wickedness. After slaying the siren, his soul would be purged of any transgressions.

Her death would be his salvation.

Chapter Thirty-One

After escaping the capital, Karmeeleon would have headed home. His palace wasn't far from the city, and he'd be too ashamed to return to Develon before confirming his enemies had been killed. Cyllene knew him entirely too well.

The palace, however, seemed empty, so Cyllene wandered into the vast gardens. A pebbled pathway coiled around flower beds and led over a stone bridge across the garden's river, fed by a small waterfall. Bright orange fish gracefully glided through the crystal-clear water, while tall white birds perched upon the river's edge, so perfectly still that, as a child, Cyllene mistook them for statues. The garden itself was enclosed within sturdy stone walls, covered in vines, and filled with an array of lush trees spanning a spectrum of colors, ranging from vibrant red to delicate pink to pristine white.

In the center of the garden was a circular, roofed platform, supported by five columns. She used to go there as a child to draw or play with Tyrell. It was a realm of pure tranquility, a world unto itself.

Captain Zylina stood atop the platform, icy eyes staring into Cyllene, her hands behind her back. She was as still as the birds perched by the river and was the color to match.

"It must have been nice growing up here." Zylina's head turned from side to side, admiring the beauty of the garden. "So much vibrance, so much light. I never saw much light when I was a child. The Omi trains its Security in training camps, concealed underground from the rest of civilization. But, of course, you wouldn't know that. While I and the other Security members spent nearly a decade being taught how to endure pain and fight like a true soldier, you were here, in a palace, being treated like royalty."

"I could still beat your ass."

Zylina descended the stairs of the platform. "No matter what savagery you learned in that arena, you could never have become one of us. The general was a fool to ever think so."

Cyllene grasped the handle of her blade.

They stood across from each other. Zylina paced towards her and raised her sword. She gently drew the weapon from the sheath, a mocking smile across her lips. Holding her sword in one hand and the casing in the other, Zylina truly looked like one of those birds as she raised her arms into the air like great wings. She dropped the casing and then pounced at Cyllene. Cyllene drew her blade and blocked Zylina's attack.

Their weapons locked, Zylina eyed Cyllene's blade. "Where did you get that?'

"It was given to me to destroy people like you," Cyllene spat. "The Omi defeated the Ichu centuries ago in order to protect Arcadia from evil, but you and Karmeeleon have corrupted it."

"No one within the Omi thinks you belong. Now even Karmeeleon has forsaken you. Once word gets out that you've handled this blade, you'll be completely out of friends."

"I don't need friends," Cyllene said. "But rest assured, word won't reach anyone, for this blade is forged from the sacred metal of the Holy World—the strongest there is. And with it, I'm going to cut off your pretty head."

Cyllene pulled away and swept her weapon forward.

Zylina ducked under the blade just in time, ensuring only a few loose strands of hair got sliced off.

Despite the extraordinary sharpness and strength of the blade, it was surprisingly light, like handling a feather. The thought occurred to her that this weapon would have been invaluable in the arena, even though Zylina surpassed any opponent she had encountered in the competition. While lacking the sheer muscular power of certain arena fighters, Zylina had been trained with a sword since a young age and handled it with ease.

Zylina stepped back and prodded her sword forward. Swiftly evading the attack, Cyllene spun to the side and retaliated by swinging her blade towards Zylina's head. Zylina skillfully defended herself, and their weapons clashed once again, creating a resounding *clank* that reverberated throughout the garden.

Despite Moise's advice, Cyllene didn't retreat after her attack. Zylina was different from those she had faced in the arena, where she relied on wearing down her opponents and using her speed to her advantage. Zylina was lighter and quicker than Cyllene, but less strong.

Cyllene applied as much pressure as she could, digging her blade into Zylina's and drawing the captain's weapon closer to her own face. Her arms ached, but Cyllene didn't let off, using every ounce of strength to push her blade forward. Their eyes locked. Zylina's face was strained and reddened, concentrated on keeping her sword at bay. Her trembling arms and the glistening beads of sweat on her forehead revealed that Zylina was struggling.

Slowly but steadily, Cyllene inched closer, until Zylina's sword touched her cheek and eventually pierced her flesh. Blood trickled down Zylina's face, staining her white attire.

Zylina kneed Cyllene in the groin, causing her to pull the blade away. Following up with another swift kick to Cyllene's stomach, Zylina forced her back.

Zylina whirled her sword into Cyllene's blade, shattering her own weapon in half. Cyllene glanced at her blade in awe, and then turned her eyes back to Zylina. The captain stepped back, holding only half a sword, frozen in terror. Cyllene thought she was about to make a run for it, but then Zylina smiled.

Cyllene furrowed her brows. "What are you grinning about?"

Then, she heard it—the sound of approaching footsteps behind her. She swiftly turned to face the source, but it was too late. A member of the Security team struck her back, causing Cyllene to crumple to the floor in pain. A squad of Security members quickly surrounded her.

Cyllene eyed Zylina. "You cheated."

"I like to win." Zylina shrugged, her grin still intact. "Anyway, there's no rules in battle."

The captain punched her in the face, flooring her. Zylina then ordered the Security members to take her to Karmeeleon, and she was dragged to his personal praying house. She should have known he'd be there.

Once inside, they dropped her on her knees before General Karmeeleon. Zylina presented Cyllene's blade to him. He ordered them to hunt down the warriors who owned the others. The door slammed shut after them, but Cyllene couldn't bring herself to look at the general.

"Welcome home," he said, sending shivers down her spine.

She raised her head. For the first time in her life, she was ready to defy him. "This is not my home."

The lizard turned away, his eyes filled with hurt. He pressed his scaly hands against the chapel's wall and leaned against it. Then his expression transformed into rage. "I provided you with a home. A sanctuary from sin. I offered you salvation!"

His words bounced off the marble walls, echoing throughout the small chapel. Cyllene stood, biting her lip, her fists tightly clenched at her sides. "You gave me a home where you spoke only of how evil the people on the outside were, but it's you who commits the most heinous sins of all! You killed my brother!"

"I had to have you to myself," he replied, and then looked as though he might have regretted those words. "What I mean to say is, I loved you. It was my duty to shield you from sin. Your brother betrayed the Omi and would have only led you astray, away from righteousness. Away from me." A brief silence hung in the air as Karmeeleon scrutinized her from head to toe. "How can you wear that outfit, after you betrayed your own people? You helped our enemies escape the capital."

"But they're not my enemies, are they?" she replied. "The old man who gave me my weapon wasn't delusional, as you claimed. That's why you tried to destroy my blade and then hid it under your floor, fearing that if anyone saw it, they'd know what I was destined to do."

"And what exactly do you think you're destined to do?" he asked.

"What the Omi tried to do and failed—protect the people of Arcadia from evil."

"What do you know about evil, you stupid girl? The Ichu are back. They've been spotted, and you know nothing of their power. Wait until you've stared one of those monsters in the eyes, and then tell me if you have truly witnessed evil before that moment. How are four idiots with blades going to defeat those creatures? Arcadia needs the Omi now more than ever."

"Idiots? They escaped you, didn't they?"

He unclenched his fists and took a breath. "Anyone else would have killed you when you were a child, knowing what you were destined to do. But I thought I could change destiny and make you see the light. Maybe I was wrong to send you to that awful arena. But when I think back on how happy we used to make each other, it makes me hope we can put our mistakes behind us."

Karmeeleon stepped towards her and reached out his scaly hand. He pulled her hand towards him and kissed it tenderly. His eyes were full of the intense, dark glare of lust she had come to recognize all too well.

She pulled her hand away. "All I remember is you taking advantage of a confused little girl." Cyllene backed away, but the general followed, his green cape swirling behind him. He caressed her cheek, evoking another shudder from her.

"I am giving you one last chance to save your soul. There is no more hope for our lives, Cyllene. Develon knows of my failure and of your betrayal. Here, in this chapel, under the watchful eye of the Creator, pledge your love to me, and I shall swear mine to you. Then, the Creator shall recognize our love and absolve us of our transgressions once we perform a final act of sacrifice." He had cornered her now, her back pressed against the room's walls. Behind him, Cyllene glimpsed the crates containing naphtha and quicklime, materials he used for his infernal fires and his miniature flamethrower.

"And what might that be?" she asked.

"To burn this chapel with us inside. Your brother's gone, and you have nothing else to live for. Like you, I also lost my baby brother. Let the Creator deliver us to the land that has been promised to us, where we can both be reunited with our brothers. There, we'll be together forever, as man and woman, as husband and wife."

Cyllene eyed the shrine of the Holy World on the wall beside her. "There's just one problem with that."

"What?"

"You're no man." She yanked the golden, circular statue from the wall and hurled it at him. "You're a big, evil lizard."

Karmeeleon fell to the floor, pinned under the weight of the shrine. She lifted her blade and dashed to the exit. Before she burst through the doors, she heard the clang of him tossing the statue and freeing himself. She turned back toward the chapel, her sword poised for defense. Suddenly, Karmeeleon burst through the doors, moving on all fours with a feral roar, like a savage beast. Fear gripped her as he lunged upon her, pinning her down.

"You're right," he said, his breath brushing against her face. "When I was a boy, I would watch the human children. I longed desperately to be like them, to be flawless and cherished by the Creator, just as they were. They labeled my kind as an abomination, and I yearned more than anything to prove them wrong. I wanted to show them that even a repugnant lizard like me could feel, learn, and love just as a human could. That was all I wanted. When I witnessed the human children attending school, I saw the boys and girls holding hands, and I yearned to do the same. I wanted to show them that, despite my hand being colder and scaly, I was just as deserving and capable of protecting and loving them, just like the human boys. Every single day, I watched and yearned for that chance."

A rock hit his head. "Get off her!" a voice yelled.

Both Karmeeleon and Cyllene turned their gaze towards the source, finding Rella standing in the garden, tightly gripping her sword.

Karmeeleon frowned. "This doesn't concern you."

"But your continued existence does," Rella replied. "That concerns me greatly. In fact, it downright bothers me."

Karmeeleon got off Cyllene and drew his sword. "You're dealing with matters you don't understand, little girl. You should have stayed at home with your daddy."

"I no longer have a home," Rella declared, stepping forward. "You destroyed it, and you killed my daddy."

Rella dashed at him. He blocked her attack and kicked her to the ground.

Cyllene quickly rolled to her side, rising to her feet and

retrieving her own sword. She leapt at Karmeeleon, plunging her sword into his back. It broke through his armor. He let out a pained squeal as blood oozed out from the wound. She pulled her weapon out. He whirled round to strike her, but his tail tripped her over and so his blade merely struck the air above her head.

Rolling swiftly to safety, Cyllene positioned herself alongside Rella, both of them facing the general.

"You followed me?" Cyllene asked Rella, without taking her eyes off their opponent.

"When hunting becomes your sole means of survival for fifteen years, you develop quite the knack for tracking."

Cyllene squinted her eyes. "You calling me an animal?"

"While I wouldn't necessarily dispute that statement, I was actually referring to him," Rella replied, her gaze unwaveringly fixed on Karmeeleon.

Karmeeleon reached for a set of bladed rings tucked into his belt and swiftly launched them towards the two. Cyllene evaded them easily, having experience from her training with the general. However, Rella lacked such experience and found herself unable to evade one of the rings in time. It grazed her side, leaving a painful mark as it sailed past.

The general took out his flamethrower and unleashed a torrent of fire upon the stone wall of the garden, shattering vines and multi-colored pebbles. To avoid the flames, both women dropped to the ground. Startled, the white birds by the river took flight, perhaps for the first time in Cyllene's memory. The flames rapidly spread, devouring the vibrant trees and plants.

Karmeeleon ripped off his cape and threw away his armor, and Cyllene knew that to mean he was about to take advantage of his camouflaging skills. In a flash, he changed his scales to match the dye of the pathway and disappeared from sight. He moved silently, slashing Cyllene's stomach with his razor-sharp claws.

Gasping in pain, she struggled to see through the thickening smoke. She swung her sword in the direction she believed Karmeeleon to be, but he had already shifted his position. Soon, she felt the cruel piercing of his nails against her cheek, then her arm. Before long, her body bore numerous claw marks, oozing crimson trails.

Rella swept her sword, hoping to strike the invisible lizard, only to receive a claw mark on her stomach.

Cyllene focused, trying to see something that would give him away. Then she saw it—a dripping of blood in mid-air from when she cut his back earlier.

She struck her weapon down, driving the blade into his shoulder. He emitted a piercing shriek and suddenly became visible, his camouflage vanishing. Cyllene swiftly withdrew her sword, and together with Rella, they relentlessly hacked and sliced at Karmeeleon, their blades penetrating his exposed, scaly skin.

The maimed lizard dropped to all fours and retreated into the dense cloud of smoke. The flames now surrounding them, Cyllene and Rella hurried to the stone platform above the garden.

Suddenly, the platform trembled beneath their feet. Cyllene glanced over the edge and saw Karmeeleon charging through the smoke, crashing into the columns that upheld the platform. One column had already succumbed to the impact, and as he collided with another, it too gave way. The platform slanted downwards into the thickening smoke. Cyllene and Rella desperately clung to the edge of the platform, fighting against the pull that threatened to drag them into the blazing inferno below. The once-lush garden was now completely consumed by the merciless flames.

Cyllene's feet dangled dangerously close to the licking flames, the scorching heat threatening to overwhelm her. The intense heat made her head spin, and sweat poured down her body. Her lungs burned from the smoke, and she coughed uncontrollably.

Karmeeleon crawled onto the platform. He dug his claws into the stone, trying to stop himself from falling.

Over her shoulder, Cyllene noticed the flames reaching the chapel, where Karmeeleon stored his supply of naphtha and quicklime. Karmeeleon must have seen this, too. His face caved into an expression of utter despair. He clawed at Cyllene and Rella's legs, desperate to get them before their inevitable fate.

Cyllene turned to Rella, her vision obscured by the thick smoke. "Hold onto me tightly and let go!"

Rella looked at her. "What?"

"Trust me. It's the only chance you've got."

Rella clutched Cyllene and they let go of the platform. They dropped, sliding past Karmeeleon, and plummeted into the river beneath the waterfall.

Even underwater, they heard and felt the explosion. The water got so hot Cyllene thought it might boil, but they endured the intense heat and remained submerged.

When they surfaced, merely debris of the palace's chapel still stood. The garden was completely gone, except for some blackened stones and the charred remains of a giant lizard. Cyllene gave a sigh of relief, feeling a newfound sense of freedom she had never felt before.

His death was her salvation.

Chapter Thirty-Two

Aaron wondered if he was a terrible person. Sometimes, he felt like he was. He constantly convinced himself that he was powerless to change things, which led him to not even try. Though he felt he had a good sense of what was right and wrong, he had never been one to express his views or to condemn someone when they said or did something he considered to be immoral.

As a child, he felt guilty that people in the world lived in squalor, while he lived in comfort, but he had never done anything to feed the hungry. He felt guilty that people were born ill, while he had been born healthy, but he had never done anything to ease the lives of the less fortunate. His grandfather had given him the gift of empathy, but what good was it if he didn't use it?

Clare had brought out the best in him. Not only did she boost his confidence and given him happiness, but she also taught him that compassionate thoughts alone were not enough to help others. To truly make a difference, he needed to take action, just like she did. Aaron felt there were limitations on what he could do. But when he looked at Clare, he couldn't help but consider that these limitations were only in his mind and that he actually had no bounds. With her by his side, he had the motivation to change the world and the confidence to believe he could. Even as a child, Clare had risked her life by spreading her father's books. She was the best person he knew, the bravest, and most heroic.

Life was a beautiful thing, and to feel the pain that others feel in their lives could also be a wonderful thing. Because, it's then, Aaron realized, that he felt closest to other people. There was nothing more human than to feel someone else's pain. The greatest asset ever gifted to humanity was empathy.

Unfortunately, Aaron's time with Clare had been cut short, and he wondered if he would ever realize his full potential without her by his side. He remembered now that the Omi had attacked the City of Eden with the help of Lord Patrick. Though his memories after that were still hazy, Aaron recalled that he had witnessed Patrick cut down his father and brother. That day, Aaron and Clare had each declared their love, but she had decided to go with Patrick in order to save her family. It would seem though that she had ended up marrying Radmir to spare her parents. Radmir was hardly a better suitor than Patrick, and he shuddered over what kind of existence she may have had to endure over the past ten years.

Aaron trailed behind Eric, venturing through the labyrinthine tunnels that supposedly led to the Omi's Sanctuary hidden within the underground city of Anubai. They each carried candles to light the way. The tunnels stretched on for what seemed like an eternity. Just as described by the Pure Bloods, the tunnels were hard and smooth to the touch, and there were long thin tracks of metal on the ground, perfectly even and as cold as ice. The tracks were old and rusty. Aaron knew that the tunnels were from the times of the heretics. He wondered about what other knowledge may have been lost across the centuries because of the Omi.

Though the tunnel broke off into several sections, Eric seemed to know where he was going. Then, a figure appeared in the corner of Aaron's eye. It was Kathe, the young Pure Blood who had told Aaron about her mother. She brought a finger to her lips, signaling him to remain silent, before vanishing into one of the connecting tunnels.

Though he was probably imagining things, Aaron had to follow her. He bolted after her, calling her name, and ignored Eric as he yelled for him to come back.

Up ahead, Aaron could see the small girl turn a corner into another tunnel. At the end of that tunnel, Aaron emerged into a ray of sunlight. It dawned on Aaron that, by traversing the tunnels, he and Eric had journeyed beneath a chain of mountains and arrived in uncharted territory. Here, in this land of wonder, lay a cluster of houses where sunlight gleamed off the glass windows. The houses had two stories and triangular roofs.

Aaron felt his heart beating in his chest and his body grow cold. He was afraid. This was a discovery he wasn't supposed to make. It was evidence of a civilization greater than his own, and proof that everything the Omi had ever said was a lie. There was more to be gained than the knowledge from the Creator's texts, and he realized then that the heights of humankind likely knew no bounds.

Aaron walked to the door of a house and thrust it open. There were so many windows; he had never seen a house so full of light. On the walls, concealed within glass, were human beings printed on pieces of paper. Too real-like to be paintings. The people were dressed weird, not in robes or dresses, but in different colored tops and pants.

In every room of the house, there were copper chains and glass orbs hanging from the ceiling. Aaron could see no candles or lanterns, and he just knew that the orbs were somehow sources of light.

Aaron looked out the window and saw Kathe standing in the middle of the street. He exited the house and ran to her, calling her name. She neither moved nor spoke, and her eyes stared back into him without once blinking. As he knelt beside her and grabbed her by the arms, he got makeup all over his hands. Confused, he rubbed her skin and realized she was wearing a concealer. Beneath the makeup, her skin was as white as snow. This girl was no Pure Blood, but an Ichu, and she was older than he was by centuries.

"I'm sorry," she said, sounding as though she wanted to cry, but emitting no tears. "I'm so, so sorry, mister. He told me I had to lure you here. Just like he told me to bring the Pure Bloods south."

"I don't understand."

"If it means anything, my mother really was killed by the Omi. I didn't lie to you about that. That was when *he* found me. I was all alone, and my mother was dead. I was so afraid. He said he could stop me from being afraid, and so I gave in to him. After that, I didn't want to listen to him, but I had no choice. I had to follow whatever he said. He gets into my head. He's in my head right now. He said if I got the Pure Bloods to go south, they would tell everyone about us. The time for hiding in the shadows is over, he said. Another war lies in front of us—a Second Great War."

"Who's *he*?"

Kathe pointed over his shoulder, and Aaron slowly turned to find a man dressed in khaki robes, his skin as pale as Kathe's. His eyes were bloodshot. The young girl then ran away.

"Don't blame Kathe," the man said. "She was only doing as commanded, as do all my subjects."

"Who are you?"

"Chief of the Ichu. In the old world, people called me Nathan."

"Old world?"

"Before the Omi's empire."

Aaron shrugged. "What do you want from me?"

"I want the same as you."

"I highly doubt that."

"Clare," Nathan said.

Aaron stepped forward. "What do you know about Clare?"

"I know the Omi have her, and that you want to get her back. It won't be easy. But if we work together, we can."

Aaron furrowed his brows. "Why would you want to help me rescue Clare? How do you even know who she is?"

"She's an important part of my plan."

"What plan?" Aaron asked.

"My plan to get everything I want. I will lead the Ichu, who have lived in hiding for centuries, against the Omi. Together, we will end humankind. A stronger race will prevail. They will follow me. Everyone follows me."

"So, why would I help you?"

"I can make you an Ichu, just like I did for Kathe. Now she no longer cries for her mother. If I grant you immortality, you will no longer feel fear, grief, shame, or anxiety. Your pain over missing Clare will dissipate. You'll no longer feel or love. The Ichu are not slaves to their emotions. There is no suffering. You can be strong like us, Aaron. If you feel nothing at all, you can finally be all that you can be."

"You think that makes you strong?" Aaron asked. "You were afraid to feel so you surrendered your humanity. That makes you nothing but weak."

Nathan's fists clenched. "I am afraid of nothing!"

He raised his whitish palm, and a wave of air flung Aaron against one of the walls of the houses.

Nathan raised Aaron into the air, and then threw him down the street. Aaron fell to the concrete, grazing his arms and legs. He crawled and found himself staring at the Ichu's Chief, a sadistic smile of glory on his face. The Chief flicked his hand. A surge of energy slammed against Aaron's head, knocking it backwards.

Aaron lay on his back, grasping his head in agony. But he

would not avert his gaze and give the Chief the victory of seeing him frightened. They stared at one another. In those seconds, Aaron realized something—he knew those eyes. Somewhere, he had seen this man before.

Nathan's stare intensified. Pain overtook Aaron, as if his entire body was burning from the inside. He clutched his stomach and vomited blood, coughing so not to choke on it. Fire burned through every inch of him, charring his bones and boiling his blood.

Then it stopped. Nathan looked over his shoulder. He turned back to Aaron and said, "Next time we meet, you will help me find Clare. I guarantee it."

Aaron staggered to his feet. Nathan turned and disappeared into a forest at the other side of the houses. Aaron wiped his mouth and followed him, stumbling to the tree line. As he entered the forest, he saw the red uniforms of Security approaching.

Chapter Thirty-Three

I

CCXXI (X Years Ago)

Rella was no longer certain about her future. She had thought she was destined to become Governor of Eden, but, now, what was she going to do? Currently, she was a prisoner. She had been told she would likely be released, but that her father would not. Even if she was freed, she would have no food or money. All of her possessions had been destroyed in the fire or claimed by the Omi. She had no clothes except the tunic she was wearing. There were no family members she could turn to for help. Other than her father, she was alone in the world.

The servants had started behaving strangely to her; they no longer brought her extra meals when she ordered them to, and they refused to send her messages to her father. Rella understood that the city was currently occupied by the Omi, so their rules had to be followed, but there were no laws against extra meals and no reason to be cruel.

When one of the maids brought her eggs for breakfast,

Rella pointed out they weren't cooked the way she liked. The maid had said to go hungry if she was too good for them and that Rella was to no longer give orders to anyone. Rella had never thought she was too good for anything. It was simply the case that father had told her she could have what she wanted.

After breakfast, one of the Omi's guards came to say that she was being released and that she could speak to her father before leaving. Rella followed the guard down the jail's hallway, lit only by candles, all the way to a cell at the end.

"Rella?" her father said once he saw her, his sullen face transforming into a smile.

At the other side of the iron bars, he sat on the straw-covered floor, still dressed in the robes he was wearing when the Omi arrested him.

"I'm being released, Father," she said.

He reached out his hand and held her. "That's wonderful news, Rella. This must be our goodbye, though. Tomorrow they're going to execute me, and I don't want you to see it."

She felt the tears stream down her cheeks but tried to remain strong. "What should I do, Father?"

"There's a town in the highlands called Culloden. Go there and find Alioth. Don't tell anyone where you're going."

"Who is he?"

"Alioth is a friend. He will look after you."

"Father, I won't give up on you. We have to get you out of here before tomorrow. Perhaps I could return here with a knife, overpower the jailer, and break you out of this cell."

"You'll do no such thing. I won't have the Omi kill you, too. You're to go to Alioth, where you'll be safe, and that's the end of it. Do you hear me, Rella?"

He spoke in such a stern tone that she couldn't defy him, and she nodded, now breaking down fully in tears.

Her father wiped her tears away. "Rella, you will need to adapt and learn to navigate a world that may not always be kind. It is my failing that you possess such unwavering trust in others. You cannot underestimate the dangers that lie beyond these walls. People will no longer obey your every command."

"You want me to be less trusting of people?" she asked, confused, having always believed that to be a virtuous quality.

Her father shook her head. "No. I want you to keep believing the best in people. However, you have to be prepared to look after yourself. If you come across someone dangerous, you need to be able to defend yourself. Alioth will help with this. He was a friend of the Queen. I want you to promise me something."

"Anything."

"One day, you will take Eden back from the Omi. I know this is a lot to ask, but you've always been able to achieve whatever you put your mind to. Life is always beautiful. You just have to look for the beauty in people and in the world. That includes having hope for the future. Hope for things to get better. So long as you have hope, there is nothing you cannot do. It may take many years, but I have no doubt that you will eventually be able to give Eden back to the people."

"I promise," she said. "One day, I will take back our home."

II

CCXXXI (Present)

Rella and Cyllene made it back to the capital, now mostly a ghost town. She was still suspicious of Cyllene, but Cyllene claimed that if Aaron was in trouble, she wanted to help, seeing as how he had saved her life. So, Cyllene offered to show Rella the way through the tunnels.

At the capital, Rella found Lukas and the other Pure Bloods, who must have tracked Commander Straumme's Enforcers. They were scavenging for weapons.

Rella ran towards Lukas and he sighed when he saw her. "What are *you* doing here?"

"I'm here to help rescue Elara and the other prisoners," she said.

"I thought my people already made it clear: We don't want your help."

"But you need it. You don't even know how to get to the Omi's Sanctuary from here, do you?"

To this, he didn't reply.

"Again, I'm sorry we led the Enforcers to you. But I can make up for it now."

Lukas turned to his people, who had been listening intently. They nodded reluctantly and Rella led them to the tunnels, carrying a lantern she had brought from Karmeeleon's palace. Before leaving, she and Cyllene had been sure to stock up, including on some ceramic balls, filled with a flame-throwing weapon, that Cyllene had called grenades.

"Are these like the tunnels you found in the uncharted lands, north of Eden?" she asked.

Lukas stroked the smooth stone and said that it was. The tunnel then echoed with the sound of boots. Ahead there was a wall of Commander Straumme's Enforcers.

"You've led us into another trap," Lukas spat.

Rella groaned and told him to be quiet. She reached for a grenade inside her pocket. One of the soldiers put out his hand and ordered the men to arrest them. Rella tossed the grenade forward and yelled for Cyllene and the Pure Bloods to take cover in one of the connecting tunnels.

"You idiot!" Cyllene yelled. "You have to light it!"

The ceramic ball landed just before the feet of the Enforcers. Rella lunged her lantern at the cracked orb of clay and it combusted the tunnel in the form of a giant fireball.

III

Eric had always been a religious man, even before being taken in by the monks. He did not pretend to have all the answers, but simply held onto the belief that there was something greater than himself in the universe, guiding him forward.

Now, as he was escorted to the end of the tunnel by Commander Straumme and his Enforcers to Develon's Chamber of Life at the Sanctuary, he felt his faith had been rewarded. Indeed, he had found meaning to his life by helping Rella and Aaron. And the weight of the tablet in his hands reassured him that he was on the right path.

Two dozen Pure Bloods stood at the edges of the room, along with Clare, surrounded by palace guards and monks. Brother Guin and Develon, recognizable by his red robe and gold mask, stood by a marble table, where a redheaded girl was gagged and bound. Develon told Straumme that he had done well in capturing Eric, causing Straumme to smile victoriously.

"Good to see you have delivered me the tablet, Brother," Develon said. "I admire your devotion."

"I want to know what it says," Eric replied.

Develon presented his hand. "Then hand it over."

Eric did so, and Develon studied the tablet's markings. Behind Develon and Guin, Eric noticed the wall of hieroglyphics. There were symbols he had never seen before, including what looked like men in spacesuits and rockets taking off from the land.

"Well?" Eric asked.

"It's a map and list of directions."

"I already knew that."

"It was written a thousand years ago by Princess Ava's protector, Daniel. It's directions over how one may access the Holy World." Develon pointed to the symbol of three pillars on the tablet. "I've seen this structure somewhere before in the deserts of Tyrin. That's where we will go first."

"We?"

"The Omi," Develon said. "Not you. You have proven to be more trouble than you're worth."

Brother Guin grinned. "Brother Eric was always a trouble-maker, Your Highness."

Develon signaled to two of the palace guards, and they grabbed Eric, shoving him to the floor. Eric looked over to the Pure Bloods. "With the tablet, you now know how to access the Holy World, so why still kill the Pure Bloods? Clearly, sacrificing their blood will make no difference."

"We will slaughter the Pure Bloods as it tells us to do in the Omi's texts," Develon said. "It's about ridding the world of the non-conformists. So long as they choose to only mate with each other, they will always be different from us. That cannot be. Under the Creator's eyes, we are all one, and there is only one way of life: the Omi's way."

"The Omi's way," the monks chanted. "We pray as one. We eat as one. We study as one. We work as one. We sleep as one. We live as one."

"Now, Brother Eric, you and the Pure Bloods will die as one."

IV

Rella, Cyllene, and the Pure Bloods ran through the blackened tunnel, knocking down any Enforcers still in their path. Cyllene led the way, claiming to know which tunnel led to the Omi's Chamber of Life within the Sanctuary, sure that was where sacrifices were held.

Eventually, they came to a doorway cut into the stone with a couple of guards standing outside. Rella and Cyllene cut down the guards and piled into the chamber with Lukas and his people. The imprisoned Pure Bloods and Clare stood at one side of the room, encircled by guards and monks, including Commander Straumme. Elara was laid down on a slab of marble, Eric standing on one side in the grasp of two Enforcers, and Develon and Brother Guin standing on the other. No sign of Aaron.

Develon had a knife placed at Elara's throat. Under the blade, Elara's chest was heaving up and down in panic. Then, they spotted each other. "Rella!"

Rella stepped forward. The guards in the room turned their attention to her and Cyllene. Both of them were ready. Develon stepped back and ordered his men to kill them.

Lukas directed his people to attack, and they leapt at the guards, batting them with whatever weapons they had scavenged in the city, many losing their lives in the process.

Without a weapon in his hand, Straumme stomped towards Rella, a furious scowl on his face, and evaded a blow of her blade. He dove his left fist into her stomach and snapped her nose with his right. She fell onto her back, dropping her blade, and he rammed his foot into her ribs. She cried in pain and reached out for her weapon, but Straumme crushed her hand with his foot and slid the weapon away.

Straumme stood above and punched her in the face several times. She felt the blood ooze from her nose and drip down her face. She kneed him in the groin, and he slumped forward, failing to omit so much as a wounded moan. Instead, he clenched his teeth, and the eyes on his wrinkled face bulged with rage. Rella pulled at one of his legs, tripping him over, and she jumped on top of him, pinning him to the marble floor. With as much might as she could muster, she launched her good fist into his face, again and again. He caught hold of her fist on the fourth blow, squeezed, and twisted her wrist until she groaned in pain.

Rella headbutted him in the face and he released her. She clasped hold of his head with both hands and slammed it against the flooring until he stopped moving and the beige marble was decorated with his blood.

From atop Straumme's body, she scanned the chamber and saw Cyllene and the Pure Bloods were keeping the guards busy. Rella wiped the blood from her nose with her hand and dashed across the room to unstrap Elara, seizing back her blade on the way. Brother Guin clasped Elara's hand to stop her, but Rella punched him in the face, flooring him. Guin crawled behind the marble table for cover, whimpering all the while.

Many of the Pure Bloods had fallen in the fight. Cyllene, Lukas, Clare, and the remaining Pure Bloods stood next to Rella. The guards encircled them. There were too many of them. Before they could make a move, Rella took out another grenade and aimed it at one of the torches fixed into the wall.

"Stop!" Develon screamed. "You'll destroy this holy place!"

"Then let Clare and Eric and the Pure Bloods go!"

Behind Develon, Rella saw a wall of hieroglyphics, containing strange symbols, including one that reminded her of that night at the observatory with Clare and Elara. Then, she realized what Eric had meant when he said he had come from a different world ten years ago. He had traveled to this world in an object like the one in the symbol—that was what she had witnessed fall from the heavens.

She pointed to the symbol. "I saw an object like that when I was a child. It's a transporter, isn't it? It transports people between worlds." She turned to Eric. "That's how you came to our world. It was your transporter I saw ten years ago, right before the monks found you. That's why they had to teach you our tongue."

"Brother Thomas found me and saved me from certain death," Eric said. "He told everyone at the Monastery that he found me alone in the desert."

"Where did you come from?" she asked. "What is your world like?"

"My world was once full of beautiful oceans and several giant continents, but we ruined it all by not caring for our world. I, and many others, were all sent in different directions to explore the cosmos and find a new planet we could make our home. We were told to send word back if we found one that was suitable, but all my equipment was destroyed in the crash."

"You must have been very important on your world to have been chosen for such a mission."

"On the contrary, I volunteered because I had nothing to stay for and no one to miss me. I hoped to be the one to find a new world for my people. Instead, I found a world that was in even greater despair."

"Word of this can never get out," Develon said. "If people's eyes are drawn to the stars, they will live unfocused lives. Our sole ambition must be to obey the Creator's texts and gain access to the Holy World. There, we will learn all the answers."

"Or we could focus on understanding the mysteries of our own world," Rella replied.

Among the symbols behind Develon were buildings, structures, and people wearing clothes that she could make no sense of. Underground, the Omi had been documenting the rise and fall of civilizations on Arcadia for centuries, and Rella wondered if any of them had ever once been similar to the society Eric came from.

"When Brother Thomas found me, I had parachuted during the crash and landed unconscious some distance away from the crash site," Eric said, turning to Develon. "I left behind comrades. What happened to them? Did they survive the crash? I have given you the tablet. Now, please tell me what you know."

"When Security found the crash site, your transporter was empty," Develon said. "Someone had already found it and looted the contents."

"No bodies inside?"

Develon shook his head.

"Was it operational?"

"No, it was completely devastated by the crash," Develon replied. He held up the tablet in his hand. "That's why this is so important. It provides directions to the transporter used by Daniel and the Pure Bloods when they first arrived on Arcadia a thousand years ago. We need to find where they stored it if we are to use it to retrace their steps to locate the Holy World."

"Don't you see? The Pure Bloods weren't divine lifeforms from a Holy World," Eric said. "They must have come from a world just like mine. They were likely in contact with the heretics that once lived here, just like the other non-human species who came here."

"We must all have a common ancestor," Develon said. "It is the Holy World that holds the key to the origins of life."

"The heretics may have had the answer, but were destroyed by the Omi, who have distorted everything," Rella replied.

"You are making a mistake. We are not the enemy. The real foe of all humankind is the Ichu. As the Omi offers security and order, the Ichu brings destruction and chaos. We will not survive the Ichu's return unless we are united as one. Evil is upon us."

Even behind his gold mask, Rella could see the fear in Develon's eyes as he spoke. Still, she told Eric and the Pure Bloods to slowly exit the chamber, and they did so, including Elara, Clare, and Cyllene. Eric took back the tablet as he left. Rella then slowly backed out, all the while holding up the grenade in her hand.

Though they were letting her leave, once Rella was at the safety of the door, she hurled the grenade at the flames regardless. Develon sprinted towards her, screaming for her to stop, but it was too late, and the chamber was engulfed by a bright explosion.

V

Rella felt like she had been brought back to life as she ran through the tunnels, Elara by her side, closely followed by Eric, Clare, Cyllene, and the Pure Bloods. The general who'd killed her father was finally dead. For so long she thought there was nothing they could do about the Omi. But now she knew she could make a difference. More than that, like Eric said, she was destined to make a difference—to end the Omi. And she had the blades to prove it.

She glanced at Eric's smile and the tablet he still carried, now knowing that the tablet's engravings told a story of ancient technology, a map to an old transporter, and a lost connection to the stars. It symbolized not just a potential escape from Arcadia but also a bridge between the past and the future.

Rella turned to the Pure Bloods and asked them if they would help with one more thing. Then, they all followed Eric, as he retraced Aaron's steps down the tunnel. Rella wasn't worried because she knew they would find him.

She was going to keep her promise to her father. Furthermore, she had managed to keep faith in people. She would not allow the act of a few men to lessen her view of people as a whole. We are only human. People are corruptible. But her father once told her to believe life was always beautiful, and she'd never let anyone change that.

Everything was going to be all right now. Somehow, with the general now dead and Develon's chamber destroyed, Rella just knew. Of course, the Omi still had Governors in control across the continent. But this was the start of something.

Killing the general and rescuing Elara had proven to her that they were destined to have the blades. It was all part of a plan, that one day would end with bringing the Omi to their knees. Not because it was written in the stars or any such nonsense, but because they had the self-belief that they could make a difference. Rella missed her father every day, as well as Alioth. But now she had come to accept she was destined to avenge them and to make Arcadia a better place in their name.

She looked over to Elara and, realizing she hadn't since finding her, embraced her. Elara, too, had the look on her face of something that Rella never again thought she'd see on Arcadia—a look of hope.

Chapter Thirty-Four

As the Security member approached, Aaron unsheathed his blade. Two more appeared, and the blade shook in Aaron's hand. The three beings stepped leisurely towards him, their expressions stone cold.

Three more appeared behind them, all dressed in their red scaly outfits to hide the spray of blood. Now, there were six after him.

Aaron put away his weapon and ran from thc forest, dashing back to the street of houses. But six Security members approached from the tunnel.

Soon, they encircled him. The twelve Security members drew nearer. Then, they halted.

A woman, dressed in white, stepped between them, and Aaron recognized her as Zylina. Her expression was as cold and serious as the others.

Aaron shook as he drew his blade. He bit his lip and tried to look brave, but he had no idea what he should do. He couldn't defeat them all. He couldn't die now that Clare was so close. Still, if he was going to go down, he was going to do so fighting. He was through with being a coward.

"Where is your friend?" Zylina asked.

Aaron ignored her, glancing around the Security members. None of them held any weapons. They knew they didn't have to.

"You and the monk were spotted entering these tunnels together. Where is he?"

"Not here," Aaron replied.

"Then who were you just speaking to?"

Aaron adjusted his footing, adopting a fighting stance. He was far from polished, but he had certainly come a long way.

Zylina turned to her squad and ordered them to take him prisoner.

All twelve of them pulled out their swords. Aaron threw himself at the nearest Security member, swinging his blade. He barely clashed weapons before one of them hit his legs from behind, knocking him to the ground. He lay on his back, still in pain from whatever Nathan had done to him.

A man placed his boot on Aaron's arm, keeping him from picking up his weapon.

Aaron looked up to meet Zylina's eyes again. Hand on hip, she was still smiling. She stepped towards him and bent down, causing a creak of her outfit.

"Eventually all our prisoners pray for death," she said. "They don't want to feel pain any longer. When I'm done with you, you too will wish you could never feel anything again."

Aaron knew she was wrong. Even in years of longing for Clare, his hope that he would find her again had kept him going through hard times. Nothing was more human than feeling love for another person and he would never wish to lose that.

As he thought about Clare as Radmir's wife and as the Omi's prisoner, he wished he had been able to feel her pain for her instead. To feel the pain of others, he decided, was a wonderful thing; it made him feel alive and human. Empathy was indeed the greatest of human assets, as well as love, because whenever he faced dark and ugly times, that was when he most felt the drive to go on. It was then that he most wanted to find the good and beauty in the world, as well as do some good.

He reached for a rock on the ground, picked it up, and bashed it against the Security member's foot. As the man flinched, Aaron retrieved his blade and jumped to his feet.

Aaron parried the attack from another man in red. Just then, they all stopped at the sound of emerging war cries. Behind his attackers, Aaron saw the whole community of Pure Bloods dash from the tunnel, led by Rella, Eric, Cyllene, and —Clare!

Zylina ordered her squad to retreat and they headed back into the forest, though a few stayed behind to try and slow down the Pure Bloods, paying for the decision with their lives.

Aaron pushed his way through the chaos and then stopped and stared as Clare approached. He went lightheaded and thought his knees might give way.

"Clare?" he asked, not sure if he was seeing things again.

"It's me," she said. "I hear you've been looking for me."

"I've missed you so much."

"I've missed you, too."

The moment she said those words and looked into his eyes, Aaron's anxieties drifted away. He had hoped to see her again for so long. It had been clinging to that hope that had pushed him forward. Now, there was finally nothing between them and whatever happened next would be up to them.

Epilogue

Mamoru's brownish hand dug into the ground as he dragged himself along.

His body was healing itself, but not quickly enough. He wheezed for breath. When he heard footsteps approaching, he used what little strength he had left to crawl to his knees to see who it was.

The identity of the man was obvious from his pale skin and projected veins. It was his old Chief—Nathan.

Mamoru lowered his head, out of both shame and respect. "I failed you once again. Please, Chief, kill me for my disgusting failure."

"As disappointing as you are, the Ichu need all the help we can get if we are to defeat our enemies."

That voice. It wasn't right. The voice wasn't fear striking. It was thin and pitiful. Mamoru raised his head to stare the man in the eyes. This wasn't Nathan. It wasn't his Chief. "I knew Nathan was dead," Mamoru said. "You're a sheep in wolf's clothing!"

The imposter clutched his hand. The air around Mamoru began to heat, and then it spread throughout his body. It was an old work of magic. Nathan knew how to do it, but how did this phony know?

His blood boiled as his heart slammed against his chest. While it was difficult to kill an Ichu, it was possible, and this was certainly one way to do it. Blood foamed from his mouth. He asked, with red spittle oozing down his jaw, "Who are you really?"

"My name is Patrick," the man said, and it was the last thing Mamoru ever heard, right before he caught fire. There was no pain as the flames burned him. Then, there was darkness.

Acknowledgments

Thanks to those who read earlier versions of the story and provided feedback, including Arran, Brooks, Emerson, Holly, Molly, Rena, and Taylor.

Lastly, thanks to my friends and family, who I can always count on for support.

About the Author

Ben Cotterill was born and raised in Stirling, Scotland. Fascinated in understanding extreme human behaviors, he studied forensic psychology. After completing his PhD on the psychology of children's eyewitness memory, he moved to the United States to teach forensic psychology to university students. When not working or writing fiction, he spends his weekends hiking the Appalachians and his vacations traveling as much as possible.

~

To learn more about Ben Cotterill and discover more Next Chapter authors, visit our website at www.nextchapter.pub.

Blades of Destiny
ISBN: 978-4-82419-318-6

Published by
Next Chapter
2-5-6 SANNO
SANNO BRIDGE
143-0023 Ota-Ku, Tokyo
+818035793528

14th April 2024

Milton Keynes UK
Ingram Content Group UK Ltd.
UKHW020058100624
443713UK00008B/330